The Body in the Fjord

Katherine Hall Page

The Body in the Fjord

WHEELER
PUBLISHING, INC.
ROCKLAND, MA

★ AN AMERICAN COMPANY ★

ACKNOWLEDGMENTS

I would like to thank my cousin Hege Farstad for the enormous amount of help she provided—finding answers to obscure questions and checking endless details. When I was growing up, I thought she could do anything, perhaps even fly—and I still do.

Thanks as well to others of my family in Norway: Aud Christensen, Camilla Farstad, and especially Olav Christensen for the jokes.

I'm also grateful to Lasse Bakke and Gerald Eiken for information regarding the west coast of Norway. Both are wonderful storytellers.

I have taken some liberty with the architectural layouts of the Stalheim, Fleischer's, and Kvikne's hotels to further the plot, but other details are accurate—especially the food!

Thanks to Zachary Schisgal, my editor, on the first of our journeys together, and to Faith Hamlin, my agent, who's been on board since the beginning, as have my dear husband and son—Alan and Nicholas—both of whom eat *fiskepudding*.

Published in Large Print by arrangement with William Morrow and Company, Inc. in the United States and Canada

Wheeler Large Print Book Series.

Set in 16 pt Plantin.

Library of Congress Cataloging-in-Publication Data

Page, Katherine Hall
   The body in the fjord / Katherine Hall, Page.
      p. (large print) cm.(Wheeler large print book series)
   ISBN 1-56895-562-6
   1. Fairchild, Faith Sibley (Fictitious character)—Fiction. 2. Americans—Travel—Norway—Fiction. 3. Women detectives—Norway—Fiction. 4. Norway—Fiction 5. Detective and mystery stories—Fiction 6. Large type books. I. Title. II. Series
[PS3566.A334.B657 1998]
813'.54—dc21

                                                                98-006711

To the Christensens and Malmgrens,
past and present,
and
To my mother, Alice Malmgreen Page,
and my aunt, Ruth Malmgreen Samenfeld,
with thanks for our voyage "home"—what a
time it was!

Look into any man's heart you please, and you will always find, in every one, at least one black spot which he has to keep concealed.

—HENRIK IBSEN, *Pillars of Society*

Prologue

"The book says, 'The Flåm train ride continues to be one of Norway's most popular tourist attractions,' " a woman with a slightly nasal voice read to her husband.

He was looking out the window at the people still waiting to board in front of the station at Myrdal.

"We'll be descending from two thousand eight hundred and forty-five feet above sea level to six feet above sea level in only twelve miles. I don't think I like the sound of it, honey, do you? Isn't that kind of steep?" She pursed her lips and tugged at his sleeve to get his attention.

He hadn't been listening—not an uncommon occurrence. But he had caught enough to know what she was talking about. He'd read the book, too.

"I'm sure it's all very safe. We're in Norway, for God's sakes. What could be safer?"

"You're right. I'm just being an old fussbudget."

He'd turned to look at her and now he turned back toward the window. He hated it when she pulled at his clothes. Hated it when she used what she thought were cute words, like *fussbudget*. Who talked like that, for God's sakes? Her voice kept going—and going.

"Anyway, it says here the train has five separate braking systems. And they couldn't possibly *all* fail, or even if they did, the train

1

would be going so slowly by then, we could jump off."

The man repressed the impulse to point out to his wife that jumping off the train as it zigzagged down the mountain to the fjord at any speed would be as suicidal as staying on with no brakes, and he merely grunted something that could be taken as either encouragement or discouragement. His wife opted for the former.

"What was I thinking of? This is going to be fun! It says the train passes through twenty tunnels. We won't be going very fast, though. It takes fifty-three minutes to go down. Fifty-three minutes for twelve miles. But wait—it says it takes forty minutes to go up. Now, that doesn't make a speck of sense. You'd think going down would be faster, wouldn't you? It must be a misprint. We can time it, then write to the guidebook people."

He didn't reply, continuing to stare out the window.

You could tell the Norwegians from the tourists, because the Norwegians of all ages carried knapsacks. The tourists had bags on wheels, bags with wheels, or bags strapped onto racks with wheels. Wheels were the thing.

He'd been in Norway long enough—this was their last day—to discover Norwegians didn't all have blond hair and blue eyes, but they did all look healthy. Good posture, too. Those knapsacks. Must be the free health care. Like to see them in the winter, he thought. Dark the whole day. Maybe they didn't look so healthy then.

The train started with a smooth exhale and they set off down the mountain.

"Get the camcorder, honey. This is fabulous! Besides, we're coming to that waterfall soon."

Kjosfossen. A photo opportunity. He got the camera ready. When the train stopped deep inside a tunnel, he dutifully trailed after his wife and the others, going outside through the dark dampness, emerging into daylight farther down the tracks.

The waterfall was everything the book promised. His wife scampered close to the edge, letting the spray from the mountain torrent hit her in the face.

"So good for your complexion! Better than Evian!" she shouted back to him. He felt vaguely embarrassed by the nymphlike antics of this middle-aged woman. He knew for a fact she never sprayed water—French or any other nationality—on her face. Who was she trying to impress? He also knew for a fact it wasn't him. Just something to say. Always something to say.

A man at his side was following his gaze.

"Kjosfossen. It's one of our best ones, one of the biggest," he said.

And it was. Tumbling down from ledge to ledge, crashing against the dark rocks, rocks that in June held pockets of snow, there was nothing delicate about the waterfall. No bridal-veil similes, no maidens in the mist, but roaring, pounding, impenetrable white water. He lowered the camera for a moment, bent down, and threw a twig in. It vanished instantly, engulfed in the powerful swirling foam so rapidly, he could not even be sure he'd seen it go in.

His wife was still capering about on the slippery rocks. Almost all the other passengers had gone back to the train. His new companion did not seem to be in any hurry.

"The water goes into the river at Flåm, then the fjord. The Aurlandsfjord. Good fishing down below. Salmon," the man said.

The train whistle blew. His wife gave a start, lost her footing, and for one brief moment...

Seconds later, she was grabbing his sleeve. "I could have killed myself!" She was indignant. "The book should have mentioned how dangerous those rocks are."

They boarded the train and he resumed his post at the window.

The journey ended at Flåm. When they got off the train, he was surprised to see people running from the platform and down the road toward the river. They were all talking at once.

"What's happening?" his wife cried out. "Ask if anyone speaks English. They all speak English."

He shook her off, wanting to know himself what was causing this uncharacteristic agitation. Wanting to run with them.

"You stay here with the bags."

He was not far behind the man he'd been talking to in the tunnel, catching up with him shortly before they reached a knot of people standing on the banks of the river. Several were crying. A few were retching in the grass.

The cause was immediately obvious.

Caught between two rocks was the body of a man—a young man, it appeared. One of the blonds, although his head was so bashed in from his turbulent journey, it was hard to tell. Some blood had turned the pool where he'd come to rest a sickly pink—salmon pink. His right arm had been wrenched back over his head, assuming a position impossible in nature. Most of the clothes had been torn from his body. Incongruously, one foot remained clad in a running shoe, the laces neatly tied.

"It's a wonder he's here at all," the man from the train said. "Usually in these waters, they're never found."

The roar of the falls high up the mountain had become the mere babbling of rushing waters emptying into the deep, still fjord. Mesmerized, he watched as the clear current rolled smoothly over the rocks, swept past the grisly impediment, and continued on to the sea. Watched it over and over again.

Never found.

"Pix, dear, I have to leave for Norway tomorrow, and I think you'd better come, too. Something rather dreadful has happened and Marit needs us."

"Norway?" Pix Miller was still breathless from catching the phone, and the name of the country was all she could get out at the moment. Norway—this was considerably farther afield than her mother's usual proposals: lunch at Boston's venerable Chilton Club, bird-watching at the Audubon Sanctuary in Lincoln. Then the rest of what her mother had said hit home and she caught her breath quickly.

"Marit! What's wrong! Is she ill?"

Marit Hansen was one of Ursula Rowe's oldest and dearest friends. They had been girls together, growing up in Aleford, Massachusetts, some eighty years ago. Marit's family had moved back to Norway when Marit was a teenager, but the two friends had always stayed in touch.

"No, Marit's fine, but it appears that Kari's boyfriend, Erik, has been killed in some sort of tragic accident."

"Oh my God! Poor Kari! How is she taking it? What a thing to have to cope with at her age. You met him last summer, didn't you?"

"Yes. He was a student at the university with Kari. They talked about getting married in a few years, when they had enough money to

6

buy an apartment." Ursula Rowe paused as the picture of the happy, carefree couple came to mind. They had taken a picnic to one of the islands near the Hansen's house in Tønsberg, on Norway's east coast. The fjord was filled with boats and the beaches filled with people eagerly storing up the summer sunshine against the long, dark winter. Kari, Marit Hansen's granddaughter, and Erik were a beautiful couple—tall, blue-eyed, blond, so alike as to be brother and sister, except Erik was trying to grow a beard. Kari had teased him about the patchy stubble. Ursula felt very tired. It seemed every time the phone rang, it brought bad news—sickness or another acquaintance gone. She knew she would never get used to it, no matter how often friends reached for the supposedly comforting platitudes, saying that it went with her age or that, in some cases, it had been a "good" death, mercifully painless, quick.

But this death was different. There was nothing good about it. Erik Sørgard was young, barely out of his teens at twenty-one. He had hardly begun his life. All those hopes and dreams. She realized Pix was speaking.

"Mother, are you still there?" It was unusual for Ursula to tune out.

"Sorry, it's all been quite upsetting and I have so much to do to get ready. And you— you'd better call Sam right away. Samantha can keep an eye on Danny, and we shouldn't be gone too long, I hope."

Ursula had returned to matters at hand, but Pix was confused. Of course Marit would

7

be upset about her granddaughter's fiancé's death, and Ursula's particular brand of care— a combination of stiff upper lip and subtle coddling—was always effective, but to drop everything and rush off to Norway now?

"Can't you give yourself a few days to get ready? Why do you have to go tomorrow? I'm sure Marit would understand, and of course I feel terrible and would like to see Kari especially, but I can't just leave." Car pools, her part-time job at her friend and neighbor Faith Fairchild's catering company, plus all the meetings scheduled for this week—the vestry, the food bank's steering committee, the PTA, the...

She heard a heavy sigh come over the wires. Ursula was not given to sighs, or vapors, or any other Victorian modes of self-expression.

"You wouldn't be able to see Kari. That's the whole point. She's missing. Now, wash your hands and come over. We'll talk about it while I pack."

Pix peeled off one of her gardening gloves and regarded the dirt that always managed to seep through.

"How did you know I was in the garden?" She had to know. Her mother's clairvoyance could be startling.

"You were out of breath and you shopped on Saturday. Tuesday morning's your Friends of the Library day and Friday's the hospital. The children are in school and you work for Faith in the afternoons, so where else would you be running in from?"

Hearing her life reduced to such a prosaic open book was depressing. Pix hung up the phone, promising to be there as soon as possible, and went to wash. She'd been thinning a patch of ribbon grass, planted as a small island for contrast in her border, and now the size of Manhattan and the boroughs, threatening to choke out the delphinium and Shasta daisies completely.

Hands clean, she reached for her car keys, then turned back to the phone and called Faith. Briefly, she related Ursula's totally absurd request and promised to stop by to fill Faith in after she'd left her mother's.

"Good," Faith replied. "This sounds interesting. What could possibly happen in quiet little Norway that would send Ursula rushing off like this, especially with you in tow? Maybe you'd better call before you come— if I'm not here, I'll be at the kitchen. And Pix, your passport hasn't expired again, has it?"

Pix had once made the mistake of revealing this lapse to Faith, who insisted she immediately rectify the situation. "I'd as soon let my driver's license expire! What if someone offered you a free trip to Paris? You wouldn't be able to go." Pix had pointed out the extreme unlikelihood of such an event, and when Faith countered with the suggestion that Sam, Pix's husband, might suddenly propose a romantic getaway to, say, Bali, Pix was forced to admit the free Paris trip would be more apt to come up first. But she had renewed her passport, exchanging one hideous picture for another. The guys at Aleford

Photo on Aleford's Main Street had managed to catch her grinning like an idiot. She would not be surprised if the next time she did use her passport she was refused entry for security reasons. She certainly looked demented.

She backed out of her driveway and turned left toward her mother's house. Norway, tomorrow! She couldn't possibly go. Just leave?

Faith Fairchild sat on the end of her friend's bed, a large four-poster, watching Pix pack what seemed like an extremely insufficient amount of clothing for a transatlantic trip. Maybe enough for an overnight somewhere. She surreptitiously tucked an extra sweater in and wondered if she could convince Pix to take another suitcase. But packing was secondary at the moment.

"All right, start at the beginning. Marit Hansen gets a call from her granddaughter, Kari, last Friday afternoon from the train station in Oslo."

"Yes. Kari and Erik were working for Scandie Sights this summer. It's one of those tour companies." Pix's tone carried an air of purity, that of someone who has never indulged in mass travel, preferring to get hopelessly lost on her own. "The tour had a brief stopover at the station in Oslo on its way to the west coast of Norway. They were coming from the airport, because the group started in Copenhagen. Marit says Kari asked her to find

10

her address book and look up the phone number of a friend of Kari's living in Bergen. She gave her grandmother the name of the hotel where the tour would be in Bergen that night, asking her to phone. She apparently didn't have time to wait while Marit looked for it then."

"Did she sound anxious or say anything else?"

"Mother didn't know. In any case, when Marit phoned the hotel that night, they said Kari wasn't there and they put her through to one of the tour guides, who was extremely put out. He told her Kari and Erik had eloped, leaving him without anyone to carry the bags, or whatever they were doing."

"How did he know this?"

"Something about a message from a stationmaster in a place called Voss."

"But why didn't they tell the tour guide in person? They were with him on the train when it left Oslo, and they must have known that they were going to run off."

Faith was on the point of packing her own bags. She had managed to solve a number of crimes in between baking soufflés and tending to her family—the Reverend Thomas Fairchild of Aleford's First Parish Church, five-year-old Ben, and almost two-year-old Amy. Sleuthing in foreign countries held a particularly seductive appeal. It wasn't that she didn't think Pix and Ursula, an impressive pair, couldn't handle the situation—well, perhaps not in Faith's own inimitable way—if there even was one. So far, nothing of a criminal nature had emerged in Pix's narrative. Only a tragic one. Still, Faith was feeling left out—and itching to go. She slipped back into the bag some of the undergarments Pix had put to one side. There was nothing worse than having to rinse out unmentionables in a hotel basin and festoon them across the towel bars.

"And Erik's body was discovered when?"

"On Sunday morning in Kjosfossen—at a river in a place called Flåm, on the west coast. Sam and I were there. It's famous for its steep railway and a beautiful waterfall up in the mountains. The tour had been there on the way to Bergen. At first, everyone assumed Kari must have drowned, too. The police were even suggesting a double suicide, but Marit refuses to believe that."

"I don't blame her. You don't kill yourselves immediately after announcing you're going to get married. Although don't those Scandinavians have the reputation for being prone to depression? Ibsen, Munch—think of *The Scream*. Those dark days of winter. Trolls."

"A myth—not just the trolls but the rest, too. Their suicide rate is no better or worse than any other European country's. Besides, this is summer." Pix deftly folded a denim wraparound skirt. "And I *know* Kari. She's been here twice—once when she was very young, then two years ago. Remember, I told you about her visit? You were on vacation. She had a bus ticket that let her go anywhere in the country and she ended up here after covering every state except Alaska and Hawaii. She'd had a terrific time and there was nothing depressive about her. The opposite, in fact.

Very outgoing." Pix remembered Kari's account of her travels, from Frito pies in the Woolworth in Santa Fe to Mount Rushmore—"It was so small! In *North by Northwest,* the noses were much larger!" They had laughed until tears ran down their cheeks.

Faith looked askance at the heavy turtleneck Pix was packing. Could it get that cold in Norway in June? Obviously Pix thought so. She continued her line of questioning. "Marit hasn't heard anything from her since the call on Friday?"

"No, and she's desperate. It's possible that Kari and Erik slipped, falling into the river, or one tried to save the other, but that doesn't explain the knapsacks—and of course Marit has no idea why they were quarreling."

It was this information that had sent Pix home from her mother's to pack after a call to Sam and nine or ten others canceling various obligations.

"Knapsacks? Quarrel?" Pix had told Faith recently that she was so afraid of repeating herself, a dreaded sign of the encroachments age made on memory, that she found she was, instead, forgetting to tell friends and family whole bunches of things. This was obviously one of those times.

"I must have left this part out." Pix was stuffing socks into the toe of a Bass Weejun. "Anyway, you know Norway is a small country, a little over four million people. The discovery of Erik Sørgard's body has been big news. The police asked anyone who might have seen either Kari or Erik to get in touch with them.

13

So far, no one has reported seeing them, except for the people on the tour, and of those, only one woman saw them after the group boarded the train in Oslo. There weren't enough seats, so Kari and Erik had gone to another car. This woman was looking for the food cart and passed Kari's and Erik's seats. She told the police they were having 'a vicious argument'—those were her words. Since she doesn't speak Norwegian, she had no idea what it was about.

"Then the knapsacks. One of the clerks in the lost-luggage bureau at the Oslo railway station noted their names on two knapsacks a conductor had turned in late Saturday. One of the clerk's jobs is to transfer names and addresses on items to a master list they keep. When he heard the news, he called the police. He remembered their names, because his last name is Hansen, too—although there are so many Hansens in Norway, I don't know why Kari's name stuck with him."

Faith ignored the Hansen conundrum. "At least this gives you a place to start. You have to find out how the knapsacks got to Oslo. It's on the east coast, right? And the train was on the west coast? Why weren't Kari and Erik carrying them? And was it a lover's spat or something more? Even if she couldn't understand what they were saying, the woman might remember what their gestures conveyed."

While appreciating Faith's advice, Pix hadn't finished. As Faith, with the wisdom of someone ten years younger, constantly told her, there was nothing wrong with Pix's memory, and if Pix occasionally had trouble dredging up details like the name of the kid who sat behind her in third grade, it was because her fertile brain was weeding out useless information to make room for new, more important facts—like these.

"There's more. Everything appeared to be in Erik's sack, but things were missing from Kari's."

"What kinds of things?"

"According to her grandmother, her passport, driver's license, and money," Pix said grimly. "The report of the quarrel—and Kari does have a quick temper, which I'm sure the police have managed to find out from someone by now—has caused them to change the bulletin from 'missing' to 'wanted for questioning.' The passport is particularly puzzling, because Norwegians don't need one to travel within Scandinavia. Erik had his passport, too. It was still in his knapsack."

Faith reached for her pocketbook, a large Coach saddlebag, dug down, and added a few things to Pix's suitcase: a penlite with fresh batteries, the ultimate Swiss army knife, a Côte d'Or dark chocolate bar, matches, surgical gloves, skeleton keys, and a small can of hair spray—tools of the trade. She wished she was going more than ever, although Norway, where boiled potatoes accompany most meals and dried cod soaked in lye is the pièce de résistance of the groaning Yule board (see recipe on page 345), had never attracted her in the past. Fjords or no fjords. You had to eat.

"Put these where you can get at them eas-

15

ily—your jacket pocket, whatever—after you land. And be sure to carry fifty dollars or more in Norwegian currency on your person, not in your bag, at all times."

"Hair spray?" Pix had eyed the other items and they made some sense, although the thought of a situation where she might have to use the gloves to avoid leaving fingerprints was not comforting. But hair spray? Her short, thick dark brown hair fell into place and stayed there.

"Because they're not about to let you into the country that awards the Nobel Peace Prize, or any other one for that matter, with a can of Mace or pepper spray, so this will have to do. Hope put me onto the brand." Faith's sister, Hope, a real estate appraiser for Citibank, and her husband, Quentin, lived in New York City, where the two sisters had been born and raised. She regularly passed on news to perennially homesick Faith, from what was hot in self-defense to the closing of the Quilted Giraffe, one of their favorite restaurants.

"Here, take this comb. It snaps into the mirror. The hair spray will feel more legitimate then." Faith knew her friend well.

For a brief moment, Pix found herself wishing Faith was coming, too. She'd never carried a weapon before. Gingerly, she picked up the spray as if it were a live grenade and slipped it into her toiletries bag. She zipped her suitcase shut and set it on the floor. She'd take that sweater out after Faith left. For now, she was ready to go.

It wasn't going to be a pleasure trip. In

fact, all thoughts of any pleasure had been shelved by Marit's call for help—help in trying to make sense of a nightmare. According to Marit, there was only one way to find Kari and she couldn't do it. Someone had to pose as a Scandie Sights tourist—as soon as possible.

Someone had to blend in with the group: "The Little Mermaid Meets the Trolls: Copenhagen to Fjord Country." The Mermaid/Troll tour. The tour where Kari and Erik had last been seen.

Pix leaned back into her seat. It was ten o'clock at night and they were still in Newark. It had already been the flight from hell and they weren't even in the air. First, the plane from Boston was delayed—something about thunderstorms in New Jersey. One of the legion of dark-suited businesspeople glued to their cell phones had pried himself away to shout to a companion that one of the tanks at the oil refineries near the turnpike had been struck by lightning and that things were totally screwed up. For some reason, they both thought this was hysterically funny.

When the flight finally was announced for boarding, the surge of humanity threatened to engulf them, until Mrs. Arnold Lyman Rowe whipped out her folding cane and parted the seas. Pix had never seen this cane before, and as they were ushered to the head of the line, Ursula flashed her a triumphant look. "I only use it when I have to," she whis-

17

pered. Clearly this was going to be a no-holds-barred trip.

Strongly citing extreme inconvenience, Ursula got them bumped to first class after they arrived at SAS in Newark, where they discovered their flight was at the gate but that the doors were closed. They would be forced to wait several hours for the next flight. She also made them call Marit. By the time they got on the plane, Pix was exhausted. Ursula was, of course, fresh as a daisy and perky to boot. Pix wondered why on earth her mother had thought she would need her daughter's help. So far, the only thing Pix had done was use one of the meal chits SAS had issued to secure a cup of tea for Ursula. The hamburgers that had been sitting wrapped in foil for many hours and fries from before that had held little appeal for either of them. Well, she could start taking charge now.

"I think the best thing to do is put on these masks and go right to sleep. That way, we'll be on Norwegian time when we arrive. I'll tell the steward we don't want the meal."

Ursula had been examining the contents of the bag thoughtfully provided to first-class passengers for many hundreds of dollars extra with all the excitement of a child opening a very large birthday present.

"Even toothpaste!" she exclaimed. The Rowe women, besides traveling light, always traveled economy class.

"I'm going to reset my watch now." Pix adjusted her footrest. They would be able to sleep in these seats, something impossible on every other flight she'd made. Fitting her long, angular frame into an airline seat was like trying to put those springy joke snakes back in the fake mixed-nuts can. Both mother and daughter were tall—and attractive, although Pix had never believed she was, despite a husband given to unrestrained, unlawyerly rhapsodies about her dark chestnut hair and deep brown eyes. Ursula's hair was white, a clean white, like new-fallen snow. It too was short, but, unlike Pix's, it curled slightly. Ursula's cheekbones had become more pronounced, yet age had not clouded her brown eyes.

Pix reached for the button to summons the steward.

"What are you doing, dear?"

"Calling the steward, so we won't be disturbed when they serve dinner. We can wear these sleep masks."

"But I want my dinner. It could be something nice." Her mother sounded uncharacteristically plaintive.

Pix had heard Faith on the subject of airplane food and thought it unlikely that SAS had whisked a cordon bleu chef aboard especially for this flight.

Ursula persevered. "It will probably be something Scandinavian. You know how much you like salmon. It could be salmon."

"All right, we'll have dinner, then go to sleep immediately after."

Her mother had pulled a menu from the pocket in front of them. "See, smoked salmon to start. Now, you don't want to miss that."

19

Pix was seeing a new side of Ursula: Ursula the traveler. Yes, mother was intrepid, still gardening, living on her own, fiercely independent. She'd asked for a kayak for her eightieth birthday and plied the waters of Maine's Penobscot Bay with aplomb. In between worrying about her children—Mark, almost twenty; Samantha, a senior in high school; Danny, a seventh grader— all worrisome ages—Pix worried about her mother, despite her self-sufficiency, or maybe because of it. But she knew her, or so she thought. The long wait in Newark Airport had revealed another Ursula: Ursula the outgoing. Pix had spent the time slumped in a tortuous molded plastic seat, trying to read the Fodor's guide Faith had insisted she bring so she'd know where to eat. Her mother, meanwhile, was making friends, and as they departed for their various destinations, she filled Pix in on the lives of these new acquaintances. Ursula's Christmas card list was growing faster than Pinocchio's nose.

"I never knew the copper in the Statue of Liberty is Norwegian copper. That interesting man I was just talking to told me all about it when I mentioned where we were going. At the time it was cast, a French company owned the copper mine in Norway and that's how it happened. I wonder if Marit knows."

Pix had been amazed. On her own turf, her mother never spoke to strangers and was even known to be reserved with friends. Talk about off the leash.

The plane bumped down the runway and

soon they were in the air. Ursula had insisted that Pix take the window seat and was now craning over to see if she could spot the Norsk Lady Liberty in the net of twinkling jewel-like lights spread below, enveloped by darkness as they gained altitude. She leaned back and was soon captivated by the map on the movie screen marked with altitude, speed, mileage, time, and their tiny plane inching along the Eastern Seaboard.

A few bursts of static, then a voice: "This is Einar Magnusson speaking. I am your captain tonight. On behalf of Scandinavian Airlines, I would like to welcome all of you on board and I'm very sorry for the long wait on the runway. I promise to make up the time. You will be in Oslo before you know it!" His voice was cheerful, sincere, contrite. He repeated the announcement in his native tongue, sounding even more cheerful, sincere, and contrite. Pix was vaguely alarmed. Exactly how did Einar propose to make up this time? Her mother's thoughts were elsewhere.

"Danish. You can always tell. You know what Marit says. They sound like they have a potato in their mouths."

Pix wasn't going to touch this one. Dane, Swede, Norwegian, Hindustani—she didn't care, so long as he got them to Oslo safely. Mother, on the other hand, seemed to have picked up some of Marit's intense nationalism—the "Forty thousand Swedes ran through the weeds chased by one Norwegian" kind, or "The only thing the Swedes have that the Norwegians don't are good neighbors." Norway had only been independent from Sweden since 1905 and feelings still ran high.

Dinner arrived. The lox was followed by decidedly non-Scandinavian sirloin tips. Pix passed on the mango mousse and turned her light off. She hadn't had to supervise Danny's homework, or deal with dinner. She was missing a meeting and Samantha's senioritis, which veered wildly from counting the days until graduation to tears at leaving. Pix *had* been able to just leave after all. She wasn't indispensable. If only it hadn't been for such a horrible reason.

"Good night, Mother."

"Good night, Pix. If you wake up, wiggle around or step over me and walk up and down. They say this helps you with jet lag."

Ursula read a lot, Pix reminded herself, and she wondered what other travel tips awaited her. Before drifting off to sleep, she lifted her mask to check on her mother. Ursula had headphones on and was watching the movie. Pix pulled the mask down. Mother didn't get to the movies much.

A horrible reason... The steward had given her two blankets and they actually had some heft to them, as opposed to the tissue-paper ones issued to economy class. She pulled one up around her shoulders and tried to let sleep, so close, claim her. Marit would be waiting for them. Marit, a Scandinavian version of Ursula, tall, poised. Pix had a hard time imagining the two stately old ladies as silly little girls, the way they described themselves when they looked at the old pictures.

The Larsens, Marit's parents, had emigrated to the United States sometime in the early 1900s. They had been intending to join relatives who had settled in Minnesota, but arriving in New York, Mr. Larsen had mistakenly purchased railway tickets for Hampton, New Hampshire, rather than Hampton, Minnesota. A thorough man, he was conscientiously following a map as they traveled, and upon hearing the names of places that did not appear on his route, he realized his error and got his wife, great with child, off the train in Boston. At this point, Mrs. Larsen had had enough of travel and enough of the United States. Unlike her husband, she did not speak any English and was already longing for herring. They decided to stay put and see how things went. Norwegians tend to be bodies that do not stay in motion once having arrived someplace. The one thing Mrs. Larsen did do was insist that her husband get on a trolley with her and ride until they found a place enough like home so she could tolerate their sojourn in this foreign land. The place turned out to be Aleford, twenty minutes west of Boston. Of course, Aleford no more resembles the rolling green meadows, deep fjords, and towering mountains of the Larsen birthplace than it does the Amazon rain forest, but it did have some birch trees and red barns. That was enough for Mrs. Larsen. After the birth of her first child, Nils, Marit's older brother, now passed away, along with her only other sibling, Lars, Mrs. Larsen started doing wash for various ladies in Ale-

ford, who promptly became "her ladies."
And her favorite lady was Ursula's mother,
Mrs. Lyman.

The Lymans lived in a sprawling old house
with a backyard that sloped down to the
Concord River, a branch of which ran through
town. Ursula had inherited the house and it
was where Pix and her brother, Arnold, had
grown up. It seemed as much a part of the family as the people who had inhabited it over the
generations. Pix didn't want to think what
would happen to the house after Ursula died.
Didn't want to think about that at all.

The Larsens' house also backed onto the
river, farther downstream. From the pictures, it seemed this generation took to the
water the way Pix and her brother had. Ursula
and Marit in a canoe, swimming, rowing.
But always Ursula and Marit. Both were the
only girls in their families and they sought each
other's company on every possible occasion.
Marit was such a frequent guest for dinner,
she had her own napkin ring.

Mr. Larsen was a carpenter and his business prospered throughout the twenties.
Ursula liked to point out all the houses he had
built in Aleford and the surrounding towns.
"There's one of Pete's," she'd announce as they
drove past. Mrs. Larsen stopped doing wash
and devoted herself to handwork, inviting
her ladies for coffee and cakes. The smell of
cardamom, Ursula once told Pix, could still
transport her instantly back to the Larsens'
kitchen. Then the Depression hit and people
weren't building houses anymore. Peter

Larsen eked out a living repairing stoops and doing other odd jobs. Mrs. Larsen started washing again. But when they finally made the big decision to return home, they told the Lymans that they had never touched their savings—savings securely tucked into the bank in Norway, where their cousin, Olav, worked in Tønsberg. The Larsen boys were grown, married, and on their own, doing as best they could. Marit had recently finished high school. It was time to go.

When that time came, Mrs. Larsen was as sorry to leave as she had been to come, but it was Marit who was the most bereft. She and Ursula swore to remain friends forever, write often, and visit as soon as they had the money. It would be a long time before the first visit, but they wrote constantly. The war years were very hard. Marit lost both her parents. Heart problems, the doctor said, but she knew it was the lack of good food. The Lymans sent packages, many that never arrived. The years after the war ended were lean, too. Pix remembered packing dried fruit and jars of peanut butter for people she'd heard so much about, she felt she knew them. Marit had married shortly before losing her parents. Her daughter, Hanna, was born during the occupation.

Now the Norwegians were the rich ones, with their black gold, the North Sea oil. Ursula had been astonished at the wealth of the country she'd observed during her trip the previous summer. No more food packages, although she wondered how people could afford anything at all, even to eat, with prices so high.

Pix awoke with a start. She had no idea where she was. The steady drone of the jet engines brought her back to reality. Reality? What was that? She was on her way to Norway to join a tour group because her mother's best friend was certain the key to her granddaughter's disappearance and the death of her fiancé lay hidden somewhere among the camera-laden, sensibly shod, indefatigable tourists Kari had been shepherding. And if Marit Hansen believed something was true, there was no arguing. The only one Pix knew more stubborn than Marit was Ursula.

"Why don't you go out and find Marit and I'll wait for the suitcases," Pix suggested. Her mother had taken her cane out again. All the better to pass through customs, although a silver-haired grandmother, especially one who had not been to South America several times in the last month, would merit no more than a smiling, passing glance from the Norwegian passport control. It was, Pix reflected, the perfect cover. She also gave a thought to why her mother was posing as an old lady again. What did she have in her hefty purse?

Captain Magnusson had been a man of his word and they were only a half hour late. It was eleven o'clock in the morning, June twelfth. June eleventh had been swallowed up by various airports and the time change. Pix felt only slightly fatigued, but she wished she could tap into Ursula's energy source. Kelp

26

pills? Ursula swore by them and all the vitamins she took.

The two bags appeared, carry-ons that SAS had still insisted be checked, much to Ursula's annoyance. "The whole notion of traveling light is to avoid having to check your luggage. Why can't they understand this? Scandinavians are usually so sensible." Pix pointed out that, judging from the name tags sported by the personnel at Newark Airport, it appeared no one working for SAS had been born anywhere near the Land of the Midnight Sun and let it go at that.

Quickly passing through customs, blushing with guilt at the thought of her hair spray, gloves, and other paraphernalia, Pix pushed open the heavy door leading to Fornebu Airport's main waiting room and was immediately embraced by Marit. Like most Norwegian women, she was well groomed, her bright white hair waving softly back from her tan face. In the winter, the color was from ski trips; now it was from the beach or the park. She was wearing a navy knitted suit and what Pix always called "the Norwegian Ladies Club necklace"—a heavy chain of gold they wore with everything from ball gowns to bathing suits. She was smiling as she greeted Pix. Pix was not surprised. Norwegians as a whole were not given to letting it all hang out. Erik was dead and Kari was missing—wanted by the police to aid them in their inquiries, as it was delicately put—but you'd never be able to tell from Marit's demeanor. A Norwegian's entire family could have been

27

wiped out by a giant meteorite and the first thing he or she would say to a visitor would be, "You must be hungry. How about some coffee and a little cake?" And Marit was doing it now.

"You are so good to come. How was the trip? Are you very tired? Or hungry? And where is Ursula? Surely she has not been stopped by customs."

"Isn't she with you?" Pix looked wildly about the waiting room. It wasn't very big. "She came out ahead while I waited for the bags."

"Now, now, don't worry. There're not so many places she could go. We'll have her paged."

Pix had lost her children any number of times, ranging from agitated seconds in the aisles of Aleford's Stop 'n Save to full terror at the Burlington Mall for five minutes before Danny emerged from beneath a sale rack at Filene's. But she had never lost her mother.

Marit was speaking to a friendly-looking woman at the SAS information counter. "Yes, of course we have Mrs. Rowe. She's having some coffee and a little cake with us in the back room. She didn't see you and we thought she'd be more comfortable here."

It was the first time Pix had heard Norwegian English in a long time and her ear welcomed the slightly singsong, lilting sound—some of the sentences ending on a questioning note—"Of course we have Mrs. Rowe?"—certain words punctuated by a quick intake of breath for emphasis, almost always with *ja* or *nei*. Marit had spoken this way, too, but Pix

28

had been too busy scanning Fornebu for some sign of Ursula to appreciate it. She remembered with a sharp stab what her children had called "Norwegian teenspeak," Kari's frequent addition of a giggle or outright laughter at the end of a remark.

Marit had tucked Ursula's arm through hers and was leading the way out of the airport. She was making determined small talk—about the flight, about the plans to move the airport from Oslo's center to Gardermoen, north of the city. "We all love Fornebu. It's so convenient, except it really is too small. You know, we used to call it a 'cafeteria with a landing strip,' and it has gotten much bigger, but still the new one will be better. It will be nice to be on the fjord and not see the jumbo jets." So far, nothing had been said about Kari or Erik.

Pix followed, carrying the bags. She blinked in the bright daylight. Like the airport, the very air seemed scrubbed clean. And the cars—they all looked like new, no dents, no grime. Marit opened hers with an automatic key, apologizing. "It came with it and now I'm so used to it." Another national trait: no bragging, no self-aggrandizement. The opposite, in fact. During the Olympics, there had been a concerted campaign to get the Norwegians to root actively for their own athletes, passionately as they might feel inside. They had to be reassured that it was quite acceptable and the world wouldn't think they were a nation of show-offs. Showing off—a Lutheran sin, right up there with adultery, lying, and murder. There was even a Norwegian word for it, *jantelaw,* which roughly translates as "Now, don't go thinking you're better than anyone else."

It was a short ride to Marit's apartment. When Marit's husband, Hans, died, she and Kari, who was a young teenager, had moved to the capital city, using the house in Tønsberg for weekends and during the summer.

Even in the car, Marit avoided the topic on everyone's mind, but the moment they entered the apartment, it was the time and place. She firmly shut the door, announcing, "You have to get the two-fifty-five train to Voss to meet the tour, and we have a lot to talk about. You will need to take a little rest, too, Ursula?"

Her friend shook her head. "I'm not at all tired, and besides, it's a long train ride and I can rest then. Why don't you tell us everything that's happened since we spoke? Has there been any more news?"

Marit led the way into the living room. The apartment wasn't large, but it felt spacious because of the plate-glass windows overlooking the Oslofjord. The walls were painted a deep blue-green. The trim was white. Artwork of all sorts hung from floor to ceiling. There was a big stone fireplace and the floors were wood. A handwoven striped rug defined the dining area as separate from the living room. Where there weren't pictures, there were bookcases crammed with books in several languages. Ursula and Marit sat on the couch, Marit motioning for Pix to sit opposite them in a comfortable-looking leather armchair. The inevitable coffee table, staple of Scandinavian home furnishing, did indeed hold coffee cups and plates.

"I know they feed you all the time on those flights, but you should have a little something. We can eat while we talk."

Pix jumped up to help Marit, who insisted she stay put, returning almost immediately with the coffee and a platter of open-faced sandwiches, *smørbrød* (see recipe on page 346). Despite the gravity of the situation, Pix felt a twinge of pleasure when she saw her favorite, the bread hidden by rows of *reker*, nestled on mayonnaise, a bit of lettuce, a curl of paper-thin lemon on top. *Reker* were tiny, succulent shrimp, only available this far north. Next to these open-facers, she liked *reker* best straight from the boats where they had been caught and cooked. One could buy them by the bag here in Oslo on the wharf in front of city hall and in the fish market in Bergen. It was the essence of being in Norway, strolling along a waterfront, eating fresh shrimp. But she doubted there would be any time for this in the days to come.

"The police call constantly. They keep asking if Kari has gotten in touch with me. I think they are watching the house, too, because they think I might try to hide her."

Ursula came straight to the point. "But why? How could they possibly believe she is responsible for Erik's death? Surely it was an accident!"

Marit shrugged. Her face now looked tired

31

and the color faded. "Probably they don't know what to believe, and the newspapers, television, and radio are full of the story from morning to night. Nothing better to do with their time." Marit was disgusted. She paused. "They have dredged up the whole business with Hanna and it worries me that Kari, wherever she is, might be seeing it." Marit had made it absolutely clear to them as they ate that in her mind Kari was alive.

"Oh no, that's disgraceful!" Pix was indignant. Hanna had been only a few years older than she was. There had been one golden summer when Ursula brought both her children to Norway and they joined the Larsens, their various cousins, and their friends on an island in the middle of the Hardangerfjord. The children all slept in one big room, the attic of an old farmhouse. They were outdoors from dawn to dusk. Pix had worshiped Hanna. Hanna swam like a fish, could climb any tree, and her arrows always hit the target. She told the younger children wonderfully scary tales of the trolls who inhabited the woodlands and came alive at night, pointing out their faces turned to stone by the sun's first rays in the mountains surrounding the fjord. Yet there was a dark side to Hanna, the night side of the trolls. She was moody and no one was ever sure what would cause her temper to flare. That summer was the first summer her parents became the same kind of targets she trained her bow and arrow on. Again, she seldom missed.

It grew worse as she got older. Tønsberg

seemed hopelessly conventional. It was the sixties and she craved new experiences. Some of them, she found through drugs. Then she met Sven and he became the most powerful addiction of them all. Throughout, her mother and father strove to stay with her, fearing a break, offering her any kind of help, whatever she wanted, trying not to be demanding. They never wavered in their love, even when it was rejected. Across the ocean, Ursula would read Marit's letters and feel helpless. She went to visit her friend alone and came back visibly upset. "This will not end well," she told her daughter, who was by then old enough to know what was going on.

Hanna took off with Sven. They went wherever their fancy took them. Marit and Hans received postcards and were grateful for them. Then the cards stopped. Hanna returned home eight months later, pregnant. Sven had abandoned her in Greece when he learned he was about to become a father. Hanna had thought he would marry her. Instead, he found another young girl and left. She was penniless and had to work to save money for a ticket home. She did not want to ask her parents for it. Maybe she wasn't even sure that was where she was headed.

When Kari was born, at first it seemed that Hanna was happy. She insisted on doing everything to take care of the golden-haired baby, a baby who always smiled, especially when her mother picked her up. It brought the Hansen family together for a brief, very special time, later a time treasured like the sal-

vaged beads of a favorite broken necklace—
not enough to string, but put away to save forever nonetheless.

Hanna killed herself on Kari's second
birthday. She went deep into the woods,
climbed high up into a tall Norwegian spruce,
made a noose, and hanged herself. Some
hikers found her.

Now all the old accounts were being res-
urrected. Had the daughter done something
similar, convincing her lover to join her?
asked the papers. Or was there some aberrant
strain in the family that erupted in madness
and Kari had pushed Erik to his doom, then
killed herself—or run away?

"None of this is true, Marit. You know
that." Ursula was polishing off a *smørbrød*
with a kind of ground meat patty and fried
onions. "Stop reading the papers and don't
turn on the radio or TV. If there's anything
you have to know, the police or someone will
tell you. Besides, you'll be meeting us on
the tour soon."

"I know, but I just wanted to tell you what's
been going on." Marit pursed her mouth.
"It makes people feel better if they think
others are worse off."

Pix had never heard Marit speak so pes-
simistically. She thought of the questions
she and Faith had raised. Now was the time
to ask them. When they met Marit at the
hotels the tour would be stopping at, they would
supposedly be meeting for the first time and
striking up a casual acquaintance. The tour.
Marit's call to Ursula had been a plea for

Ursula to pose as a tourist, but the two women had quickly decided Pix would be useful. "You'll be the *hund*," Marit had told Pix earlier. "The dog—you know, like for the blind. You will be our *hund,* since we are now such old women and can't do everything we once did." Pix wasn't sure how she felt about her new role, but it was true that, while in terrific shape, Marit and Ursula just might not be able to do things like the trip by horseback they'd taken across the vast Hardangervidda some thirty years ago.

The Mermaid/Troll tour. It reminded Pix of her first question—actually, two questions.

She had wondered from the beginning why Marit was adamant they join the tour to investigate, eliminating all other possibilities.

"You seem so sure that whatever has happened is linked to the tour. I know it was where they were last seen, but couldn't the explanation for all this lie somewhere else? A situation with a friend, someone they know at the university?" Pix was trying to ask her question delicately, avoiding words like *drugs.* She added, "Or a senseless attack by a stranger?"

"I thought of those things—of everything. I have told myself enough stories for many novels." Marit sounded bleak. "I think I have spoken to everyone Kari ever knew, gone through her address book, reached friends of friends. Nothing. Everyone seemed genuinely puzzled about where she might be and what could have happened to Erik. The only thing left is the tour.

"Erik's parents have believed from the beginning that it was suicide after a quarrel, and they blame Kari. They are very religious people and Erik seemed rebellious to them, although it was only normal growing-up behavior. Now, perhaps they feel he has been punished. I cannot pretend to understand, only grieve for them. They won't talk to me any longer. But I don't agree. I knew Erik and I'm sure he wouldn't have taken his life. Kari and Erik were very happy together. As for a stranger, we do not have many of these random crimes in Norway, although I suppose it could have occurred. But why? They weren't robbed. No, the tour is the only hope, and I have such a strong feeling about it. Almost as if Kari herself is telling me what to do."

She stopped, her lips set in a firm line. Pix knew there had never been any doubt about going on the tour. She'd just had to ask. This settled, or unsettled, the next question followed.

"Isn't it going to seem odd for us to be joining the tour so near to the end? Wouldn't we have waited for the next one? What did you say when you made the reservations?"

"Remember, Erik worked for this company last year, so I know a lot about it. Apparently, the most popular part is the fjord cruise. If there's room, they let people sign up just for those four days. You can leave either from Bergen or Oslo and meet the rest at Voss. You won't be the only ones, I'm sure."

"Also, can you tell us exactly what Kari said when she called Friday night?"

Marit closed her eyes for a moment, then opened them and recited from memory, a memory she had obviously been over many times. "She said the tour was going well. No rain—they'd had rain with the first one and everyone complained. I asked her where she was and she told me she was about to get on the train to Bergen. She was in the main train station, Oslo S, not the smaller one at the National Theater. She said, 'I don't have much time, *Bestemor,* and I'd like you to do a favor for me.' 'Anything,' I told her. 'Could you go into the top middle drawer of my desk, get my address book, and give me Annelise Christensen's phone number? No, wait—they're boarding and I have to go. There isn't time. Call me with it tonight. The tour is staying at the Augustin Hotel; you know it.' I said no problem and that I'd talk with her later. 'How is Erik?' I asked, and she said, 'He's fine, but there's something else.... I can't talk now. I'll tell you tonight.' She hung up without even saying good-bye. At the time, I thought the train must have started to move, but now I think maybe someone came along, someone she didn't want overhearing what she was about to say."

Pix nodded. "Two more things. Did she say anything about eloping? And who is Annelise Christensen?"

"I've told you everything she said as exactly as I can remember. And if she had planned to elope, I know she would have said something. But she never *would* have eloped. It was always her dream to get married in the

37

domkirken in Tønsberg where she had been christened and confirmed. Erik, too. They spoke of it when you were here, Ursula, and we went to that concert there."

"Yes, I remember. Kari was joking about how often she had been a bridesmaid lately. And you were reminiscing about your own wedding there during the war, wearing your grandmother's dress and drinking the toast with some sort of raw alcohol mixed with orange soda your father concocted."

"And Annelise?" Pix persisted.

"She was at school with Kari and now she lives and works in Bergen. She hasn't been there very long, and you know how it is for us on the east coast. We cannot get used to the rain—and if you are not from Bergen, you are really an outsider to many people there. You know they always say Bergen, not Norway, when someone asks them where they're from. I think Kari wanted to see how Annelise was doing—if she'd found friends."

"Why couldn't she just look her name up in the telephone book when she got there, or ask information? Why would she call you for it?"

"There are not so many names in Norway and there are as many Hansens as Christensens, I'm sure. That's why we put our professions as part of our names so often. Without Annelise's address, Kari would have had to call many A. Christensens, and she wouldn't want to bother people."

Heaven forbid, Pix thought. Bothering people was another sin in this very polite society.

"I phoned Annelise after I spoke to Carl, the tour guide. I thought maybe Kari had been in touch with her some way, but she hadn't heard from Kari and was as surprised as I was that they had eloped. When the news of Erik's death came, she called right away. She, too, is worried about Kari, of course, and if she hears anything at all, she said she would let me know at once."

Pix nodded.

"I think you're looking a little peaked, dear," Ursula said to her daughter. "I'm sure Marit wouldn't mind if you took a short nap before we leave for the station."

Pix was about to protest that, like her mother, she could sleep on the long train ride, but she closed her mouth when she felt the meaningful glance from Ursula hit her full force in the face. Her mother wanted to be alone with her old friend. To comfort, console... plot?

"You can lie down in Kari's room. I'll show you." Marit led the way out of the living room and down the narrow hall. "The bathroom is just here." She nodded at a closed door marked with the traditional heart.

Kari's room also overlooked the bustling Oslofjord, and the thin muslin curtains let in the sunlight. Pix noted the heavy roller shades, necessary at this time of year, when the sky could still be bright at midnight. The walls of the room were covered with blue-flowered wallpaper that Pix recognized as Laura Ashley. Kari was something of an Anglophile after working as an au pair outside

London one summer. Bracelets and necklaces hung from an assortment of wooden pegs. A bookshelf held childhood books, in addition to her university texts. She was studying to be an occupational therapist. The shelves also held a piggy bank, photo albums, and a funny-looking troll. There was a full stereo system, stacks of cassettes and CDs, and headphones—presumably for Marit's sake. The antique pine bed was covered with a *dyne,* the down-filled comforter that served as bedding in Scandinavia, its crisp white cover changed, instead of a top sheet. Two fluffy pillows were at the head, and for a brief moment, Pix thought she might crawl in and pull the comforter over her head for a few minutes of blissful unconsciousness. But she didn't like to sleep in the daytime. It made her groggy, cranky—and she had a lot to think about after talking to Marit.

Most important, though, was the realization that here she was in Kari's room. What would Faith do in a similar situation? She'd snoop, of course. Pix felt fully justified in opening any and all drawers if it would give her a clue to where Kari might be and what could have happened. Kari's small chest of drawers was covered with framed photographs, makeup, a silver comb and brush set. Pix picked up a photo of Erik and Kari. They were wearing their student caps. Erik, twenty-one—only a year older than Pix's own son. The thought stabbed her and she put the photograph down.

She walked over to a print on the wall. It wasn't by an artist she recognized—Munch or Kittelsen. It was of a small country house with trees, flowers, and animals, done in a naïve folk-art style. Very charming. She couldn't read the artist's signature, so she took it down to get a closer look. Marianne Arneberg. Moving to replace it, Pix realized that something was taped to the back.

It was an envelope.

She lifted the flap and removed the contents. There wasn't much: a few letters, some photographs. One picture tumbled to the floor. It was of Kari—Kari arm in arm with a very handsome dark-haired man.

Kari with someone other than Erik.

2

But she was wrong. It wasn't Kari. It was Hanna.

The resemblance was remarkable. Mother and daughter looked almost identical. But the clothes were the giveaway. Hanna was wearing a long flowered dress, the kind love children made in the sixties from their Indian-print bedspreads. She had beads around her neck, as did the man in bell-bottom jeans. On the back, only one word was written—the name Sven—and no date. The couple was standing in front of a Volkswagen Beetle parked alongside an olive grove. Olives did not grow in Norway. Not much of anything grew in Norway, where only 3 percent of the land was arable. It must have been taken in Italy, or France, some other place far from home. The two were smiling. Pix searched her memory for an image of Hanna. She had never seen her at this age. She had never seen her smiling so happily.

Pix felt relieved. The fleeting notion that Kari—with a secret love other than Erik—might not be who she seemed had made Pix feel unsteady. She knew she was on unfamiliar turf, but that this turf might suddenly suck her down into some sort of underground even more complicated than what was presently before her eyes was frightening. She reminded herself that Kari and Erik were students, good students, in love, planning for the future. Honest, loyal to each other.

She looked at the letters and the other photos. More pictures of Hanna. Hanna and a baby, Hanna and a toddler—Hanna and Kari.

The letters were written in a childish hand, the script rounded. Pix could recognize only a few of the Norwegian words. "*Kjære Mor og Far*"—*mor* meant "mother"; "grandmother" was *bestemor,* your best mother, an appellation Ursula heartily applauded. *Far* meant "father." "Dear Mother and Father." The letters were signed "Hanna." Hanna writing to her parents from some early trips with friends or her school? She'd drawn a little horse in the margin of one, a garland of roses in another.

Why weren't these pictures framed and on Kari's bureau with the rest, the letters in the big antique wooden box, ornately painted, that Pix had discovered held postcards and other letters? She thought a moment. There had been some photographs on the mantel in the living room, their silver frames well polished, like everything else in the apartment—Marit and Hans's wedding picture, Kari's graduation photo, Hans's and one of Marit's parents. But none of Hanna. Marit didn't seem the type to be ashamed of her daughter's suicide. Was it too painful to be reminded of what might have been? Or something else? Whatever it was, Kari had kept these links to her mother hidden. Pix imagined her sitting on the bed, reading the letters, looking at the faces, wondering. Long ago, a two-year-old would have asked many questions. Where did *Mor* go? When will she be back? How had her grandparents answered them? And *Far*? What about him?

There was a gentle knock on the door and Pix jumped a mile. "Pix, are you awake? We have to get ready to leave soon."

Marit pushed the door open a crack. Pix shoved the envelope under the pillows. She was glad she was sitting on the bed and she hoped Marit wouldn't notice the picture was off the wall. She answered quickly. "I'll just wash up and be right with you."

"Fine. You don't need to hurry too much. I have your tickets, but Ursula thinks it would be better to get to the station a little early."

Pix knew what this meant. The Rowes considered being on time being wherever you had to go at least thirty minutes before. If this meant driving around a neighborhood until the doorbell could be rung precisely on the hour, then so be it. It was a trait Marit and her compatriots shared. In Norway, on time meant on time.

The moment the door closed, Pix put everything back in the envelope. It had been frustrating searching the room when she didn't know the language. The letters and postcards in the box might have revealed something. On impulse, she took the photo of Hanna and Sven out of the envelope. She also removed the one of Kari and Erik from its frame and put both pictures in her wallet, tucked behind her passport. It seemed like something Faith would do. She smoothed the bed, fluffed up the pillows, and hung the picture back on the wall. It looked exactly the way it had before Pix had entered. Faith would have done this, too.

Ursula Rowe was sound asleep. Sitting across the aisle, Pix felt a pang. Her mother looked so vulnerable, her mouth slightly open. With her dark, lively eyes closed, she looked like the old lady she was. Pix had been dozing, too, but fear of drooling in public and troubled dreams had kept her from real sleep.

The sunshine of Oslo had given way to gray skies as they crossed the Hardangervidda. When he punched their tickets, the conductor had cheerfully assured them they would see much nature on the five-and-a-half-hour trip, but Pix was finding the vast empty stretches of landscape bleak and forbidding. It was also unsettling to plunge constantly in and out of the strings of snow tunnels, necessary to keep the line from east to west open during the harsh winter. The *vidda* was the site of that horseback trip Marit, Ursula, and a group of Marit's friends had taken so many years earlier. They had called themselves the "Cartwright sisters." *Bonanza* was wildly popular in Norway at the time, as later *Dallas* proved to be—well before the country became a Dallas itself.

After the horseback trip, Ursula had returned to Aleford, uncharacteristically restless and touchy. She had raved about the wild beauty of the *vidda*, the lakes, the reindeer. Looking out the window, Pix suddenly understood why her mother might have chafed at Aleford's tidy village green after this seemingly endless plain high in the mountains, so near to the sky—a sky whose horizon was broken not by trees but only an occasional hut, *hytte*, once used by herders, now by hikers, or converted to summer houses. Before the train, the paths that crossed and recrossed the *vidda* were well worn, essential connections between villages on the two coasts. Now the train eliminated the need, but the Norwegians were still walkers, taking pleasure in hiking across the lonely plateau from one isolated hut to another. She was seeing much nature. The conductor had been right. *Whoosh.* Another tunnel. The light flickered through the slats like a strobe. Pix closed her eyes.

Why did Kari and Erik have their passports? She had to find a moment to ask Marit when they struck up their "new" friendship tomorrow. It was the one thing that suggested they had planned to elope. Get married in Norway, then take off—for olive groves? Or had they simply packed them the way one does all sorts of things—to be prepared—penlites, rubber gloves, hair spray.

They were out of the tunnel. A red-faced young woman was having trouble negotiating a heavily laden food cart through the connecting compartment doors. Two passengers immediately leapt up to help her. Pix didn't think this would happen on Amtrak. The Norwegian state railway system was clean, too—even the bathroom.

Ursula woke up. "Coffee, don't you think? And maybe one of those pastries."

Two coffees and two pastries, wrapped in plastic and tasting like train food everywhere, cost about what dinner at Legal Seafoods in Boston would. If they had opted for Cokes, it would have been dinner at Olives. The exchange rate was terrible and things cost the earth here. She'd have to stop converting to dollars or she might starve.

"We should be there soon." Ursula moved over to sit next to her daughter. "Isn't it beautiful?" Pix was about to confess that she was not as taken with the view as Ursula and that perhaps it was her mother's fond memories coloring her opinions, when the sun broke through the dark clouds. Beams of light, so precise as to suggest the hand of some unseen Bergmanesque director, brought the surface of a lake in the distance to life, the colors of the moss-covered ground appeared, and a flock of birds took flight. A solitary hiker was silhouetted against the glow. It was beautiful.

"We had such a wonderful guide. We all loved him. Dead now, I should imagine. We all thought he was such an old man then, and he was probably only about sixty."

The loudspeaker announced that Voss was next, and the message was thoughtfully repeated in several languages.

"I think I'll go make myself tidy," Ursula said. "We'll be meeting the group soon." She eyed Pix's outfit with approval. It was similar to what she had on herself, except she wore a skirt. Her daughter was wearing navy cotton pants, a blue-and-white-striped shirt, and a bright blue cotton cardigan. Pix normally liked to travel in jeans, but she knew her mother did not approve of women Pix's age wearing what Ursula persisted in calling "dungarees." It was all right when they were in Maine on Sanpere Island, but not on a trip like this.

"I'll go after you." Pix wanted to comb her hair and wash her face, too. The group— she wanted to look her best for them. First impressions...

While she was waiting, she realized that many miles away her family hadn't even had lunch yet. They'd be out of sync for the duration. She felt suspended in time, as if she'd been gone from home for days, rather than a day. The trip across the *vidda* has produced strange sensations of total removal. She reminded herself she was a wife, mother—and daughter. Someone with responsibilities. Someone, a voice inside said, with too many.

What on earth was she doing here?

It wasn't hard to locate the tour. An extremely tired-looking man with a mop of unruly blond hair and dark-rimmed glasses stood holding a flag with the Scandie Sights logo—a giant pair of binoculars with a snaggletoothed troll in one lens and Hans Christian Andersen's Little Mermaid in the other.

"I'm Pix Miller, and this is my mother, Mrs. Ursula Rowe," Pix said, noting that her mother had the cane out again.

He put the flag down and checked their names off on the list attached to the clipboard he was holding in his other hand. Pix wondered where the other guide was. Marit had said there were two.

"I hope we haven't kept you waiting," Pix apologized, realizing as soon as she said it that since this was the train the people meeting the tour from Oslo were supposed to take, there was no way they could be late.

Her remark produced a smile. "I'm Jan Ekhart, one of your tour guides. You are on vacation now. You don't need to worry about things like this. There are still people getting off the train, and we won't leave for the hotel for fifteen minutes or so. Carl—he's the other leader—said they would hold dinner for us."

Pix realized that of course most members of the tour, the ones who had started in

Copenhagen, were already at the hotel. She also realized that she was at the station in Voss, the place where Kari and Erik had left the message with the stationmaster about eloping.

"What should we do with our luggage?" she asked Jan, eager to get inside the station.

"You leave it on the cart here"—he pointed off to the side—"and we take care of everything." That sounded fine to Pix. Ursula's bag was as compact as her own and she could easily carry both of them, but it would be nice to let someone else do it for the next few days. They had put the Scandie Sights tags on but had failed to find a way to wrap the bright red Scandie luggage straps around their modest bags. The tags would have to do.

"Why don't you wait here," Pix told her mother. "There's a bench by the door and you can keep an eye on Jan so he doesn't leave without me."

"What are you going to do?" her mother asked. "Never mind. Just hurry. You can tell me later."

Pix went inside. It was crowded, but since everything was conveniently translated, she soon found the information booth.

She was about to approach the genial-looking man behind the counter when she realized she didn't have a plan, or much time. She'd simply have to bluster her way through.

"Excuse me, but isn't this the place where that poor young man was last seen? You know, the boy who drowned and has been in all the newspapers? They're saying his girlfriend

49

had something to do with it. She was here, too, right?"

The man looked startled. Maybe he recognized Pix's attempt at a complete personality change for the phony one it was. Or perhaps it was the southern accent she'd unaccountably found herself assuming.

"Seen? No, no one saw them here."

"But I thought the papers said something about Voss. This is Voss, isn't it?" she said with the unsure air of a tourist about to find out she might have joined the wrong group and should be in Stockholm instead.

"Yes, this is Voss," he told her patiently. Then, aware that she wasn't going to leave until she'd heard some detail about the sad case that she could use to impress her friends back home, he added, "They left a message here saying they were running away together to get married."

"How on earth could they leave a message if no one saw them?" Pix asked plaintively. Could this possibly work?

It did. "We got the message by phone. They were already someplace on the road."

Pix feigned excitement, which wasn't hard. Her first actual clue!

"And were you the one who spoke to the girl? What's her name? Karen? Something like that."

For a moment, the man seemed to succumb to Pix's blandishments. He would be quoted someplace in the United States. He wondered if she lived near Minnesota and knew his cousin. "It wasn't Kari—that's her name.

It was the man, Erik. He just told me to write the message down for the Scandie Sights tour guides who would be arriving by bus to take the train to Bergen."

"I never dreamed that things like this could happen in Norway." Pix as Blanche DuBois continued: "It's such a calm and happy place. People are so kind."

"Sad things can happen anywhere," he told her solemnly. He was so nice, Pix felt a twinge of guilt as she thanked him, said good-bye, and raced for the door. She didn't want to miss the bus. Or dinner.

Pix felt like a new girl. It was true that others had joined the tour at Voss, but the group that had been traveling together since the beginning was the in group, the popular kids. It wasn't that they excluded the latecomers—just the opposite. As Pix and Ursula walked into the dining room at Fleischer's Hotel and headed for the tables with the Scandie Sights cards, they were immediately urged by several people to join them. The veterans exuded an all-knowing air that became even more apparent as the meal progressed. Advice ran rampant. It was a table of six.

"*Velkommen*. That's 'welcome' in Norwegian," a plump woman with tightly permed curls said. "I'm Erna Dahl and this is my sister, Louise. Twins, although you'd never guess! We're from Virginia. What about you?"

Ursula extended her hand across the table. "How nice to meet you. I'm Ursula Rowe and this is my daughter, Pix Miller. We're from Massachusetts."

"Oh, I just love Boston!" the woman seated next to Pix exclaimed. "We're the Bradys— no relation to the Bunch—Marge and Don." The introduction was so pat, Pix knew it had been repeated hundreds, maybe even thousands of times.

"Pix—is that a particularly New England name?" asked Louise Dahl. You *would* never guess the Dahls were twins. Unlike her sister, she was thin and her hair was straight and fine, falling slightly below her ears in what had been a bad cut and was getting worse as it grew out. The women appeared to be in their mid-forties.

Ursula gave her daughter a little pat on the hand. Think of Marit, it said. Think of Kari. You don't get information if you don't give, and this is no time to be standoffish, however much you dislike hearing this story in particular over and over again.

"No, it's a nickname that stuck. Pix was the tiniest little girl when she was born. We called her our 'little pixie.' That became Pix, and most people don't even know her given name, Myrtle—I am very partial to the ground cover; it has such lovely purple flowers."

Pix flashed a game smile at the table. "Of course, I didn't stay a pixie for too long, but by then, even I was so used to the name, we couldn't imagine changing it." She did leave out two facts—that Pix was definitely the lesser of two evils and that when she suddenly shot up to her adult height of five eleven in junior high school, she desperately wished her family could leave town and start over in a new place where she would be known as Jane.

"I hope you like fish," Don Brady said. "I'm about to start sprouting gills." Again, the Bradys seemed to have a set repertoire of remarks. His wife's smile was a bit thin-lipped.

"I'm very fond of fish, and it should be done well here. This is a famous old hotel," Ursula commented.

Her mistake was apparent in the looks the others gave one another. How come *she* knows so much? This upstart. Ursula quickly made amends. Pix and she had decided not to reveal their intimate knowledge of the country, all the better to find things out, and she'd slipped up. Hastily she added, "At least that's what it says in the brochure. I'm sure the guides and other staff have been giving you more details."

Peace reigned.

"It *is* a famous old hotel and it's still run by the same family, fourth generation. All these old hotels were built before World War One for the German and English who came here to fish and hunt," Marge reported. Pix noted the large tote bag beside Marge's chair, filled with guidebooks. The woman could lead the tour herself, hands down. But at the moment, Pix wasn't interested in the hotel's history. She was concerned with more recent events, and Ursula had given her an opening.

"How has the Scandie staff been? Someone on the train told us there had been a problem. A guide left or something like that?"

A waitress was bringing the first course, a Jarlsberg cheese tartlet, she told them.

Pix wasn't sure whether the silence that had fallen was due to the desire for food at this fashionably late dinner hour or uneasiness. Erna Dahl answered her question.

"The staff has been wonderful, especially Carl and Jan, the guides. They can't do enough for you and they are so informative."

"They don't talk too much, though," her sister pointed out. "I couldn't stand the type of tour where someone is constantly urging you to look at something, keeping up a stream of meaningless chatter." She took a bite of her tartlet. Pix was sure she gave her sister a look that had more to do with the subject Pix had raised than the flakiness of the crust. Erna sighed and her curls quivered slightly.

"We did have two staff members who left the tour and it made things a little awkward in Bergen."

"No one to carry the bags," grumbled Don Brady. "Irresponsible kids."

"They were running off together, eloping," Erna continued. "But something must have happened on the way. The boy—his name was Erik—drowned. A terrible accident."

Pix had no trouble voicing authentic concern. "How horrible! The poor girl!"

"Well, we don't really know how she's taking it," Marge said brightly. "She didn't come back, as you might expect, and we have two darlings now, Anders and Sonja. They're over there at the staff table."

Kari's and Erik's replacements were also blue-eyed, blond, and about the same age. Pix imagined that many of the people on the tour might have trouble telling them apart from Kari and Erik. Generic Nordics.

"When did all this happen?" Pix persisted. "It must have put a damper on the trip."

"We don't have any dampers on Scandie Sights tours," announced a pleasant voice speaking English with the slightly British accent many Norwegians have, which with the lilt makes the clipped speech sound like a whole new dialect. "I'm Carl Bjørnson, and you must be Mrs. Rowe and Mrs. Miller." He flashed a grin at Jan, who was by his side. "I must admit, I had some coaching. Welcome to the tour." He stretched out his hand.

"Is everything all right? Enjoying your dinner?" Jan asked. He still looked tired, yet some sort of liquid refreshment had bolstered his spirits. His voice was hearty and his cheeks flushed. His hair had been combed, but now the back of his shirt was untucked. He reminded Pix of her youngest child, Danny, almost thirteen, who could never seem to keep everything in place or clean all at once. If his shirt was tucked in, then a shoelace was untied. Hair combed, his hands would be dirty.

Carl was a head taller than Jan and would look younger longer, Pix instantly decided. Both men appeared to be in their mid- to late twenties, though Jan had already developed love handles that would no doubt continue to grow as his hair receded. Carl was lean, his eyes standard-issue blue, but his hair wasn't blond. Instead, dark curls covered his head, curls that even the close cut he sported couldn't quite tame. It gave him a slightly Mediterranean air, Norway by way of Barcelona. Definitely nice to look at.

He handed Pix and Ursula some sheets of paper. "This is our itinerary and we'll confirm all the times as we go along. No one has missed the bus, train, or boat yet." He sounded relieved. "The other page is a list of your fellow travelers and where they're from." He handed this single sheet to the rest of the table. "At the bottom, we've added the people who just joined us. Now everyone can get to know one another!"

Exactly, thought Pix, and thank you, Scandie Sights, for making my job a little easier. She was not interested in the new arrivals, since they wouldn't have been on the tour when Kari and Erik were with it. She'd need to find some way to figure out where the list divided, since the alphabetizing seemed erratic. Voluble Marge "Information, Please" Brady was the place to start.

Pix turned to her. "I wonder how many of us joined for the fjord cruise." It was enough.

"Oh, that's easy." Marge picked up her list. "Let's see. Oscar Melling is at the end of our list—I mean the group that started in Copenhagen." Clearly, Marge was sensitive to issues of exclusion. "That makes fifteen who joined at Voss."

"It seems like an extremely congenial group," Ursula said. "I'm sure we're going to have a lovely time together."

Mother paving the way for future conversation. Pix nodded in agreement—and approval.

"Yes, it has been a good bunch," Don agreed. Then, as a ruddy-faced elderly man strode by, he modified his statement. "Of course, you always have a rotten apple or two."

"Oh honey, not rotten! That's not the right word for Oscar!" She appeared embarrassed by her husband's bluntness.

Louise Dahl quickly began talking about the weather. "Only one day of rain in Bergen. And even that didn't last long."

Marge jumped in, a veritable geyser of facts, "Bergen's on the coast. You know if you measured it in a direct line, it would be about two thousand miles long, but it's really over twelve thousand five hundred with all the ins and outs. Plus, there are a hundred and fifty thousand islets offshore that protect the coast and make a kind of passageway for ships. The route was called the North Way—get it, Norway?"

They got it. Pix made a mental note to get Marge alone and find out more about Oscar. She scanned the list next to her plate—Oscar Melling, New Jersey. No town listed. Meanwhile, she held up her end by contributing a few meteorological comments of her own. How did people live in rainy places? Seattle was another, and so on.

The rest of the meal was uneventful: poached cod, boiled potatoes, apple cake. Because of the lateness of the hour, there was no evening program planned, although, Jan announced, the bar would stay open. He also urged a walk by the shores of Lake Vangsvatnet.

"And tomorrow, we don't bother you too early. No wake-up calls." A few people clapped. Pix hadn't thought about this aspect of the tour. "You have a nice breakfast, explore the village"—his *v* was a *w*—"and we'll leave for Stalheim at eleven o'clock."

Ursula and Pix said good night to the Dahls and the Bradys.

"Bed, yes?" Pix didn't know whether it was the time difference finally catching up with her or the situation she found herself in, but extreme fatigue had arrived.

"Yes, but first why don't you come to my room? We need to talk."

Pix had assumed she and her mother would be bunking down together. Yankee thrift would seem to preclude the hefty supplement for a room of one's own, but her mother had declared, "I like my own bath, dear. You'll be fine."

Marit had supplied them with a flask. "It's scandalous what they charge for a drink at the hotels," she'd said.

Ursula poured some scotch and the two sat by the window.

"Maybe we should make some notes," she suggested.

Pix shook her head. "Nothing written down. We aren't going to be handling our own bags, and even if we keep notes in our pocketbooks, it's a bit chancy."

"All right, then, what have we learned?"

"Not much," Pix said dismally. Her head was spinning. She really was tired and slightly disoriented. It was five o'clock in the afternoon eastern standard time and soon it would be tomorrow here.

"I thought the man at the station told you something," Ursula said. Pix had whispered words to that effect as they boarded the bus for the hotel.

"Yes, but I'm not sure where it fits in. No one saw Kari or Erik at Voss. They—or rather, Erik—phoned the station with the message that they were eloping."

"So they could have been anywhere."

"Yes. From what Marit said, the last place anyone actually saw either of them was on the train from Oslo to Flåm."

"I've taken it dozens of times," Ursula said. "It stops at an enormous waterfall, Kjosfossen, so people can take pictures. Kari and Erik would have gotten off the train then, wouldn't they, to make sure the tour group got back on again?"

"I remember Kjosfossen, too. Given that Erik was found in the river below, the waterfall would have been the most likely place for him to have fallen in, or whatever."

"Whatever," said her mother. Neither woman liked the other possible scenario, involving his fiancée and a mighty push.

"They weren't on the bus from Flåm to Aurland. Carl, the guide who spoke to Marit, was very specific about that." Ursula tipped her glass back and finished her drink.

"So Kari may have gotten off at Flåm and

taken another train or met someone there."
Pix had practically memorized the Scandie
Sights Mermaid/Troll brochure on the train
from Oslo. This particular tour, once having
reached Norway, tried to give its members the
quintessential Viking experience, which meant
plenty of fjords, folk museums, salmon, and
the Flåm railway. They took it down the
mountain, changed to a bus for the short
ride to Aurland, where their fjord cruiser
was waiting at the dock, took a ride up the Aurlandsfjord, an arm of the spectacular Sognefjord, then got on a bus to Voss and the train
to Bergen for several days. Now they were back
to fjord country again for a perfect finish.

Ursula stood up, opened her window to let
in the cool night air, and closed the shades
against the daylight.

"We have a lot to do tomorrow. We'd better divide up and talk to as many people as
we can. I thought that man at dinner tonight
seemed a little ill at ease, but it could have been
his wife—all those plans."

Marge Brady had told them that since her
husband's retirement, they were working
their way down her own personal list of the
wonders of the world. They'd already "done"
the pyramids, the Rock of Gibraltar, the
châteaux of the Loire, the Great Wall of
China, and gondolas in Venice. Fjords had been
next, to be followed by Mount Kilimanjaro.
Pix only just prevented herself from suggesting Marge send her list in to the Letter-
man show.

Pix kissed her mother good night. It was all

she could do to keep from crawling fully clothed under the *dyne* mounded on the bed in front of her. She hoped she could make it across the hall.

"Good night, dear. Sleep well." Her mother kissed her back and shut the door.

In bed, teeth brushed—the scotch would produce extremely unpleasant morning mouth—Pix had just enough mental energy for a nagging fear. Erik never made it to Flåm. Had Kari?

Was she dreaming or was she still on the train? Pix sat up in bed, confused. And what was that knocking sound? She looked at the clock. It was 2:00 A.M. and the knocking was at her door.

Mother! She ran to open it. What could be wrong?

But it wasn't her mother. It was a woman about her own age, but with radically different taste in night wear. Pix's was L. L. Bean, while the woman's was straight from the pages of Victoria's Secret.

"A man just tried to get from the balcony into my room and I can't make the phone work!" She was wide-eyed with fright.

Pix dashed to her own phone, the woman following closely. "I'm in the next room, one oh five. I thought Norway was supposed to be safe for women traveling alone!"

"But he didn't get in, right?" Pix asked as she waited for the front desk to answer.

"No. I screamed and he started to climb back

over. I didn't wait to see if he made it."

The front desk finally answered. Scarcely had Pix hung up when they heard the sound of running footsteps in the hall, voices, and, after a few moments, a knock on the door.

"Can you tell me what happened?" asked the young security guard standing outside in the hall. He looked like one of the Viking gods—tall, broad shoulders, fair hair, and deep blue eyes. For a fleeting moment, Pix wished she had opted for other than a granny gown. The woman from next door didn't have to worry.

"I was sound asleep." The damsel in distress stepped forward, earnestly beginning her tale. "I'm not sure what woke me, but the room felt stuffy and I got up to open a window. When I moved the curtain, I saw a man standing on the balcony. I screamed and he turned around, putting his leg up to climb out, I suppose. I was at the phone by then, but it wasn't working, so I came here."

The security guard said something into the walkie-talkie he was carrying. "Can you describe him?"

"He was tall, dark hair, a beard, and his clothes were dark. I couldn't tell how old he was. He was carrying some sort of bag. He'd thrown it to the balcony floor."

Carl and Jan appeared in the doorway, summoned by the hotel.

"Miss Olsen, are you all right?" Carl asked. "What happened?"

She went through it again.

Jan shook his head. "These rooms are quite

low to the ground and apparently someone thought he could get into the hotel this way. Maybe he thought the room was empty."

"Or maybe he thought you had something worth stealing," Carl said soberly. "But you had locked your balcony door, yes?"

"Yes, of course, and as for anything worth stealing—the most valuable thing I have is a Sony Walkman for jogging, and if that's what he wanted, he'd have been welcome to it, so long as he didn't do anything worse!"

The guard hastened to reassure her. "Crimes against individuals are very, very rare here."

The walkie-talkie sputtered and he put it to his ear.

"I'm afraid whoever he was, he's disappeared, but we will still be searching the grounds—and the hotel. He may have gotten in someplace else. Will you be all right in your room for the rest of the night?"

Pix looked at the other bed in her room. The poor woman. "You can stay here if you feel uneasy about going back into yours," she offered. "I know I would."

The woman gave her a grateful look. "Thank you. I would appreciate that."

Everyone cleared out and Pix went to secure the door. Her mother had apparently slept through the whole thing. She opened the door again and took a step into the hall, debating whether to check on Ursula, which would mean waking her up. She watched Jan and Carl go into their rooms, on the other side of Miss Olsen's. They were close by. It made her feel safe. She was sure Mother was fine.

Besides, there weren't any balconies on that side.

Inside the room, Miss Olsen was already in bed. There was quite a bit of gray mixed with her light brown hair, but she was very attractive. All that jogging had definitely paid off. She was slim and her complexion glowed, even at this hour.

"I'm Jennifer Olsen, by the way. Not a very good way to meet."

"No. I'm Pix Miller. I'm on the tour with my mother, Ursula Rowe. Are you sure you're all right? I have some scotch. Would you like some?"

Jennifer didn't seem to be too shaken up now, merely sleepy, but a little scotch never hurt.

"No thank you. I'm fine. It was unpleasant, but I knew he couldn't get in, and now it's the destruction of my ideal Norway that's upsetting me. You know, the perfect place to live, where you are taken care of from cradle to grave, everyone is honest, and everything is clean."

"I think the WATCH OUT FOR PICKPOCKETS sign in the train station reminded me Norwegians are like everyone else—good, bad, and in between." Pix didn't mention Erik and Kari. Not yet, anyway. Having Jennifer Olsen as a roommate for the night created an instant bond. Pix would wait and ask her questions in the morning, though. Now all she wanted was to go to sleep.

Pix rolled over and pulled the down comforter up to her chin. The other bed was empty. Damn! she thought. She'd missed a

64

golden opportunity to find out more about Jennifer Olsen and what Miss Olsen thought about the tour. She looked at the clock. It was past eight. In her family, anything past 6:30 meant you were ill or incredibly decadent. Fortunately, Pix had married a man who set her straight on early rising, but she was traveling with her mother at the moment. She jumped out of bed, skipped a shower, threw on some clothes, and went across the hall. He mother opened the door, fully dressed, and, from the strong scent of Neutrogena lotion that filled the air, fully showered.

"You must have been very tired, dear," she said in a not-too-accusatory voice. "Shall we have breakfast?"

Pix started to apologize, then remembered how many exhausting things she'd done in the last twenty-four hours, like fly across the ocean, travel across the *vidda,* and provide refuge in the middle of the night. She told her mother all about Jennifer as they went to the dining room.

"Do you think this man could have any possible connection to Erik's death and Kari's disappearance?" Ursula asked.

"Not really, but something out of the ordinary has already happened on this tour and we need to keep track of any other unusual events."

There is nothing quite like a Norwegian breakfast—the *smørgåsbord* laden with everything Pix liked to eat best: fruit compotes and pitchers of heavy cream; a cheese board; homemade breads and rolls; *knakkebrød,* thick, crisp whole-wheat crackers; *flatbrød,* paper-thin crackers; *wienerbrød,* Danish pastries; hot and cold cereals; a platter of *gravlaks,* fresh-cured salmon and smoked salmon; *leverpostei,* a kind of liver pâté; bowls of boiled eggs, hard and soft; sliced meats; and herring. Herring in cream sauce, herring in mustard sauce, herring in dill sauce, herring with onions and peppercorns. Herring, the "silver of the sea." The Norwegians largely survived on herring during the German occupation, drying, pickling, smoking, frying, and boiling it. Pix watched as an elderly group, speaking Norwegian, piled their plates high. One would have thought this generation would never want to see a herring again, but the opposite was true. They must feel grateful, she thought. Herring do run in cycles, returning each winter like clockwork for years—during which time, an old law stated, no lawsuits may be conducted, and everyone should fish—then the fish inexplicably disappear for twenty or thirty years. The group was laughing heartily. The herring hadn't deserted them and they were alive.

A young waitress was making heart-shaped waffles, "*vafler,*" and the smell was intoxicating (see recipe on page 349). Norwegians eat *vafler* with coffee and other cakes in the afternoon and thought the introduction of them to the breakfast menu—for the tourists— very funny. Pix noticed a tiny bottle of maple syrup. She didn't care when she ate them, but she would stick to the traditional way—a little butter and raspberry preserves.

Their plates laden, Ursula and Pix looked about the room for the Scandie Sights flags.

Most of the tables were filled, but they spotted places at a table for four. Two women of a certain age were already there, chatting away. Every once in a while, one would nibble a corner of a pastry or take a sip of coffee.

"May we join you?" Pix asked.

"Yes," said one, "I'm afraid my English is very poor, but please come." She was French. As Pix searched her mind for the remnants of Madame Durand's earnest efforts, grades seven through twelve, Ursula fluently introduced herself and her tongue-tied daughter, then proceeded to elicit the following information. The women lived outside Paris, were cousins, and took a trip together every year to break the routine. "We escape our husbands," the woman who had spoken before added in English for Pix's benefit. Her name was Sophie and Valerie was her *cousine*. "*C'est bizarre, le petit déjeuner norvégien,*" Valerie contributed to the conversation, fork poised above a fish cake. Pix had never thought of these splendid repasts as bizarre, but if one was used to a croissant and café au lait, this spread would definitely appear strange.

Carl strolled by. He and Jan wore matching Norwegian sweaters each day, it seemed. Jan's had a few pulls, but Carl's looked like new. Maybe he hadn't worked for the tour group that long. Maybe he was neater.

"How is everything, ladies?"

Mouths full, they all nodded. Pix found her voice first. "Do you know anything more about what happened last night?"

Carl gave a worried glance at the Frenchwomen. Obviously, Jennifer Olsen's adventure was not being posted with the day's events.

"No, nothing. But all's well that ends well," he said brightly and moved on.

One of your staff dead, one missing, and an intruder in the night. Pix did not think that all was well.

She tuned back in to the table conversation. Mother must have been listening to her French tapes again while she rode her Exercycle, Pix thought.

"They knew the tour would be in English, but they didn't think they needed to understand everything. It's all nature, and who needs words for that?" Ursula laughed. The cousins were smiling agreement. From what Pix knew of the French, she was sure the two believed that compared to their own history, art, and culture, the Norwegians were savages, so if they missed what year a particular stave church was built in, it would be no great loss.

After a second cup of coffee, Pix left her mother to her new friends and went back to the room to shower. But first she stepped out onto her own balcony. The door was equipped with a heavy drape to keep the light out, and since it had been partially drawn, she hadn't realized the balcony was there. It was furnished with two chairs and a small table. Pix peered over the edge. It was an easy climb up or down to the ground—or to Jennifer's room. The balconies were joined together. Tour groups were easy targets for thieves, even in Norway, and Pix was inclined to think that was all there was to it.

Feeling greatly refreshed by the shower, Pix got her things together, placing her bag outside the door as they had been instructed. Her mother's was already out and there was no answer to her knock. She decided to go down to the lobby and see if Ursula was there or if she might have decided to take a walk.

A bright voice greeted her as she entered the elevator. "I see you're another of the Scandie Sights group."

"Why yes, I am." Pix wondered how the woman knew.

"I saw you last night. Is that your mother with you? I told my husband it must be. You're like two peas in a pod. I'm Carol Peterson, from Duluth. In Minnesota. My husband, Roy, is with me and my son, Roy junior, and his new bride, Lynette. Lynette's not Norwegian, probably not a drop of Scandinavian blood in her body, but we love her anyway, and she wanted to take her honeymoon here to get to know our roots just as much as Roy junior did."

The elevator doors opened. They stepped out into the lobby and Carol finally came up for a breath. Pix knew she was expected to make a comment, and the one running through her head—something like wouldn't Lynette have rather had root canal work than come to Norway with her in-laws on her honeymoon—was not appropriate. She settled for a straightforward introduction.

"I'm Pix Miller, and yes, I am traveling with my mother, Ursula Rowe. We're from Aleford, Massachusetts."

"Massachusetts, now that *is* a coincidence. Roy was there for a convention in 1985. It was in Boston. That's the capital, right?"

"Yes, it is."

"I watch *Jeopardy!* a lot. I know all the state capitals. Everyone tells me I ought to go on, but I'd be too nervous, and besides, I don't think it's fair. Those buzzer things don't always seem to work right to me."

"Have you been with the tour since Copenhagen?" Pix was pretty sure she hadn't seen the name Peterson among the new arrivals, and the woman was a gift, a veritable font of information.

"Oh, yes, and it's been a dream come true. We're going to Kristiansand at the end of the tour. I have some cousins there I've never met. We wanted to stay in a hotel, but they just wouldn't hear of it."

Pix interrupted. It was close to 10:30 and she didn't want another chance to slip by. The buses would board at eleven.

"One of the people at our table last night was telling us about some trouble. That one of the staff drowned. It must have been horrible."

"Well, we didn't see him drown"—Carol Peterson was clearly of the "out of sight, out of mind" school—"and none of us really knew him." She paused, but Pix was sure she'd go on. There was empty air to fill. "The young people who took their place are much,

much better. More efficient and, believe me, much nicer." She punctuated the last comment with an extremely knowing look.

"Them? I thought it was just one person."

"He had this girlfriend. She was working on the tour, too. They slipped off to get married, which, I told Lynette, was very irresponsible, because if you elope, you're always sorry later. No gown and no presents. Oh, maybe a few, but nothing good."

"So, you thought it was irresponsible of them?" Pix tried to get her back on track, prying her away from place settings and a lifetime supply of Tupperware.

"Of course it was! To leave us all in the lurch like that. Why, Jan and Carl couldn't manage all the bags, and we got delayed while they tried to find out what happened to them, so we missed dinner in Bergen the first night!"

Pix tried to appear sympathetic, but it was hard. Very hard.

"You said the new people are nicer?"

"The boy was all right, although he seemed a little moody. I think when you're working on a tour like this, you should at least try to look cheerful. But the girl was a witch, if you know what I mean." Another look.

Pix did know and she was glad her mother wasn't there. All restraint might have vanished and Ursula could very well have clocked Carol Peterson one.

"Oh dear. It sounds as if you had a problem with her."

"I'll say I did. First off, we had this poky little room in the hotel in Copenhagen—the staff hands out the keys—and she wouldn't change it."

"Maybe all the keys had been given out," Pix said before she could stop herself. She wanted information and that meant not interrupting the silly woman's tirade, and certainly not sympathizing with Kari. "Although," she added quickly, "they can usually do something."

"Exactly!" Carol said triumphantly. "We did get switched, but I had to go over her head, and after that she really had it in for me. Every time I asked her to do something, she either took her sweet time or pretended not to hear me. She knew what I'd said, too, because she heard me telling Carl and Jan about her. I thought they should know—for the good of the tour."

The greater good, Pix thought dismally. Lord preserve us from all the things large and small resulting from this particular rationalization. She asked another question.

"How did you hear that the boy had drowned?"

"Jan told everyone and the police came. We were in Bergen. They wanted to know if anyone had seen anything. The girl has disappeared—or her body hasn't turned up yet. I think they had a fight and she pushed him in, then realized what she'd done and jumped after him. We know they'd been fighting. Helene Feld saw them when she went to get something to eat."

Bingo. Now Pix knew who had been the last to see them. She felt a warm—but brief—rush of gratitude toward Carol Peterson.

"There you are, dear." It was Ursula. Pix made the introductions, heard again what a small world it was, Roy senior having been to Boston in 1985, and vowed to stand back until she saw which bus the Peterson clan boarded.

Carol was the type who asked questions. Lots of questions.

3

The Petersons got on one bus and Pix steered Ursula onto the other. Jan was standing in the aisle at the front with a microphone.

"Now we are on our way to the famous Stalheim Hotel, making one stop for a 'photo opportunity' and time to eat our box lunches either on or off the bus, as you choose. Do I have any German-speaking people aboard?" He repeated the request in German. No one answered. "This is advertised as a bilingual tour, but so far, I have not had to use both languages."

Pix looked at the itinerary sheet. The bus trip would take them through a "wonderland of waterfalls and mountains," after which they would arrive at the hotel, "famous for its spectacular location and folk museum." After dinner, there would be a "program of traditional Norwegian folk dancing and music performed in native costume." The tour did not leave one at a loss for things to do. What with admiring the view, touring the museum, eating, and then clapping along—or whatever one did to the sounds of a Hardanger fiddle—it could be a very late night indeed. Pix sighed. At least Jan wasn't making a lot of inane comments, and the scenery was breathtaking. The waterfalls cascaded down the mountains in one long, sheer teardrop. They were passing through a beautiful densely wooded forest now and Jan picked up the microphone, resuming his position in the aisle.

"During the war, the Germans literally blew up Voss, and to this day, no one will buy wood cut from around here, because no factory will cut it. There are still so many bullets and pieces of metal embedded in the trees that it would break the machinery. Soon we will be coming to Tvindenfossen, a nice waterfall, and you can all take some pictures."

Ursula raised her eyebrows at her daughter. "Now we know why Jan wanted to be sure there weren't any Germans on board. Whenever I'm in Norway, I always feel as if the war ended only a short time ago. The Occupation was a terrible time."

The bus was stopping.

"Do you want to walk up to the *foss*?" Pix asked.

"I think I'll look at it from the parking lot and eat whatever this is at one of those picnic tables. You go and take a picture."

Pix had brought her camera to Norway as part of the disguise and also in case she needed to record something. She got out, following the rest of the herd up a well-worn path to look at the falls. They were not so dramatic as the one she remembered from Flåm, but steeper, starting far up in the mountains. She waited until almost everyone had gone to eat their lunches, so she could get a shot without people posing in front. Jennifer Olsen had apparently had the same idea and they walked back down together.

"Thank you so much for last night. I know I would have been fine in my room, but I was feeling a little shook."

In the light of day, Jennifer looked much less exotic than she did at night. She was wearing jeans, running shoes, a turtleneck, and a sweatshirt. The sweatshirt had NO PAIN, NO GAIN in script letters across the front.

"Well, you won't have to worry about anything happening tonight," Pix said. "The odds of something like that occurring twice in a row, or even in a year, must be infinitesimal in Norway."

"True. The funny thing is, I'm always looking over my shoulder at home. I live in Manhattan, but, knock wood, nothing has ever happened. I come here and... Well, I'm just going to put it out of my head. I don't want to spoil the rest of the trip with negative thoughts. It's been wonderful."

Pix wished she could shelve her negative thoughts. Even the beauty of Norway couldn't blot out the image of Erik's death and Kari's disappearance. She wasn't here for pleasure and she slowed her pace. Jennifer, traveling alone, might have observed more than, say, Carol Peterson.

"But I understood there was trouble earlier in the trip—a staff problem?"

Jennifer stopped in the middle of the path. Her face darkened. "It was horrible. All some people could think about when someone was dead was having to carry their own luggage."

"Dead?" It was easy for Pix to sound alarmed.

"We don't really know what happened. Kari and Erik were a young couple working for Scandie Sights—doing what Anders and Sonja do now. They ran away to get married and somehow he was swept into a river and drowned. Her body hasn't been found yet." Jennifer sounded very sure that Kari had drowned, too. Pix felt her stomach turn. Could it be just that? The two of them running off and then a terrible accident? But what about Kari's last words to Marit, the words that had been interrupted?

"Such a tragedy," she said inadequately.

"Yes, life's a bitch," replied Jennifer, walking rapidly now, as if she feared all the food would be gone. Pix felt a little guilty as she sat down next to her mother and opened the box lunch. So much for helping Jennifer avoid negative thoughts.

"You have seen Tvindenfossen and now we have the Tvinde River." On the way again, Jan had resumed his role, after eating his lunch alone. "It's a very good salmon river, and in Norway, anyone can fish anywhere— even private property is open to the public—but you need to ask and maybe pay a small fee, about ten kroner. There're plenty of places to fish for everyone without overcrowding. Norway has so many lakes that we figure there are about two fishermen for each one. We fish all year long, and Lake Vangsvatnet, the one we just left in Voss, is the site of a large ice-fishing festival every winter. Not for people with thin skins." Somehow Jan managed to make all this sound unrehearsed. A kind of stream of consciousness, like the waters rushing past them outside. He gazed out the window, thought of something, and spoke. "We have a legend about the Tvinde River, too. If you drink its water every day of your life, you'll never get old. It's just a legend, of course." He sounded disappointed.

"No thank you," Ursula announced firmly. "One of the pleasures of being old is that you don't have to be young again, especially a teenager."

Pix and her friend Faith tended to think that their lives were destined to be an endless repetition of junior high school, so this was good news, but Pix did wonder what her mother was referring to. She'd always imagined her mother's adolescent years as happy times—picnics in the countryside, rowing on the river. She realized that whatever Ursula might be recalling was obviously not in the family photograph albums.

The rest of the ride was quiet and Pix spent the time thinking about her fellow Scandie tourists. The Bradys, the Petersons, the Dahl sisters, the French cousins, and Jennifer Olsen had all been on the tour since the beginning. They seemed to be a run-of-the-mill group, maybe a little heavy on the

Scandinavian surnames, but from the look of the list, half the tour seemed to be in search of roots. Pix remembered Marit telling her that in the nineteenth century and the early years of the twentieth, almost 900,000 Norwegians emigrated to North America because of the growth in population in Norway and scarcity of resources. At one time or another, almost everyone has had a cousin in Minneapolis or Brooklyn.

Jan was talking about the Stalheim Hotel as the bus climbed up the steep road. "It's the fourth hotel built on this spot. The first one was erected in 1885. The Nærøy Valley, which you will see far below you when we stop, and the surrounding area have always been a favorite place for holidays. The kaiser liked it so much, he came twenty-five summers in a row."

"The kaiser is not quite the villain on the west coast as he is elsewhere," Ursula whispered to Pix. "I've been to these places before with Marit and it's kind of like 'Washington slept here.' "

"But why?" Pix was puzzled.

"Oh, he was always giving stained glass to the churches or statues to towns, even helping to rebuild an entire one in the case of A∞lesund, after a fire destroyed it. Benevolent. Had to keep his vacation land pleasant, and he really liked to fish and hunt."

Pix was listening to Jan; surprisingly, she found it pleasant to be picking up these tidbits of information.

"Finally after the first three buildings

burned down, they got smarter and built the present hotel out of concrete in 1960." It was painted red and appeared not unattractive, Pix thought. And given its location perched on the mountaintop, putting out a blaze would prove difficult. Jan had a few more morsels. "The same family, the Tønnebergs, has been running it now for sixty years. During the war, the Germans took it over."

Of course, Pix said to herself, and she began wondering if there was a particular reason why Jan was so intent on refreshing their memories. Had his family suffered a particularly severe loss?

"They used the hotel for one of their *Lebensborn* homes, Himmler's little experiment to repopulate the world after the war with only the best stock."

He didn't elaborate and Pix felt a chill. Not exactly what she wanted to hear about the place she would be staying, although the wartime structure was in ashes far below the present foundation. Her mother was looking out the window as the bus pulled up to the entrance and she turned to speak to Pix.

"You should go see the houses in the folk museum if there's time. I'm sure you remember the one in Oslo, but even though these houses have been moved, they're from the area around here and more or less in their natural setting."

"I'll try," Pix said, "but I want to talk to some more people and, if possible, squeeze in a sauna."

"All right. I'm going to lie down for a

while; then I'll write postcards in the lobby and see if I can make some friends, too."

Pix had no doubt the gregarious traveler Ursula, aka Mother, would.

She wished people wore name tags, much as she would hate to sport a "Hello, I'm Pix" badge herself. She wanted to search out Helene Feld and hear about the quarrel she'd witnessed on the train between Kari and Erik. Reminding herself that if you don't ask, you don't get, she went up to Carl. If the Petersons weren't on his bus, or maybe even if they were, she thought they should switch to it tomorrow and compare the two guides. The guides, after all, had been on the tour since Copenhagen, too.

"I wonder if you would mind pointing out the Felds to me. I have a friend who lives in the same town and I wonder if they know her." The Felds were from Mount Vernon, New York, and Pix did know someone from there—but she'd moved years ago. Still…

Carl seemed delighted to have something to do for her. He really was terribly attractive. She wondered how many broken hearts there were at the end of each Scandie Sights tour.

He looked around. "The Felds must already have gone to their rooms, but I will point them out to you at dinner and let them know you'd like to meet them. Perhaps you can sit together. They are quite friendly."

Pix had the feeling he was talking about approachable pets. "That would be lovely. Thank you."

The lobby was empty, but the gift shop

was full. Pix decided it was not conducive to an exchange of intimacies. Hard to fit in a pointed question when someone was intent on a hand-knit sweater. The sauna would give her a chance to collect her thoughts.

Demurely wrapped in a towel, Pix sat in the sauna and sweated. There were several other occupants, all men, none of whom she recognized from the tour. Every once in a while, someone would leave to take a cold shower, reenter, and throw some more water from the wooden bucket on the hot rocks, creating a sudden hiss of steam. Pix was doing the same. The fragrance of the hot wood and the intense heat was soporific. She found herself battling sleep. It was so relaxing. So very, very relaxing.

Someone shook her. "It's not a good idea to fall asleep in here. You shouldn't stay in too long, especially if you haven't taken one in a while." It was Lynette Peterson, and Pix couldn't help but think how much more flattering the towel was on the young bride than on her own middle-aged body.

"Thank you. I'm only going to stay in a little longer. My name is Pix Miller. My mother and I are on the Scandie tour, too. I met your mother-in-law this morning at the hotel." Pix felt obliged to explain how she had recognized the woman. Lynette was not surprised.

"Oh, I know all about you. Carol told us. You're from Boston."

"Actually, about twenty minutes outside the city."

A slightly wicked smile appeared. "Carol

thinks it's Boston. She likes to know things. That's the main activity of my mother-in-law's life—besides organizing things. I'll let her know she's wrong."

Pix didn't envy Roy junior. The Battle of the Titans was getting under way and it would go on for his entire married life, until his mother died or his wife walked out, both acts certain to be interpreted as victory by the other side.

"Are you enjoying the trip?" Pix thought it was worth a try to question Mrs. Roy Peterson, Jr. She might have picked up on something between Kari and Erik that the others had missed. Lynette took her time responding to the opening.

Pix had teenagers. Lynette's face had "Give me a break" written all over it.

"Look, Mrs. Miller"—Pix instantly felt ten years older—"is fish for every meal, a million museums, and your in-laws along your idea of what a honeymoon should be?" She answered her own question. "Of course it isn't. We should be in Bermuda, but we're not, because Carol decides this is her golden opportunity to show Roy the land of his people. It was his great-grandparents who came from here! He never even knew them! And it's not as if we live in... well, Boston. Duluth is about as close as you can get to Norway without hopping on a plane. But I agreed. There's something Carol doesn't know, and when she does, she'll be ripping. As I said, Carol likes to know things. Nosiest woman I ever met. She was even asking Roy whether he'd moved his bowels every morning until the third time, I said he'd let her know if he didn't and let's drop the subject. She didn't like that, not one little bit. And she's not going to like what's coming, either."

Pix was finding the daughter-in-law as loquacious as the mother-in-law, more even. Although the tone was the same. Who said men don't marry their mothers? Pix quickly focused on Sam's mother, a charming lady who'd died several years ago, much mourned by everyone.

"I'm sorry things aren't going well. This should be a very happy time for you." It was all she could think of to say, and she stood up as she said it, ready to leave while some remnants of the lack of tension the sauna had induced remained.

"Oh, I'm happy, very happy." She spoke through slightly clenched teeth. Her towel had slipped. From the appearance of her firm young breasts, Roy junior was probably happy, too, at least in bed. Lynette tugged at the towel, then, irritated, took it off, either oblivious or indifferent to the sauna's other occupants. Pix closed the door behind her and headed for the showers. What surprise did Lynette have for her mother-in-law? Suddenly, it didn't seem like a fair fight at all.

Ursula was sitting by the wall of glass at the end of the hotel lobby, a wall that served to magnify the view. The mountains appeared to be a few steps away, especially the tallest, its rocky summit high above the timberline. The peak had a slight purple cast to it. Pix walked toward her mother. The mountains were in fact close, the hotel surrounded by them, and only a large well-kept flat green lawn separated the front of the hotel from the precipitous drop to the valley far below.

Ursula had made friends, two slightly grizzled-looking older men, faces reddened from working outdoors, and something else perhaps. Mother was drinking coffee. Her new friends were sticking to beer.

"Oh, there's my daughter now." Ursula waved Pix over. "This is Mr. Knudsen and that's Mr. Arnulfson. My daughter, Pix Miller." The men stood and shook hands. "We were just talking about how we all came to be on the tour. Mr. Knudsen and Mr. Arnulfson are from North Dakota. Such a long way from home!"

Mother was sounding perky, even slightly coquettish. It was working.

"You must call me Ole—everyone does— and he's Henry. Anyway, as I was saying, the whole thing was that fool Svenson's fault."

Henry nodded solemnly and drained half his glass.

"My sister read about a tour of Norwegian farms in the Sons of Norway newsletter and thought the lodge might want to go. 'See how they're doing things over there,' she said. 'Be a good chance and very cheap.' So at the next meeting, we counted heads and decided to do it."

This explained the large number of males

84

from Fargo on the list—Norwegian bachelor farmers. Pix had seen them sticking together like glue and assumed they were some sort of group. Sons of Norway, of course.

"But I don't think this tour has many farms. Just one, on the fjord after we reach Balestrand," Ursula commented.

Henry nodded slowly and finished his beer.

"That fool Svenson"—the three words had become his full name—"wrote down the wrong tour number on the form when he sent in our deposits. He's our treasurer, or was, and when we found out the money was nonrefundable, we decided to go. No sense in wasting it. They make a big-enough profit. So we came."

Henry joined the conversation briefly. "We never should have put that fool Svenson in charge, his mother being Swedish and all. Anyone want another drink?"

No one did and the farmers ambled along. As soon as they were out of sight, Pix began to laugh until she thought she'd cry.

"I think we can eliminate them from whatever it is we're listing," she said.

"Yes, they seem to travel in a pack, poor things. You notice they're always first on the bus, by the door, or in the dining room. They must be terrified of getting lost or left behind."

"Have you made any other friends?"

"I chatted some more with Valerie and Sophie. I have the feeling their English is much better than they're letting on. Marge Brady joined us and they had no trouble speaking with her. She was telling them all about French châteaux."

"How nice for them."

"Don't be naughty, Pix. But I did learn something interesting. Don Brady is retired from the oil business. And there's another man on the tour, a Mr. Harding from Connecticut, who's currently working for an oil company."

Pix was slow on the uptake. "Why is this interesting?"

"Mr. Harding's is a Norwegian-owned company and Don Brady's had ties to the industry here. You do know about the North Sea oil?"

"Now, don't *you* be naughty. Of course I do. It's what catapulted the country from getting by to just about the world's highest standard of living. But how does it all connect to Kari and Erik?"

"When I was here last summer, there was a great deal of talk about what they call the Russian mafia operating in Norway, using any means necessary to learn exactly where the Norwegian oil fields are and the technology that located them. There's been a dispute for years over the Russian/Norwegian border in the Barents Sea, up north. The Russians are desperate to find some oil or natural gas of their own there and the stakes are very high, I read recently."

There is nothing like *The Christian Science Monitor* every day to keep you informed, Pix reflected. Maybe she should switch from *The Boston Globe*. Faith, of course, clung to *The New York Times* and was always borrowing the Millers' paper to find out what was on

86

television. But this was all interesting. If someone was using the tour groups to pass secret information concerning the oil industry and Erik or Kari had learned of it... Any means necessary.

"All right, we'll add oil to everything else—and Russians. I'd almost forgotten that Norway has a common border with them in the north. Maybe Marit has some idea about how this might fit in. The tour didn't go to Stavanger, but Bergen is as big an oil town."

"I wonder if she's heard any more from the police. I bought *Aftenposten* and took it to my room. I couldn't read it, but Kari's name wasn't anywhere, so there hasn't been anything new in the press."

"That's good. They're onto something else and Marit doesn't have to see her life distorted. It must have been horrendous."

Pix told her mother about the encounter with Lynette in the sauna and Pix's request to Carl for an introduction to the Felds at dinner. She didn't want her mother to think she'd been idling away in the steam.

"Then we should certainly make it a point to be on time for the meal," Ursula said, leading the way. As if there was any question.

Not surprisingly, the Felds had never heard of Pix's friend, but they were a friendly, outgoing couple. Arnie was an intellectual properties lawyer and Helene was an art historian. They had no children and had traveled extensively. This was their second trip to Norway.

Pix was sure that Helene, who seemed quite intelligent, would be able to give her some idea of the nature of the quarrel between Kari and Erik. The question was how to bring it up. For the moment, the big decision was over poached salmon or smoked pork. The whole table took the salmon, as well as the wild mushroom soup first and "fruits of the woods" with vanilla sauce for dessert.

Spooning a large, ubiquitous boiled potato onto her plate, Pix asked the Felds how they had liked the tour so far.

"It's been very well organized," Helene answered. "I wanted to spend extra time in the Norsk Folkemuseum on Bygdøy, the peninsula across the fjord from Oslo. I'm sure you've heard of it. It's where both the Viking ships and *Kon-Tiki* are. Anyway, there was no problem. Some tours make you stick rigidly to their schedule. The same in Bergen. I had never visited the Museum of Decorative Arts and wanted to go there instead of some of the other places on the itinerary. I missed the tram ride up to Fløyen, but people said it was misty and they didn't get such a clear view of the city. What has also made the tour interesting is that both Carl and Jan are extremely knowledgeable guides. They must bone up on things during the winter."

"What kind of art are you particularly interested in?" Ursula asked.

"Originally, it was wood carving—especially those wonderful Romanesque vines and ribbons combined with the zoomorphic forms that descended from Viking times and are still influencing Norwegian art today. Those lovely dragons!" Helene's glasses had slipped down her nose and she was gesturing expansively. "At first, I disliked rosemaling, overly influenced by the bad imitations in all the gift shops—those overblown roses and swirls painted in garish colors on everything from rolling pins to toilet seats!"

Ursula nodded. "I know, but the older work is very beautiful."

"Exactly," Helene agreed. "And all that color and decoration are more in character with the exuberant Norwegian temperament than the constraint of the Early Christian carved wooden forms." The glasses inched down a little farther. Pix watched in fascination, wondering if the spectacles would tumble into Helene's soup with the next folk-art era.

"It's good to hear someone refer to the Norwegians as exuberant," Ursula commented. "I get so tired of all those other adjectives—*staid, placid.* You know what I mean. The Norwegians I've met seem fully capable of kicking up their heels." Pix noticed her mother was drawing back from details, but scenes of uproarious parties and joke telling crowded into Pix's mind. She and Sam had visited shortly after they were married. Every relative of Hans's and Marit's had been bent on welcoming them. Even now, many years later, when Sam imbibed a bit too much, he'd tell his wife he was merely getting in training for Norway.

Arnie Feld agreed. "Somebody was having

an anniversary party in one of the private dining rooms at the hotel in Oslo, and from the sounds of mirth, I'd definitely say Norwegians know how to have a good time. And remember that couple we met on the train, honey?"

His wife nodded, still lost in contemplation of carved butter boxes and painted rooms.

"They were singing, not too loudly, and writing furiously on the back of an envelope. They were having so much fun, I finally had to ask them what was going on. They were composing a song for her sister's fortieth birthday, and after we talked awhile, they invited us to come along! I wish we could have." He sounded genuinely disappointed, and Pix could understand why. Helene was still eager to talk about her passion for the folk arts of the country, though.

"Now I've become fascinated with the jewelry," she continued.

"She's always been fascinated with jewelry. Don't let her fool you," Arnie said good-naturedly.

She made a face at him. "Don't worry. Even if we were millionaires, we couldn't take the kind of jewelry I love out of the country. Norway has very strict laws about exporting antiques."

Carl and Jan came by the table for their nightly check, picking up on the last word.

"Antiques?" said Carl. "Mrs. Feld's favorite subject! I hope you have been having a good time with Mr. Tønneberg's collection. By the way, don't miss the Hardanger bridal crown in the hallway. It's in a glass case high up on the wall. This one is extremely elaborate and very rare. During the 1800s in Norway, silver became scarce and many families turned their old heirlooms over to the state to be melted down. Brass was used instead for jewelry."

"I did see it," Helene enthused. "It's gorgeous. Is the collection cataloged? I saw a bowl that looks like it was painted by the 'Sogndal painter'—this area around the Sognefjord has spectacular natural beauty, but it hasn't produced the art that other areas have, particularly those on the east coast and in Telemark. Too rugged a life, too poor, but this painter—we don't even know his name—is the exception. He traveled all over the region in the mid-eighteenth century, which must have been difficult, and no other rosemaling has ever equaled his."

"I know the bowl you mean," Carl said. "The colors are so bright and the background is very soft, the blue-green he traditionally used. Very beautiful."

"And worth a fortune," Jan added. "If we had anything like it in my family, we probably used it for kindling. I grew up in the district and life was strictly practical!" He laughed.

Helene looked pained. "I hope not." The salmon arrived on a huge platter. There was enough for two tables.

"Of course I am teasing you," Jan told Helene. "My mother has her great-grand-mother's engagement spoons, and if there was a fire, she'd grab those, then think of us!" It seemed impossible for the young man not to make a joke out of most remarks.

"Engagement spoons are two spoons connected by a long chain all elaborately carved
out of one piece of wood," Helene explained.

"I like the symbolism." Ursula was busy helping herself to the fish. Pix could see it was perfectly poached, moist flakes falling to one side.
There was hollandaise sauce, but Pix knew
she wanted hers plain.

"We will leave you to enjoy your dinner,"
Carl said. "We have a few announcements we'll
make during dessert."

Pix tried in vain during the rest of the
meal to turn the conversation to Kari and Erik's
quarrel on the train, but short of rudeness,
it proved impossible to get Helene off her
favorite subject. They heard a great deal
about *tiner,* the butter and pudding boxes
used to bring gifts of food to relatives or
friends at weddings or other occasions, and
much more about jewelry, especially *bunads-
solv,* wedding jewelry.

"I wonder if modern Norwegians are as
superstitious as their ancestors," Ursula
mused after a treatise from Helene about
the use of silver to keep the trolls, those
direct descendants of the Viking pagan gods,
from harming mortals.

"There is certainly a renewed interest in the
old jewelry and its use and legends. Saga
makes wonderful reproductions, with an
explanation accompanying each piece. As
for warding off evil, I'm not sure. I know I said
Norwegians are exuberant, but they also
seem remarkably down-to-earth and even-tem-
pered."

It was now or never.

Pix put down her fork. Her plate was clean; so was the fish platter. "Yet not without passion. I understand the tour had some sort of tragic incident before we joined you, a double suicide by two lovers." She stifled the urge to give Ursula an apologetic glance. "They ran away together, then apparently took their own lives."

Helene stiffened and the color drained from her face. Arnie looked annoyed.

"Well," he said.

"No, we can't not talk about it, Arnie. Apparently rumors abound." She pushed a stray strand of gray hair behind her ear to join the others loosely gathered in an ornate barrette at the nape of her neck. Then she waited while their plates were cleared and the table was swept clean of the crumbs their crusty dinner rolls had produced.

"Kari and Erik were working as stewards for the tour, handling the luggage, helping people find their rooms, that sort of thing. What Anders and Sonja are doing now. First we heard that they had eloped, and while it was a bit inconvenient, these things happen and we could only wish them well, but then the police arrived at the hotel to question all of us. Erik's body was found in the river by Flåm. Kari is still missing."

"How sad," Ursula said, "and how difficult for all of you, being questioned, I mean."

Thank you, Mother.

"Well, yes—yes, it was. It turned out I was the last person from the tour to have seen them and the police talked to me three times. It was a bit nerve-racking, especially as I didn't have much to tell them."

"They must have thought you did." Pix was eager to keep the woman talking. She'd been unstoppable on antiques but was understandably reticent now.

"I was looking for something to eat and thought I'd see if one of those carts was in another car. I came up behind them and was all set to greet them when I realized they were arguing."

"A lovers' spat?" Ursula was holding her own.

"I don't speak Norwegian, so I have no idea what they were quarreling about, but Kari's face was very red and she had tears in her eyes. She was doing most of the talking. Erik was sitting there. He didn't look angry, just... Well, I think what I told the police was that he looked determined. Like someone who has made up his mind. And Kari seemed to be trying to get him to change it."

"Do you think he was contemplating suicide?" Pix asked. She could see Kari so clearly. The girl did have a temper, and when she lost it, the words flowed like lava.

"I couldn't say for sure, but I think if he had been, Kari would have looked more sad, more desperate than angry. She was shaking her finger at him, and somehow if he had been planning to kill himself, she would have perhaps had her arms around him. The whole thing looked... looked like she was scolding him."

Pix had been right. The woman had taken note of the body language.

"It was very awkward. I didn't want to intrude and go past them, yet I really was terribly hungry. Sometimes my blood sugar gets very low, and usually I carry some granola bars, but I'd used them up and needed something to eat."

So, Helene Feld had stood in the aisle for some time, Pix thought. Long enough to form a lasting impression.

"Then what happened? Did they make up?"

"The food cart came through the door. Kari got up to help the woman, saw me, and was immediately concerned that I find something to eat. She warned me that the *lefse*—you know, that flatbread that has potatoes in it—would taste like cardboard and recommended the yogurt with muesli. She was a very sweet girl. The whole thing is such a mystery."

The "fruits of the woods" arrived: blackberries, tiny strawberries, and a few precious *multer*—cloudberries—a delicacy that grew only above the timberline. Helene sighed. "I hope we find out what happened before we go home. I hate it when things are left up in the air."

Pix felt exactly the same way.

Jan was clanking the side of his empty glass. Drinks were extra, even bottled water, milk, and soft drinks. Pix and Ursula had stuck to whatever was coming out of the tap at Stalheim after being reminded by the Felds. She'd have to wire home for more

95

money or find an ATM somewhere in these mountains if she didn't watch her kroner carefully, Pix realized.

"Tomorrow we will board our Viking fjord cruiser and spend the day on the water, with one short stop to see a stave church, after which, we will arrive at the famous Kvikne's Hotel in Balestrand. Then the following day, a stop in the afternoon to visit a farmer and taste his *gjetost,* delicious Norwegian goat cheese."

There were a few groans. Pix was tempted to add hers. She'd tasted the cheese, caramel-colored and sweet, sticking like peanut butter to the roof of one's mouth, but with far greater tenacity. Marit used it in everything, even gravy. She'd given Ursula a recipe for pheasant in *gjetost* cream sauce that Pix, as a joke, had passed on to Faith, who still refused to believe it was real.

Ursula tapped her daughter on the shoulder. "Look at Mr. Arnulfson and his friends."

The bachelor farmers were beaming. It was definite. A farm. Well, well, well, they'd have to have a look at this. Maybe set the man straight on a few things. Pix found herself giggling. She knew that in Norwegian spinsters were called "old girls." She wondered what the term was for unmarried men. These were certainly "old boys."

"We will be spending the next two nights at Kvikne's Hotel, as you know from your itinerary. Now the bad news. We have a wake-up call ordered for six A.M."

Groans again.

"So, if you'll please have your luggage outside your doors by seven, we'll have breakfast and be on our way."

Pix had been forgetting she was on a tour. It all had been so pleasant and relaxed, except for the reason she was there. Still, six in the morning was nothing for the Rowe family. Ursula would no doubt be ready well before then.

"When you have finished your dinner, we will take coffee in the lobby and watch a program of Norwegian folk dancing. They are very good and I think you will like it. Any questions?"

"If we can get ready really fast, do we have to have the call at six?" asked Jennifer Olsen.

"No, of course not. You can inform the desk and make any arrangement you want," Jan answered.

They had been talking so much, they were among the last tables to leave the dining room, and Pix had the odd sensation that she was watching a play as the whole cast of characters walked past, nodding at them or saying a few words. The Bradys, the Petersons— with a playful injunction from Carol to hurry up or they'd miss the show—the North Dakota farmers, Valerie and Sophie, the Dahl sisters, and an older man who stopped to chat.

Arnie Feld made the introductions. "This is Oscar Melling. Mrs. Rowe and her daughter, Mrs. Miller. Is there a game tonight, Oscar? He's been playing pinochle with the group from the Sons of Norway almost every evening," he explained.

"Oh, they're a bunch of sour losers. Said I can't play anymore. That I was cheating too much." He winked at Ursula. "You notice they said 'too much.' That's because all of them were cheating like crazy. They'll get over it and we'll probably have a game tomorrow. They've been playing with one another so long, they're desperate to play with anyone new. Do either of you ladies play?"

He was a barrel-chested man of medium height, his bald head fringed with steel gray hair. The same hair protruded over his upper lip, from his ears, and snaked across his forehead in one long, scraggy brow. Oscar seemed intent on displaying any and all of a hirsute nature left to him. His eyes were deep blue and he had probably been quite handsome in his youth. He was not without charm now, partially because he worked so hard displaying it. Pix had noticed him before. He was never without a smile—or a companion. The tiny fretwork of red veins on his face indicated he was fond of supplementing this bonhomie with a glass or two.

"Sorry, I never learned the game."

"I knew it once, but it's been many years since I've played," Ursula revealed.

"You'll remember in no time. I'll let you know if we get enough people for a game," Oscar promised, then bowed slightly and left.

"What is Mr. Melling's occupation?" Ursula asked the Felds.

"He had a grocery store in New Jersey that specialized in Scandinavian foods. He started doing mail order and now that's the entire business, I gather. He was talking about going on the Internet this fall. A pretty astute businessman, I'd imagine," Arnie answered.

The picture of her mother sitting in a smoke-filled room of pinochle players—the farmers all smoked pipes and Oscar had a cigar peeking out of his shirt pocket—was too much for Pix. She started to laugh, tried to explain, and gave it up. "I think I'll go get some places for the dancing." She assumed the Felds would sit with them.

"You do that. We'll catch the end of the program. I want to take some pictures of the buildings in the folk museum. The light is perfect now," Helene said.

Pix and Ursula had no sooner sat down with their coffee when three young couples dressed in their traditional regional costumes—*bunad*—came dancing across the slate floor of the Stalheim Hotel's lobby, accompanied by a seventh young woman vigorously playing the fiddle. It was wonderful. The boys were wearing dark knee britches with long white socks, silver buckles on their shoes, and silver buttons on their red wool vests, their white shirts starched crisply. The girls' costumes were more elaborate, dark full skirts, long white aprons with intricate Hardanger lace panels, silver-buckled belts, red wool sleeveless bodices with bright, beautifully embroidered inserts and long, full-sleeved white blouses. The necks of the blouses were fastened with large silver brooches. As they danced to the lively music, Pix found herself missing Samantha in particular. She could imagine her daughter swirling around gracefully, a bright smile for the crowd. Not a bad summer job, although if it ever got hot, the costumes would be unbearable. As it was, one of the boys had taken his handkerchief out several times to mop his brow. One couple in particular danced beautifully, their steps in perfect synchrony. They reminded Pix of the older couples one saw at weddings whose steps, meshed by time, executed flawless fox-trots, rumbas, all those dances no one knew anymore. Vernon and Irene, Fred and Ginger, Kathryn and Arthur—the sixties had put a stop to the steps.

She was amused to note the twentieth-century encroachments on the scene, which at first glance could have been a wedding celebration from the last century. One boy had a slightly purple streak in his hair. Two of the girls had multiple holes in each ear.

"Now, we need your help," the fiddler said, giving her instrument to one of the dancers to hold and then tapping six people quickly. One was Jennifer Olsen, who sprang to her feet, not making even the token protest of the others.

"We call this the 'Jealousy Dance.' The two dancers on either side are trying to win the favor of the one in the middle. My friends will demonstrate; then you will do it!"

It was really very funny. As the dancers moved forward, they nodded and smiled to the person in the middle; then, moving back, they turned their heads and scowled at each other, shook their fists, and then, as the music changed, put on a pleasant face again.

Jennifer was very agile and dramatic. She was enjoying herself—positive vibes.

Pix watched and thought idly, Public faces, private faces. Which is real? What does that public mask hide? He was such a nice, quiet man, we never dreamed he... So many news accounts contained slight variations of those words. Behind one's back. She watched Jennifer shake her fist at her competitor. Jealousy, powerful emotion. Erik and Kari, the two lovers. Was there someone in the middle—or at the side?

"Pix, dear, I think when they're finished, I'll go to bed early tonight. I want to be on time in the morning." Her mother's words broke into her thoughts.

Pix wasn't tired at all. "I may stay down here or take a walk."

The dancers finished to huge applause. Jennifer flopped into a chair next to Pix's. "That was fun!"

One of the girls had stepped forward and was explaining the significance of her costume. "I have three rows of velvet on my skirt because I'm not married yet." The boy she'd been dancing with looked very smug. She tossed her head.

"And if you want one like it"—she was referring to her elaborate brooch—"you will find them for sale all over Norway, and here, too, in the shop"—she gestured—"but not the real ones, of course. They are very old." She wagged her finger playfully. "Norway is a small country and we don't have very many old things, so we need to keep them here!"

"They are strict," Jennifer said. "You can't take anything out of the country that's over a hundred years old unless you can prove it was in your family. If you get caught, it's a very stiff fine for you and the person who sold it to you."

Pix nodded. "Helene Feld was telling us about this at dinner."

A man on the other side of Jennifer joined the conversation. "You can't blame them. Look at what's happened to other countries. If you're Greek, you have to go to London to look at your past. Norway also holds on to her land. It's pretty impossible to buy property if you're not Norwegian." He mimicked the girl, "Norway is a small country and needs to keep everything here!" He laughed. "Doesn't want to become a European vacation colony is more like it."

Pix was glad. In a very short period of time, she had become remarkably partisan.

Another kind of music was coming from the bar, but Pix was intoxicated by her unusual freedom and the long light outside, not Ringnes beer or aquavit. She knew she would not be able to sleep for some time and so she strolled outdoors in the direction of the folk museum. It was farther up the steep road and separated from the hotel by a wooden gate.

She assumed at this time of night, it would be locked, but it yielded at her touch. Soon she was admiring the old dark wooden farm buildings with their sod or slate roofs. The slate roofs looked like fish scales and when she stumbled across a pile of tiles leaning against a tree, she noted the shape of each one did indeed look like a whole fish. Lichen clung to the slate, touching the gray with yellow ocher and varied shades of green. One of the sod roofs was so overgrown with tiny fir trees and other vegetation that it wasn't until Pix noticed a chimney that she realized there was a house below her on the mountain.

She climbed and climbed, smelling the sweet night air, air heavy with moisture. The moss beneath her feet was like a sponge. Her footsteps were silent. She peeked in the small windows, tried a few doors, only to find them locked, and spotted a small nest in the sod. Far above the hotel, but still on the path, the air was colder. The character of these woods would have been the same during the war. She imagined those women, inhabitants of—what had Jan called it, a *Lebensborn* home, one of Himmler's projects? Pix shuddered. Had it been a kind of brothel then or what? Women here willingly or unwillingly. They must have walked this mountainside, though, accompanied by what thoughts—guilt, fear, shame? She tried not to think about these shadows from the past and concentrated on the view. Through a gap in the trees, she could see the Nærøy River far below, looking like a snake, the way rivers always did in aerial shots. Snakes: another unwelcome thought, but surely all were benign in Norway.

She started down the path and was surprised to hear voices ahead—loud voices, Norwegian voices. Two men were shouting at each other. That much was certain, but as to the nature of the dispute, Pix didn't have a clue. Not knowing the language made everything so difficult. Who was it? Oscar Melling and one of the farmers who had caught him cheating at cards? She was determined to find out who it was, yet she didn't care to be seen snooping herself. She climbed down closer, staying in the woods, well away from the path. But the trees were so dense, she still couldn't make out who it was, although the voices were much closer now. Another problem with eavesdropping on a totally foreign language was that one couldn't recognize voices. If they had been speaking English, she would be able to guess who it was from their accents, but all she was able to determine in native speakers was gender and some idea of age. Well, these were not children.

The argument was heated and she stopped suddenly. It didn't sound like cheating at cards—or if it was, a lot of money had been lost. One man was doing most of the talking now. His words came so rapidly, he seemed not to draw a breath. Words, words flung out like a barrage of machine-gun fire. She thought if she could get down the next incline, she'd be able to see through some birches growing not too far from the path. She started down and stumbled, her leg doubling under her. She almost cried out. That's all she needed to do, twist an ankle. As she fell, she grabbed instinctively and her hand hit a pile of Hardanger roof tiles, sending them tumbling down. The moss cushioned her fall, but the tiles kept going, crashing against one another and the trees. The voices stopped. The fallen tiles were silent now. A bird cried. It was the only sound, then a muffled voice. Then nothing. Her heart was beating rapidly. She stood up. This is absurd, she told herself. She was not far from the hotel. If she screamed, someone was sure to hear her, and why would she scream? Two men were having some sort of disagreement. That was all. She climbed back up to the path and resolutely started back the way she had come. She tried to shake the feeling she was being watched. She wished Jan had never told them about the hotel's past. This was what was producing all these fearful thoughts.

At the hotel, there was no sign of anyone. She crossed the parking lot, full of empty tour buses, like so many beached whales, dwarfing the few cars in between. A door slammed and an engine started. She stood to one side to let the car pass. It was going fast. She tried to see the driver but glimpsed only a profile—a dark profile with a beard.

Ursula hadn't said anything when Pix woke her up from a sound sleep asking for the scotch. Pix didn't say anything, either. What was there to say? I went for a walk behind the hotel in the folk museum and got scared by an argument?

And the scotch wasn't really what she wanted, either. What she wanted was her husband, Sam, in bed with her, his familiar shape curved to hers. They were like puzzle pieces after all these years. Her eyes closed and she slept.

Pix sat up, wide-awake. It wasn't even five o'clock. She wondered what the dawn light looked like and got out of bed, drawing back the heavy curtains. She opened the door and stepped out onto the balcony. It was cold and suddenly the warmth she'd just left seemed very attractive. She could get another hour's sleep. The mountains had an even more intense lavender cast at this time of day, especially the largest at the end of the valley. It had been rounded by the melting snows of time, older than the rough peaks to its side. The timberline was jagged, a lush green, that slender birches growing farther down interrupted in exclamation points. The Norwegian flag at the front of the hotel was fluttering in the early-morning breeze. Her eyes moved across the picture-postcard scene, lingering over the view just beneath her window—a view that turned her gaze to stone as surely as if she had been a troll, caught by the sun's first rays, an incarnation of those early pagan evil spirits, not the latter-day gift-shop item. Her stomach turned and she started to cry out.

For there had been an addition since last night—an addition to the lawn, smooth as velvet, shimmering with dew, stretching from the front of the hotel to the edge of the cliff. The addition was a swastika. A huge blood-red swastika right in the middle.

4

For an instant, Pix thought the swastika *had* been painted in blood, but as she dashed for the phone to call the desk, she realized it was extremely unlikely. Of course it was spray paint. She didn't even want to think about a possible alternative. Her call was answered on the first ring, and from the sound of the excited voices in the background—spoken Norwegian played at 45 instead of 33⅓— she assumed she was not the first to see the gruesome graffiti.

"Hello, this is Pix Miller in room one oh seven. I've just noticed a large swastika painted on the front lawn."

The clerk interrupted her. "*Ja, ja,* Mrs. Miller. A terrible thing. We are trying to think how to remove it now. Thank you for telling us." The woman hung up abruptly, obviously very disturbed.

How to remove it? Pix slipped on a sweater and went to the balcony. A knot of people stared at the symbol, some bending down and touching the paint. Then someone on one of those riding mowers came around the corner of the hotel and they all stepped back. The grass was short, but not that short. Mowing removed all but the faintest traces. Afterward another crew raked and removed the grisly grass clippings. Then three people came out with some sort of solution in large pails that they proceeded to slosh on the paint that was left and then scrub with cloths. Everyone moved rapidly. Guests would be making their way to breakfast soon and people like Jennifer Olsen were probably already up and about for their morning run. Fortunately, the road was behind the hotel—the main entrance was at the opposite end from the large picture windows, as was the dining room.

The phone rang. Pix was surprised and went in quickly. It was the six o'clock wake-up call, the clerk's voice cheerful. Everything back to normal. Before Pix jumped in the shower, she took a last look outside. Not exactly a bright golden haze on the meadow— there was definitely a reddish cast to the lawn, which nature would soon obliterate.

While she let the warm water hit her full force, Pix tried to think what the act meant and who could have done it? The Germans had used the hotel during the war for some sort of eugenics experiment. This was the most obvious connection. Yet why the protest now? Or had it happened before? Other swastikas? Other reminders? She would ask at the desk. Since she had seen it, she thought she was entitled to ask some questions. As for the who, there was a hotel full of guests and it wouldn't have been too difficult to slip out when it finally did get dark. Spray-painting the symbol wouldn't have taken long.

She packed quickly and went across the hall

to knock on her mother's door, noting that Ursula's bags were already outside.

"Good morning, dear. Did you sleep well?" Her mother looked concerned. She hadn't asked why her daughter had awakened her the night before in search of the flask, but clearly she hoped for an explanation now.

"Things seem to be happening, but I'll be darned if I can figure out what any of them have to do with Kari and Erik—or anything else," Pix said. She told her mother about overhearing the argument while walking among the buildings in the folk museum and the uneasy feelings she'd experienced.

"Then early this morning, when I pulled back my curtains, I saw a bright red swastika painted on the front lawn."

Ursula gasped. "How strange? Because of Stalheim being used as a *Lebensborn* home? But if you wanted to make a statement, why deface this beautiful place, and now, after so many years? It seems crazy."

"Exactly. They've managed to get rid of it. I mean, unless you knew it was there, you wouldn't see it. Well, why don't we have breakfast. I have the feeling we may need all the sustenance we can get."

Her mother gave her a slightly sardonic smile. "Don't wish for things. They might happen."

After another ample *smörgåsbord,* Scandie Sights boarded the two buses at 8:15 and proceeded straight down the Stalheim Canyon by way of a series of breathtaking hairpin turns.

"What could this be like in the winter?" Pix wondered.

"Or years ago. This is the new road," her mother reminded her. They were on Carl's *tour-buss* and he had much the same style as Jan, a few well-chosen comments rather than an obnoxious stream of chatter. The Petersons were on the bus, but surprisingly Carol did not bombard the guide with questions as Pix had expected. Carol looked a bit somber, or angry, Pix noticed. A run-in with her new daughter-in-law? Or had she seen the swastika and been upset? There was no question that word of something untoward had leaked out, and the group was not quite as jovial as it had been the day before.

Pix had asked discreetly at the desk if there had ever been an incident like this before, and, looking shocked at the suggestion, the clerk had replied, "Absolutely not!"

Carl was trying hard to lighten the mood, though. His voice was determinedly upbeat and he smiled with every word.

"Now that we have come down Norway's steepest road, it is just a short ride through the Nærøy Valley to Gudvangen, where we will meet our fjord cruiser. The tallest mountain you see is called Jordalsnuten. Today with the sun, it is looking particularly fine, and we have heard a weather report promising several more days of this good weather. We are very lucky, so relax and enjoy the views!"

"We *are* lucky," a woman across the aisle said to Pix. "Friends of ours did this very same trip and the moment they hit the west coast, it rained every day."

Pix had noticed her. She and a man, probably her husband, appeared to be traveling with another couple. They ate all their meals together, sat together, and had been playing cards when Pix had left for her walk the night before.

"My name is Pix Miller and this is my mother, Ursula Rowe."

"Nice to meet you. I'm Eloise Harding. The man with the video camera glued to the window is my husband, Sidney, and"—she gestured over her shoulder to the seat behind her—"these are our friends, Paula and Marvin Golub."

She sank back into her seat. Having taken care of the social amenities, she did not appear eager to strike up a lifelong friendship. Pix had more friends than she had time to see, so it was no loss, but she planned to get to know Eloise better. Sidney Harding, she remembered, was the man working for the Norwegian oil company.

The viking fjord cruiser was a nice little boat, not one of the behemoths that provided a maximum amount of tourists with a minimum of fjord exposure. The boat had an upper deck with a small lounge, then on the lower deck, open areas at the bow and stern, separated by a large cabin with a galley and tables and chairs. The group immediately rushed forward to stake out their territories. Carol Peterson commandeered a bunch of chairs on the upper deck; the Golubs and Hardings situated themselves at a table in the middle of the large cabin and started playing bridge. The farmers stood in an uneasy clump at the stern. The Dahl sisters sat in the smaller cabin and took out their handwork. The Bradys went into the large cabin and grabbed the first table with windows to the side and front. The French cousins made several forays from the top to lower decks before choosing the top, liberally applying sun lotion, closing their eyes to the view, and lifting their faces to the sky. Pix settled Ursula next to a window in the large cabin and then went out to the bow. The only other person there was Jennifer, who was perched like a figurehead, leaning over the water and staring into its depths. Carl had just told them that at this point the Nærøyfjord was four thousand feet deep—and it was by no means the deepest fjord. Pix resisted the impulse to grab the waistband of Jennifer's jeans. She is not my child, she told herself firmly. She's an adult. My age.

"You'd never be able to find anything—anything you dropped overboard, that is," Jennifer commented to Pix.

Pix transferred her camera from her shoulder to around her neck and changed the subject. There was something definitely odd in the way Jennifer had spoken—dreamy, not her usual straightforward speech.

"I knew it would be beautiful, but this is far beyond that," Pix said. "The water is so green, and look at that waterfall!" She was tempted to go on and on. The mountains were so steep, screeching to a halt at the water's edge, it was almost as if a line had been drawn, beyond which the land could not go. The same with the sky. The densely wooded mountains soared toward the heavens; then there was a sudden break and the peaks became clouds. The air was so clear that everything was in sharp focus, intensifying the effect. The Nærøyfjord was the narrowest fjord in Europe, and if Jennifer had not been there, Pix would have stretched her arms wide, sure her fingertips would not touch the sides, but still needing to make the gesture.

"Azure." Jennifer had spoken again and Pix wasn't sure she'd heard correctly. She moved to the prow and sat down on the deck, next to the woman.

"Excuse me, I didn't quite hear what you said."

"Azure—that's the color of the fjord. It comes from the Jostedal glacier. I'm going there after the tour. The glacial ice is supposed to look blue, but the deposits color the water green. It's moving, faster than they thought. I read that the little gift shop and restaurant at the foot of it won't be there in ten years. It's the largest glacier in Europe, so I thought I should see it. There's a new glacier center in Fjærland and it's supposed to be worth seeing, too."

"It sounds as if you're enjoying Norway." And what was not to like? Pix thought as the boat slowly made its way down the center of the fjord, a few tiny farms clinging to the mountainsides, docks and sheds close to the water, all the buildings painted bright red and yellow—most with that typical up-and-down siding, so upright, so vertical. Cows and goats grazed nimbly on the inclines, defying gravity.

"I assume from your name that you are of Scandinavian descent?" she asked after Jennifer had merely nodded to Pix's previous conversational opener.

"You ask a lot of questions." Jennifer's tone was not antagonistic, but back to her normal matter-of-fact way of speaking. Still, it was slightly aggressive.

"I've always been interested in people, where they're from, what they think, what they do." This was true—and on this trip, more than true—absolutely essential.

"I grew up in New Jersey, but both my parents were born here." She sat cross-legged opposite Pix. The landscape glided behind her head, a slowly moving backdrop. She picked at a coil of heavy rope on the deck, then turned her gaze full force on Pix. "Like I said yesterday, life's a bitch. My father was in the Resistance and had the dumb luck to get captured. The Nazis shot him and the rest of the men he was with right where they caught them, in the woods. So much for the Geneva Convention. Then they came for my mother, who was pregnant with me. The Resistance got to her first and smuggled her out of the country. She skied across to Sweden and went by boat to England, eventually ending up in the States, where she had some relatives. His mother was not so lucky. The Nazis put her in Grini—that was the concentration camp outside Oslo. She died there."

"I'm so sorry." The words sounded hollow and inadequate. Pix put her hand on Jennifer's arm.

"I never wanted to come back here, although my mother was homesick every day of her life. I should have come with her, but I didn't, and it's too late now." Jennifer shaded her brow and looked up. "That must be our captain."

Pix followed her gaze. She hadn't stopped to wonder who might be piloting the boat so expertly, but of course there had to be somebody at the helm. He was staring straight ahead, a tall man—a tall man with a bushy black beard. She looked at Jennifer. Her face was wiped of all expression. Jennifer Olsen had cause to hate the Nazis, had cause to want people to remember the atrocities they'd committed. Had she done some artwork last night?

And what was it with all these dark beards?

"I think I'll stay on board, if that's all right. I'm a bit tired and I've seen a stave church in the museum in Oslo," Ursula said to Carl. She didn't mention that she had also seen this very stave church, the Hopperstad stave church, here in Vik, as well as every other one Marit had thought worth a detour.

"No problem, Mrs. Rowe. We will not be too long, and the crew will be back after they pick up some things that have been left here for us."

Ursula Rowe smiled serenely and watched the group board two buses for the ride to the church. She also watched the two stewards, Sonja and Anders, leave. Then the captain left, too. Immediately, she went to work, starting with the small upstairs lounge. She wasn't sure what she was looking for. Something out of the ordinary. Something that would mean the tour was not simply a tour. Nothing. She worked her way downstairs, hurrying in case the crew came back early, even though she doubted they would. Time off was precious, and Sonja and Anders seemed as attached to each other as Kari and Erik—as Kari and Erik had been.

The galley yielded nothing other than the fact that there would be *vafler* in the tour's future—a large waffle iron that made the heart shapes was stored in one of the cupboards. There was a small room off the galley with a table and chairs, a place for the crew to relax. Apparently nothing. A few paperbacks lay on one shelf next to a coffee mug. There was a box of brochures and maps. She opened the closet opposite the door. Knapsacks. The guides' and the stewards', according to the name tags. Kari's and Erik's would have been here. Kari's and Erik's knapsacks, which unaccountably turned up in Oslo. She pushed the bags to one side and searched the rest of the small closet. She emerged beaming. So there was something after all. But Pix would have to do the rest.

Voices.

"Do you mind if we smoke?" Anders asked the elderly woman sitting just where they'd left her.

"No, not at all," she replied.

"Maybe we should open the window. It seems a little stuffy," Sonja offered solicitously. Mrs. Rowe's cheeks were red.

"That would be very kind. Thank you."

"This church dates to only about one hundred years after the introduction of Christianity into Norway by King Olav. He was very convincing, offering a choice between adopting his religion or death. Still, people were not completely sure about this new religion, so they kept some of the old superstitions, like this circle with a cross in the middle. You had to have at least seven of these on the walls or the old gods might reclaim the church. There were no pews or seats in stave churches. Everyone stood, the women on the north side, to protect the men from evil spirits."

Pix wanted to ask the church's guide whether this was because the women were thought to be powerful or expendable, but she was moving on to further details.

"And you have seen the carved Viking ship dragon prows on the roof, another safeguard. Here inside if you look straight up, you will see the roof appears to be the underside of the hull of a Viking ship. These churches are called 'stave' churches because of these large

117

pillars holding the roof up. All of the carving and paintings also exhibit the mixture of Christian symbolism and the older Viking traditions. Notice particularly the intricate design around the three doors. Men entered through the front door, women again through a door on the north side, and the priest through this one." She gestured toward the door. "The exterior porch was used for processions and it was also where the lepers and pregnant women had to stay during the service."

"Lepers and pregnant women." Jennifer nudged Pix. "Same ole, same ole."

"We are very lucky to have this church. Between the eleventh and thirteenth centuries, about nine hundred churches were built, but so many were destroyed that we have only around thirty complete ones today. At one time in our history, many people thought the stave churches should be taken down because of their association with the pagan Viking times. Other kinds of churches were built. Just before this one was going to be sold for the wood, an Englishman bought it and saved it. Unfortunately, the owner had already washed the walls to remove the paint, so it is hard to see what it once must have looked like. You have to imagine the bright colors."

Pix wandered out to the small cemetery. A huge copper beech stood in front, its top branches even with the carved dragon's heads jutting out from the roof of the church. The spreading branches below cast feathery shadows on the red wood of the church and shaded the tombstones. Some of these had pitched forward, the weathered names faint; others were new and upright, their inhabitants known, the letters still sharply incised on the stone. Bright bunches of flowers were scattered about in small vases. She wondered how old the tree was, how many interments it had witnessed. In Aleford, antiquity meant 1775. Here, that was only yesterday.

"Wasn't that interesting? Especially about keeping the Viking ways. *Viking* is Old Norse for 'pirate raid.' " It was Marge Brady speaking. She sat down under the tree and Pix joined her. Marge was madly scribbling away in her journal. "I don't want to forget a thing. None of the guidebooks mentioned that business about the pastor having to take care of his predecessor's widow. I can tell you that would not go over big at home."

Pix had missed this. "What was the custom? I was out here."

"Well, when one died, the new one had to support the widow, so it was easier just to marry her. The woman in that portrait on the wall was married to three pastors; then she died before the last one and he married a seventeen-year-old and it all started over again. I guess it was sort of a career for these women. Do you suppose they still do this in Norway today?"

"I would doubt it. Women—and men— don't have to worry about a steady income, health care, or old age. I think I'll go back and have a closer look at that portrait, though." Pix thought of the portraits of the priests she'd seen, with their wide starched ruffs encircling their throats above their somber black robes. Her friend Faith was married to a man of the cloth, but Tom Fairchild was neither starched nor somber. Nor could Pix see Faith transferred like the parish Bible and Communion silver to Tom's successor. This old Norwegian custom—was it a reflection of their practicality, frugality, or concern for the widow? Perhaps all three—and besides, having someone around who knew the drill must have been a help to the new pastor.

But she didn't get a chance to gaze at the portrait after all. They were being urged gently but firmly to get on the buses for a quick ride to a scenic mountaintop viewpoint, then back to the boat.

Sonja and Anders had been busy setting out things for lunch—a huge steaming vat of pea soup, *boller*—rolls—salad, and plenty of sliced meats and cheese. Ursula sat at a table near the galley and the three were chatting. Like Kari and Erik, these stewards were also students. Sonja had grown up in Undredal. "It is not so far from here. We are famous for our old church. It is the oldest one in Scandinavia still in use. Undredal is a very good place to live, but I will probably stay in Oslo. These villages are very small, you know."

Ursula did know. She had been to Undredal one spring with Marit and it was tiny—but beautiful. The cherry trees had been in blossom and the church, which only held thirty people, was indeed special. Twelfth-century paintings had been discovered beneath many layers of paint on the walls and restored. There was also an intricate wooden chandelier of stag's heads, yet what she could still visualize most clearly, and with some amusement, was the pulpit with the inscription informing all who should pass by that it was painted by an Olsen, but above that proclaimed that it had been paid for by Peter Hansen. Marit had pointed it out and later teased her husband about the priorities of his forebearers.

Now Ursula turned to her task as investigator and asked the two young people, "Are you enjoying your jobs? It seems like quite a bit of work, with very little time off."

"Oh, we don't mind. The pay is good and we meet so many nice people?" Anders' voice went up and down in the typical pattern, ending on that questioning note. He continued. "Sonja worked for the company last summer, and when I met her this winter, she convinced me to give it a try, and I'm glad I did. We are seeing more of each other now than we do all year." He smiled expansively.

"I heard there was some problem with the other stewards on this trip. Did you know them?"

Sonja frowned. "I knew Erik from last summer and met Kari a few times. It's a sad thing. I don't know what they could have been thinking of. Erik was not the type to do something like this."

But Kari was? Ursula caught the unspoken thought and was about to ask, Like what? when the rest of the tour poured into the cabin, famished after a morning of sight-seeing. Pix went over to her mother. "Everything all right?"

"Better than that, dear."

Pix sighed. While she'd been sidetracked by pastors' wives and carved acanthus leaves, Mother had probably figured everything out.

"We'll have time for a chat at the hotel," Ursula said firmly.

"How big do you think it is?" Pix asked. The two women were sitting in Pix's room at Kvikne's Hotel in Balestrand.

"Hard to say—and I didn't have much time to investigate. There were some rain jackets and other things hanging in the closet. I pushed them to the side and moved the knapsacks. I'd already tapped on the walls of most of the boat—this cane is really remarkably useful—but everything felt very solid, except in the closet. The rear wall definitely sounded hollow, as if there was some sort of compartment behind it."

"But it could just be that the closet was put in later and fitted to an awkward space. Did you see any way of getting into it?"

"No. There isn't any light in the closet, and my old eyes aren't what they used to be. Besides, I'd have needed a flashlight."

Considering Ursula still did intricate counted cross-stitch without the aid of spectacles, her old eyes were holding up fine. Yet Pix knew what was coming next.

"You'll just have to get on the boat tonight

and see if you can open it. It's the only lead we have so far."

This was true. "What made you think there was some kind of hiding place on our fjord cruiser?" Pix also wanted to add, And why didn't you tell me? But a mother's mind often worked in strange and mysterious ways.

"I didn't think of it until after you all left," Ursula confessed. Hearing that, Pix felt a bit better. "I stayed behind to have a look around—you probably guessed that—but when I asked myself what I was looking for, a hiding place was the only thing that made sense. What can boats be used for? Smuggling, of course, and Norway has its drug problems, the same as the rest of the world."

"So, it's possible Erik and Kari discovered some scheme that involved using the boat to transfer drugs, or"—Pix recalled her mother's earlier remarks about the Russians—"oil secrets."

Ursula nodded. Neither she nor Pix gave voice to the corollary—discovered it or were part of it.

"We'd better go down to the lobby and pretend to meet Marit. She must surely be here by now," Pix suggested.

And she had a lot of questions for Kari's grandmother.

Kvikne's Hotel occupied the most beautiful site for lodging that Pix had ever seen. Even the incongruity of the 1877 Swiss chalet style of the original building and the high-rise modern addition could not detract from the breathtaking splendor of the view. She'd begun to think in guidebook language—"breathtaking splendor"; it was hard to avoid superlatives. The hotel was set on a peninsula jutting out into the Sognefjord, and when one was sitting on the long porch in front, as she, Marit, and Ursula were now, one was surrounded on three sides by smooth waters and snowcapped mountains. Off in the distance, the glacier, the Jostedalsbreen, glistened. There were no bad seats in the house.

It was a Swiss chalet by way of Bergen, though, and the gingerbread had a marked Viking flavor inside and out. Carl had announced before they left the boat at the small dock in Balestrand, a few steps from the hotel's entrance, that dinner would be at 7:00 P.M. "And afterward we will take coffee in the *Høiviksalen,* famous for the carvings in the dragon style by Ivar Høivik. The hotel has many fine artworks and interesting objects. Be sure to see the chair where Kaiser Wilhelm was sitting when he got the news about World War One. I think he must have been quite annoyed to have his fishing interrupted. He was a well-known sight in the village here. He used to walk his six dogs, all with bells on their collars, every day himself. When you look at the fjord now, it seems so calm and peaceful, but imagine it in 1914 with the kaiser's steamer accompanied by a flotilla of twenty-four warships—all just by the dock here."

Maybe Norway should have KAISER WILHELM FISHED HERE plaques. Pix hadn't thought much about the kaiser since modern European history at Pembroke, yet his luxuriously mustached face seemed to be before her at every turn. And come to think of it, why were they called kaiser rolls? It was incredible to think of the fjord with all those warships.

"I think we can assume if we talk softly, we will not be overheard out here," Ursula was saying. They'd ordered coffee, of course. It was impossible to have a conversation in Norway without it, especially before the sun went over the yardarm.

"I'm afraid I don't have much to tell you," Marit replied. "The police haven't turned up any new leads. The only thing they did find out was that a member of the maintenance crew found the knapsacks under the seats where Kari and Erik had been sitting when he was cleaning the train that night in Oslo. It had made the return trip. He turned them in to lost luggage."

"So, nothing there. Except who removed Kari's things? Kari, or someone else?" Pix asked.

Marit shrugged.

Pix asked another question. "I know you said Kari was probably calling Annelise, her friend in Bergen, to find out how she was. But could there have been any other reason? Had Annelise ever worked for Scandie Sights?"

"No. Annelise moved to Bergen to take a job at the Vestlandske Kunstindustrimuseum—the West Norway Museum of Decorative Arts. I'm sure if she'd worked for the tour group, Kari would have mentioned it."

The Museum of Decorative Arts—the one Helene Feld had been so eager to see, the one where she'd spent her time in Bergen instead of sticking to the tour's itinerary. Pix filed the thought away.

"But what about you?" Marit asked anxiously. "Have you found out anything at all? I feel at times I am going mad. That Kari will walk in the door and that this will be a bad dream."

Pix and Ursula told her the few facts they'd managed to ferret out—Pix's conversation with the stationmaster in Voss, Helene's account of the argument. Pix omitted Carol Peterson's description of Kari, but she related their other attempts to get information from the guests. Ursula told of the possibility that there was some kind of secret compartment on the boat.

"You have done so well." Marit was impressed. "Now all Pix has to do is go see what's in it."

Pix had been thinking of this very thing. It seemed so simple to her elders. Piece of cake. Let Pix do it. Pix the *hund*. But it was not simple at all. She'd have to wait until it got dark, which meant another sleepless night, and then she'd have to be sure there was no one else around or likely to come upon her. How could she possibly explain her presence on the boat? Sleepwalking?

They finished with some more random impressions and an account of the intruder on Jennifer Olsen's balcony at the Stalheim Hotel.

126

"Oh, and last but not least, when we woke up this morning, someone had painted a giant red swastika on the lawn in front of the hotel, just before you get to the edge of the cliff," Pix told her. She was amazed to see the powerful effect her words had on their old friend.

Marit looked as if she'd seen a ghost.

"A swastika?" she whispered. "At Stalheim?"

"Yes." Ursula reached for her friend's hand. "What's wrong? What does it mean?"

"I can't tell you here." Marit seemed very close to tears. "Meet me in my room. It's three oh seven."

Puzzled, Pix and Ursula waited five minutes before crossing the lobby to the elevator. A Japanese tour bus had arrived and the two women were forced to wait for the next elevator. As soon as one had arrived, the group rushed on and there had been no more room.

"The Japanese are perhaps the most polite people on the planet, the most aware of social ceremonies. The only reason I've ever been able to come up with for their kind of lemminglike behavior abroad is that they're terrified of getting separated—or, worse still, getting left behind forever."

"Like the North Dakota farmers."

"Precisely."

Neither woman had referred to Marit since she'd made her dramatic exit.

They exited the elevator into a deserted hallway and quickly went to room 307. Marit opened the door at their knock. She must have been standing just inside.

The room was spacious and had a comfortable sitting area. Ursula drew Marit next to her on the love seat. "Now, what is it?"

"It's so complicated and it was so long ago. Hans and I were going to tell you; then we thought it better to tell no one. We were trying to erase the past, and you can never do that."

"What are you talking about, Marit?" Ursula's direct question hadn't worked. Maybe a second one would do it, Pix thought.

"The Stalheim Hotel was used in the war for something the Germans called a *Lebensborn* home. We had nine of them in Norway. They were breeding places for the world the Germans envisioned after the war. We Norwegian women were especially prized because of what they thought was our pure blood. That all the children we produced with their soldiers would be tall, strong, and blond. After the Occupation, German soldiers were encouraged to father children with Norwegian women. It was their duty to the Reich. When they got pregnant, some of the women went to Germany. Some stayed where they were and had the children, yet that was very hard. You have to understand, I make no judgments of them, but others did, often their own parents, and it was terrible for them. Most went to have the babies in these homes."

"But what would happen to all these babies? Who would raise them?" Pix asked.

"They were sent to Germany or in some cases

adopted by parents here, people who were sympathetic to the Germans. We were not all in the Resistance, remember. Quisling had his supporters."

"Why are you telling us this?" Ursula asked quietly. She had taken her friend's hand again when they had entered the room, and she still held it.

"After the war, the children who remained in the homes were claimed by their mothers or adopted by Norwegian families. Some of the children who had been sent to Germany were traced by refugee organizations and brought back here for adoption if the mother did not want them, which was usually the case. The fathers, of course, were known only to the mothers, and mostly their names were not recorded. The children were given two names at birth, a Norwegian one and a German one. They used to have mass christenings, twenty-five babies at a time. The babies were well looked after, but it was horrible—the whole idea and raising them like so many prize sheep. There is a story that one of the women soldiers assigned to Stalheim refused to be there and ended up at the bottom of the canyon." Marit stopped speaking and seemed to be gathering energy to go on. Pix was trying to blot out the image of a body spiraling down, down to the river that looked like a snake.

"Hanna was a *Lebensborn* baby. She was born at Stalheim."

"Oh, Marit, you should have told me years ago. It wouldn't have made any difference!" Ursula cried out.

"I know that, yet Hans and I thought it was something we shouldn't talk about. Nobody mentioned these children. Of course, our families knew we had adopted a baby. We knew when we got married that we couldn't have children. The war years were so hard and Hanna seemed like our reward for getting through them. No one asked us where she had come from, and she looked just like us. Not a very large gene pool," she said, glancing at Pix.

"Did Hanna know?"

Marit nodded. "We were stupid there, too. We should have told her as soon as she was old enough to understand, first that she was adopted and later how—but we waited until she was fifteen. I sometimes wonder about how our memories work. She was eight months old when we got her, but she was always asking questions. Where was she born? Why didn't we have other children? When we made our first trip to the west coast and came by Stalheim, she was very small, but she cried and said the big mountains frightened her."

Fifteen, Pix thought. Between the ages of her own Danny and Samantha. The time when adolescents are forming the identities that will travel with them throughout their lives, making the choices that determine the journey's path. Hanna must have been so confused. To find your mother was not your mother and your father not your father. And later she did virtually the same thing to her own daughter, not providing her with a father, then abandoning her.

"Nothing was ever right after that. We never should have told her," Marit said bitterly.

"It would have come out," Ursula said. "These things always do."

"And Kari?" Pix was asking all the hard questions. "Did she know about her mother?"

"This winter, there was a show about the *Lebensborn* babies on television. Now fifty years later, it's out in the open—all the problems these children have had, how they have searched trying to find out who they are. I wanted to change the channel, but Kari wanted to watch it. I had to leave the room, and she followed me out to the kitchen. Before I knew it, I was telling her everything. I thought she was old enough, that she could accept it. Kari is not Hanna. Emotionally, they are very different."

"What did she say?" asked Pix.

"She said, 'Then you're not really my *bestemor?*' "

Marit had wanted to lie down and reluctantly they'd left her, but not before she'd told them that Kari wanted to find her mother's family and that Marit had agreed to help her. "I don't want another grandmother," she'd told Marit. "It's a matter of the truth. I have to find out the truth."

Pix and Ursula were walking into the dining room at Kvikne's, passing through several pretty Victorian-style sitting rooms all oriented toward the view and, unlike most Victoriana, comfortable-looking—inviting couches, light-colored walls, and the drapes pulled back. Oil paintings, genre landscapes of what appeared out the windows, hung in tiers on the walls. The surfaces of many of the tables were crowded with bric-a-brac, potted plants, and dozens of signed photographs dating back to the hotel's early years. In pride of place stood those of the Norwegian royal family, starting with King Haakon VII, the Danish prince Karl, whom the Norwegians elected as their first constitutional monarch when they broke away from Sweden in 1905. He took a Norwegian name and reigned for fifty-two years. His grandson, Harald V, is king now. Small Norwegian flags on silver flag posts stood by the photographs. Bright red, with a blue-and-white cross off center, it seemed admirably suited to its surroundings, streaming out in a long banner from the porch at Kvikne's, picking up the breeze from the fjord, or flying high in front of most houses all over the country, plus being scattered throughout Norwegian interiors as an indispensable objet d'art. The Norwegians are exceedingly proud of this flag.

"My God, Mother, did you ever see so much food!" It was the *smörgåsbord* to end all *smörgåsbords*. There wasn't one long table, but many—and side tables—one just for cheese, one for non-alcoholic drinks, a very large one just for desserts.

"Where should we start?" Pix was bewildered, a feeling intensified by the behavior of the diners, who were descending on the food like predators, the only variation being in motion: Some were piling their plates as rapidly as possible; others were circling quietly before pouncing.

"With a seat," Ursula suggested, and led the way to the tables with the Scandie flags.

"We have the window seats tonight," Carol Peterson called out triumphantly as they passed. Her table was full. There was to be no tête-à-tête for the newlyweds.

"Would you care to join us?" Louise Dahl asked.

"Thank you so much," Ursula responded, and motioned toward the groaning boards. "It's hard to know where to begin."

"We start with herring, then a plate of other fish—shrimp and *laks*—there's also *gravlaks* here. Do you know what that is? Fresh salmon is cured with dill and a mixture of salt, sugar, and white peppercorns, then placed under a weight for some days and—oh, maybe it's simpler if I come with you. Everything is delicious and you may not know what it is."

"I don't want to trouble you," Ursula protested.

"It's no trouble. I want to get some smoked eel before I have my meat course."

"This is the food we grew up with and we still cook it, although nothing so elaborate as these dishes. Kvikne's is known for its *koldtbord*—that's what it's called in Norwegian, although most use the Swedish word, *smörgåsbord*. Anyway, it's the best food in the world to me! Let Louise show you what to do," her sister, Erna, advised.

Pix was only too happy. She'd eaten her share of Norwegian food, but this was a whole new level. Even Faith would be impressed by Kvikne's.

"We start with the herring by itself, because it's salty and we don't fill our plates too full, so we can appreciate the flavors."

And not look too greedy, Pix thought. Nothing in excess.

As they strolled by the tables, Pix was delighted to see how much the Japanese were enjoying all the Nordic variations on sushi.

"After your herring, I'd advise some *laks* and a little of this smoked eel, which is eaten with a bit of scrambled egg at room temperature. Maybe some shrimp, and the mussel salad looked good." She then pointed out the enormous variety of cold meats, ranging from pâtés to slices of ham, salami, and roast beef. There were also *salats*—thinly sliced cucumbers with dill (see recipe on page 344), cabbage with caraway, beets and sardines.

"The last course before dessert is hot. I'm not sure I'll have more than a meatball—they're made of veal and beef, bound with egg and bread crumbs, a little nutmeg, and fried in salt pork—but you should definitely have some *fiskepudding* (see recipe on page 341)."

"*Fiskepudding?*" Pix had never encountered this particular delicacy before. Some kind of piscatorial Norsk dessert? They did have a sense of humor.

"It's a bit like a fish mousse. You just have to try it, and be sure to have some of the cream sauce with shrimp on top, and take some *tyttebær*—lingonberries."

"Lingonberries!" Pix knew what they were—a kind of small Nordic cranberry. You ate them with reindeer meat.

Louise nodded vigorously. "You can't eat *fiskepudding* without lingonberries."

Pix looked at Louise's angular body. She would have expected plump Erna to be the one interested in food, but here was Louise, her eyes shining with delight as she contemplated the notion of *bløt kake*—layer cake—and some kind of fruit *grøt*—compote—to end her meal. Essential Norwegian food names tended to be monosyllabic and atonal: Bread was *brød*, butter was *smør*, cheese was *ost,* steak was *stek,* and above all, fish was *fisk*.

"It's not a combination I would have thought of, but it works," said Pix after polishing off her *fiskepudding,* cream sauce, lingonberries on the side. "They are not too sweet, not too tart, and the taste cuts the richness of the fish." Since going to work at Have Faith, Faith Fairchild's catering business, Pix had picked up some of the nuances of food pairings, although not even the barest whisper of any food preparation. When Faith had offered her a job, Pix had made it clear that accounts or activities such as counting salad plates would be fine, but not even turning on an oven or stirring a pot. Faith had assured her friend that this was the furthest thought from her mind. She knew the Miller kitchen well, and from the look of Pix's cupboards, the family could have been mistaken for major stockholders in General Foods, et cetera. Many of the boxes had HELPER printed on the front.

"I'm glad you like it. We make it at Christmas. It was our mother's favorite dish," Louise Dahl said.

Ursula noticed the past tense. "Has your mother been gone long?"

The two sisters put down their forks simultaneously. "A year this January," Erna replied. They both still seemed devastated.

A household of women. Obviously, the two sisters had never married, and Pix had a hunch all three women had lived together.

"Your mother was Norwegian, then? You know so much about the food..." her voice trailed off.

"We are all three born in Norway, but Louise and I don't remember it very well. This is the first trip for either of us."

"It's a shame your mother wasn't able to go back for a visit," Pix commented. It had been her experience that every Norwegian-American not only longs to visit the land of his ancestors but considers it a sacred duty, as well.

"She didn't want to go," Louise said sternly, and for a moment the conversation came to a grinding halt; then Ursula picked up the ball.

"The newlyweds have disappeared and Mrs. Peterson doesn't look too pleased." She laughed.

A cartoonist would have had a fine time drawing the mother-in-law with steam coming out of her ears, arms folded across her chest, jutting elbows like the spikes on a mace. Her voice carried across the room loud and clear. "You know very well what they're up to, and they can do that anytime. How often in their lives are they going to be at Kvikne's Hotel? I ask you that." Roy senior didn't appear to have an answer and he wisely concentrated on his third helping of dessert.

"I thought they were going for more food. At least that's where they headed. We might just as well have gone to Thunder Bay like we always do, but I wanted to make this trip special. It didn't matter how much planning it took, and believe me, I had to give up a lot of things to do all that, but do they care? I ask you.... Roy, did you hear what I said!"

His mumbled reply was inaudible, whether from discretion or cake.

The Dahls giggled appreciatively. "It's been like this since the beginning of the trip—a contest—and I think Lynette is ahead."

Pix thought of how the young woman had looked in the sauna at Stalheim and compared her with Carol, who had been going in rather heavily for boiled potatoes over the years. Lynette was definitely ahead in some departments, but the older woman had genetic guilt induction honed to a fare-thee-well. Pix would still say it was even money.

The Dahls were telling Ursula about their jobs. Erna was a hairdresser and Louise worked as a secretary in a lawyer's office. The dining room was beginning to clear. Sophie and Valerie walked by the table.

"Dancing in the lounge tonight. You must

come," Sophie urged. "*Très amusant, n'est-ce pas?*"

Ursula explained in fluent French that her dancing days were over but that she was sure her daughter, *la jeune fille,* would be tripping the light fantastic. The Dahl sisters also seemed inclined to join the merriment. Although she gave a pleasant nod to Mother's fait accompli, Pix had plans of her own. Dancing or no dancing, she wanted to work in another sauna. She had to have some time to herself to think about Marit's revelation, and the macarena was not apt to provide an opportunity for contemplation of this sort.

But first there was coffee in the Dragon Room.

The dragon style harked back to the decorated prows of the Viking ships, translating the fierce beasts and other creatures into romantic works of art, a nostalgic nod to the past. Tapestrylike weavings, more landscapes, and several huge paintings of Norsk legends hung on the room's warm red walls. But it was the carved furniture, wooden floor, and ceiling that gave the room its particular beauty.

"It's hard to imagine how someone could have done such intricate work," Pix said to Erna Dahl. Jennifer Olsen, who had joined them, agreed. "Some people think it's really tacky—all these dragons and swirls, overdone, but I love it. Only in Norway."

Erna was apparently about to add her own words of appreciation, having nodded vigorously at Jennifer's words, when they were distracted by a heated argument behind them. A coffee cup was slammed down on the table, hard. It didn't break.

"I started with nothing and nobody ever gave me anything. What these young people today want are free handouts. They have babies so they can get money from the government, and nobody wants to work!" It was Oscar Melling and his face was redder than ever. The fringe around his bald head bristled.

"All I said was that the Norwegian health-care system could be a model for us. I'm not talking about welfare," Arnie Feld protested.

"You don't know what you're talking about! That's your trouble," Oscar blustered.

Don Brady walked into the fray. "Keep it down, Melling. We're here for a vacation."

"Are you telling me to shut up?" Oscar was ready for a fight and even assumed a pugilistic posture.

"Yes, I am!" Don was red in the face now, too. Wives were appearing like magic from their contemplation of carved rosettes.

"Honey," Marge said to Don, her hand on his elbow as Helene linked her arm through Arnie's and took a step backward. But equally by magic, Carl and Jan materialized.

"I thought you were going to buy us a beer, Mr. Melling." Carl stood directly in front of the man, blocking the others.

"We get very thirsty talking all day," Jan said. Both young men were smiling. Oscar muttered something and left with them, but not before casting a foul glance at his opponents.

"What do you suppose that was all about?" Pix was surprised. The group had seemed so friendly.

"I hate that man," Jennifer said vehemently. "He's a bully and would say anything to get a rise out of someone. He's been a pain since we started."

The rotten apple. Pix remembered Don Brady's remark at dinner at the Stalheim Hotel.

Carl was back, working the crowd, a word here, a word there, more smiles all around. At the end of a tour, the guides must have aching facial muscles for days. Jan was presumably hoisting some flagons with the troublemaker. Soon everyone was talking and laughing again. Oscar had been relegated to an anecdote: "The trip was wonderful, except for..."

The Dahl sisters excused themselves to titivate before the ball, or, as Louise put it, "We'll just go freshen up a bit before the music starts."

Pix finished her coffee. It was impossible to get a weak cup in Norway, and this should keep her wide-awake for the night's exploit. Searching their fjord cruiser for drugs or stolen oil-rig plans was not something she wanted to broadcast, however. So instead, she said to Jennifer, "I think I'll go and see if my mother needs anything, then look in on the dancing. After that, I want to find the sauna. It should be a great one here." What she really wanted to do was head straight for the sauna, but she wanted to check out who was dancing, and there might be a chance to talk to some of the people she hadn't been able to talk to yet, or those she wanted to speak to further.

Ursula answered the door. Marit was sitting on the balcony; the flask and two glasses were on a small table. Marit was laughing. Nobody needed anything, especially not Pix. She didn't even bother to go in.

"*God natt, god natt,*" Marit called.

"Don't forget about getting on board the boat" was Mother's good night.

As if, Pix thought, her children's speech patterns having long ago invaded her own.

5

"I got my thriilll on Blueberry Hiilll."

The music was blasting from the smoke-filled lounge and dancers crowded the floor. The air was warm and faces glowed, shining from exertion and alcohol. Pix wanted to keep alert and awake, although with all the coffee she'd drunk, she'd have to drink an enormous amount of beer to put a dent in the caffeine. By the end of the trip, her blood type would probably be arabica instead of B-positive. She ordered a Coke and sat down at a small table off to the side, where she was content to observe and not participate as tourists from every corner of the earth twisted and shouted their way through the group's next spirited number. It was an interesting rendition of the old classic. The female vocalist didn't sing at all like Chubby Checker and her accent occasionally made the English words sound Norwegian, but when she belted out "like we did last summer," the dancers went nuts, gyrating even more madly. Thoughts of hip-huggers. Thoughts of blankets at the beach. Thoughts of youth.

Pix was surprised to see Oscar Melling back in good graces, or at least with some of the tour. He was panting away opposite Carol Peterson, who was managing to stay with the beat even as her eyes scanned the room for her wayward daughter-in-law and poor benighted son. Pix could see Carol intoning the words over cups of coffee stretching end-lessly into a future of neighborhood coffee klatches: "He was such a good boy, until he met up with her. Not that I'm criticizing, mind you, but..." Roy senior was talking to Don Brady. It was apparently a very serious subject. Their heads were bent close together and Don, who was speaking at the moment, had locked his fellow Scandie sightseer's eyes in his own intense gaze. Suddenly, the two burst out laughing. What on earth could they be discussing? Pix tried to think how she could move closer to eavesdrop.

The Hardings and the Golubs were, of course, playing cards, although the table was partially out the door—so they could hear each other. Pix wondered if they played for money. There was no sign of the bachelor farmers. No doubt, they stuck to their routines and had all gone to bed at what would have been sun-down, to arise at sunup.

The number ended and Pix was debating whether to have another Coke or not. Skip-ping it meant a week's tuition for Samantha at Wellesley, where she was going to be a

142

freshman in the fall. But Pix needed to have some reason for lingering and she had absent-mindedly drunk the first small glass down while she was looking about. She ordered another one, wished she was on an expense account, and continued her surveillance.

The group played a slow number. Pix didn't recognize the song, but she did recognize the tempo. It was make-out music. All those couples in her teen years embracing on the dance floor, rocking from side to side, maybe taking a step to the rear or the front to provide a semblance of motion. "What fun is that?" her mother had asked. "That's not dancing! Why bother?" Pix, besotted over Sam Miller, two years older and two inches taller, had not explained. There were some things mothers would never get.

"All those dancing-school years with Miss Pat and Miss Nancy," Ursula had complained. Yes, the adolescents of Aleford had been taught to dance properly. Girls wore party dresses and white gloves. Boys had to struggle into suits and ties. Pix, with the arrogance of youth, had reminded her mother that people disapproved of the waltz when it was first introduced. "Nice eighteenth-century girls didn't dance that way."

But Ursula had the last word. "Someday you'll be glad you learned to dance." Many weddings, bar mitzvahs, and fund-raisers later, Pix was indeed glad she had.

The French cousins were dancing together. They had the air of professionals—impersonal smiles, eyes ahead, perfectly coordinated steps. They acknowledged her by dipping slightly as they passed.

Carol Peterson was still dancing with Oscar Melling, who was grasping her so tightly, Pix was sure the buttons on his sports shirt were embossing her flesh. She had changed from the brightly colored polyester pants suits she favored during the day to a wide-skirted floral-print cocktail dress—cruise wear. It was accessorized by matching beads, earrings, and several bangle bracelets. A white Orlon cardigan with plastic pearl buttons fluttered from her shoulders like a tiny cape, the gold-plated sweater guard threatening to choke her. She was chattering feverishly and Pix thought she heard her say, "You naughty man, you," as they, too, passed by. Her hair, uniformly light brown, was styled in what Pix vaguely recalled as an "artichoke" cut from her youth. Carol's leaves were all firmly lacquered in place, down to the wispy ones over her brow.

Pix noted again that jogging and whatever else Jennifer Olsen did to stay in shape had paid off. She was wearing a cotton-knit dress that clung to her body. It was very short and Pix remembered the equally provocative night wear Jennifer favored. Her dancing style fit these fashions. She was twisting, but not grinding gears to the floor and jumping up again, as the jack-in-the-boxes surrounding her were. Instead, her whole body seemed to shimmy and slither seductively, pulsating with the rhythm. Pix didn't recognize her partner from the tour. She must have met him at the hotel. He couldn't keep his eyes off her—

and the slight smile on her lips clearly stated she knew it. More power to her, thought Pix. Over fifty didn't mean Ovaltine and early to bed these days. Well, maybe it meant early to bed, but not Ovaltine. Clearly, Jennifer was a boomer and proud of it.

She was beginning to feel as if she was watching a film, Fellini by way of Oslo. From the look of the crowd, intent on wresting every last drop of pleasure from their tour—they'd paid for it, after all—it would be many hours before she could count on slipping out of the hotel to search the boat.

And what if she did find something? Something Kari and Erik had also found out about. Something with which they confronted someone. Pix shuddered as she thought of the repercussions of such knowledge. If it concerned oil secrets, that meant big money, and the lives of two young Norwegians wouldn't count for much.

What a strange tour this was, though—secret compartment or no secret compartment. Kari and Erik's disappearance. Erik's death. Then after Pix's arrival, there had been the man on Jennifer's balcony and the swastika on the lawn at Stalheim. That reminded her of Marit's revelation. Did the war have anything to do with all this? She stared hard at the dancers, the Scandie Sights members in particular. There weren't any young people on the tour, with the exception of Roy junior and Lynette Peterson. Then came Pix. She hadn't been at this end of the age range for years. The check marks she'd been making on questionnaires were getting alarmingly higher and higher: 20–30, 30–40, 40–50!

So, a large number of the tour members would have been the newlyweds' age during the war, young people whose youth was clouded by fear and deprivation. The swastika had been meant as a reminder, a reminder of the war and the *Lebensborn* homes. All the Norwegian-Americans on the trip—had one of them come from Stalheim or one of the other homes, a *Lebensborn* baby? Had there been memories of the war that were so bad, they had driven someone to deface the lawn—and maybe to something else? Something Kari and Erik had discovered? Pix thought of Jennifer. She was certainly bitter, and with ample cause. Had she come to Norway to seek revenge for her father, her grandmother, and now in memory of her mother? Her mother, who had always been homesick but had never come back? There were many Norwegians during the war who had stood by and done nothing. And there were those who hadn't been content to stand by, but who actively collaborated. Still, she hadn't mentioned anything about Stalheim, and it had been Pix's impression that Jennifer's family came from the east coast. But then the woman hadn't been explicit.

The swastika. At the time of the war, Norway had very few Jews, still didn't. Jews, monks, and Jesuits were not even allowed into the country under the 1814 constitution, which named the Church of Norway, Evangelical Lutheran, as the religion of the government. The prohibition against Jews was repealed in 1851. The monks had to wait until the end of the century and the Jesuits until some time in the 1950s. From Marit, Pix knew that not too many Norwegians actually attended church services, although they belonged to the church. It had also been a surprise to find out some years back that only about half of Norway's Jews had survived the war—those who escaped to Sweden at the very beginning of the Occupation, about seven hundred. Had the swastika been meant to symbolize collective guilt?

And what about the man in the beard on the balcony? A thief? All these beards. She was very aware of the photograph tucked away in her pocketbook, the picture of Sven and Hanna, Kari's mother and father. Hanna, definitely a *Lebensborn* baby. Kari had been deeply upset at the discovery. Marit had said Kari wanted to find out about her family and that she had agreed to help. Pix would have to ask her if they'd started to search, and if so, how? Poor Kari. To discover suddenly that both sides were a mystery. She'd grown up with no knowledge of her father or his people. Did she want to search for him, too? Or maybe she had found him? The beards. Pix had discovered the name of their hirsute captain, Captain Hagen, but his first name was Nils, not Sven. Still, people changed their names. Captain Hagen? But if Kari had found her father, why would she and Erik have gone off? And surely she would have said something to Marit. Could this have been what she wanted to talk about?

Pix was tired. And muddled. The chanteuse was crooning "Dream, Dream, Dream" and the couples on the floor slowly swayed. Pix liked the Everly Brothers better. She was in a grumpy mood. Time to hit the sauna and sweat all the bad vibes out. Sonja and Anders were directly in front of her table. She couldn't get up without disturbing them. Their eyes were closed and they weren't moving at all, her arms around his neck, his about her waist. The music stopped and they broke apart, seemingly startled to find themselves at the Kvikne's Hotel and not whatever private neverland they shared.

Back on the job, Anders was polite and cordial. "Mrs. Miller, are you enjoying the music?"

Before she could answer, the drummer stood up, grabbed the mike, and exclaimed in several languages, "Time for everyone to wet their whistles. We'll be right back."

Roy senior, looking none too pleased, reclaimed his wife, and Oscar, whose whistle seemed drenched already, presumably went in search of more.

"May I get you something?" Anders asked, and Sonja sat down next to Pix.

"That's very kind of you, but I still have some Coke, thank you," Pix answered, realizing that in her effort to nurse the drink, she'd scarcely touched it.

"A beer for you?" he asked Sonja.

"*Ja, takk,*" she answered, and he walked away toward the bar to join the long queue already formed.

Sonja repeated Anders's question, but she broadened it. "So, are you enjoying the tour?"

"Very much," Pix replied. "It's so beautiful. I loved being on the boat, watching the mountains and waterfalls. I hadn't wanted to dock, but this is lovely, too." It was true. In the front of the ship, sailing along the fjord, she had felt so calm and all things had seemed possible. Kari would be found. There would be some sad but logical explanation for Erik's tragic death. Draw your strength from mountains. If true, then the Norwegians must be the mightiest people on earth. Well, at one time, she supposed they might have been, if pillaging and far-flung travel counted. Even now, with a system that cared for all, they had managed things quite well. But on land, lovely as Balestrand was, the dark thoughts came and she recalled herself to her task.

"Only I can't help but think of that poor young man, the one who was killed, and the girl who has disappeared. Those must have been difficult days in Bergen."

Sonja's cheeks flamed, and it was not the warmth of the room, or Ringnes beer.

"Better to put it out of your mind. Yes, it was hard in Bergen, but Anders and I were there already and could start work right away, so none of the guests suffered too much."

"I mean everyone must have been upset. I heard Erik and Kari were very well liked."

"I wouldn't know about that," Sonja almost snapped. Would have snapped if the soft inflection her accent gave to her words allowed for emphasis.

149

"They weren't well liked? But I thought..."

"*He* was a nice boy and we all thought very much of him. As for Kari, she did not deserve him. Last summer, he was always worried about what she was doing when he wasn't there. I was only with her a few times, but I knew the type. I don't know what the English word is for it—Kari liked to tease the boys, not that she wanted anyone but Erik. Oh no, she had him where she wanted—with a ring through his nose for her to lead him around until she got the ring on her finger."

Pix was taken aback at the vehemence of Sonja's tone. She asked her, "Was Erik one of Anders's friends, too?"

"No. Anders never met him. This is his first time working for the tour."

Pix started to ask another question, but Sonja forestalled her. "You will enjoy the visit to the farm tomorrow. The farmer's wife makes pancakes for everyone and usually serves little cakes, too. Their goat herd is not too far away. You can get some nice pictures."

Anders sat down with the drinks and Pix realized that the girl had seen him approaching before Pix had.

"The band is going to start again soon. Have you ladies been having a nice chat?"

Neither lady said a word; then both said yes at once. Sonja burst into giggles and seemed once more sweet and unaffected—just like Pix's notion of Kari.

Carl and Jan stood in the doorway. No rest for the weary, Pix thought. Tour guide was not the job for her, although she had been functioning as such unofficially for years during every family vacation. "And now you will see the famous Anasazi cliff dwellings, where we will spend some hours walking in their footsteps...." Carl and Jan didn't have to cope with the "Oh, Moms" that greeted her efforts. Maybe being on a payroll wasn't so bad.

The two young men were making for her table.

"Are you having a good time, Mrs. Miller?" Jan asked. "And your mother? She's okay?"

"Oh, yes, we're both enjoying the trip very much. Mother went up to bed after coffee."

"Good, good." Carl beamed. Pix was curious about what they did during the winter. The two guides had come in search of the stewards and the four were conversing rapidly in Norwegian. It must have to do with arrangements for tomorrow. Anders kept nodding and saying, "*Ja.*" Sonja added a word or two and the four seemed to have finished their business.

"What do you do in the winter?" Pix asked. "I think someone mentioned you and Anders are at the University of Oslo," she added, addressing Sonja.

"Yes, we are still students. I am studying economics and Anders is in a business course. We want to make a lot of money," she quipped.

"And you?" Pix asked Carl.

"I work for Scandie Sights all year. We have many tours during the winter—ski holidays, trips to warmer places. We even go to the United States. The Norwegian Farmers Tour."

Pix assumed he was joking and laughed.

"No, really. In the early spring, we go to Bismarck, Fargo, and places in Minnesota. I must admit, though," he said ruefully, "I enjoy the summer tours more. The farmers all treat me like a city boy. Well, I am a city boy. I've never worked on a farm in my life. They give me quite a hard time and nothing impresses them. They visit each farm, rub some dirt through their fingers, and shake their heads. The most fun I've ever had on one of these trips was when I took them to the Mall of America. I didn't know what it was and the weather was bad. It was the only thing I could think of to do with them. They weren't interested in the art museum. They were like terrified children—it was so huge—and suddenly I was the big man. They clung to me like glue!"

Pix got the picture, and "Prairie Home Companion" 's Garrison Keillor was ringing in her ears.

"And you, Jan? Do you work for Scandie Sights all year, too?"

"*Nei,* My family is in the oil business, and as soon as summer is over, it's back to the office for me. I live now in Stavanger."

The band returned; before they started, Pix decided to call it a night—at least close this chapter.

"I think I'll see if the sauna is open," Pix said, and stood up. Anders, Carl, and Jan stood up also.

"We'll say good night, then," Jan said. "It

should be another good day tomorrow. You'll like the farm."

Sonja said, "I was telling Mrs. Miller about the pancakes."

Anders smiled at his girlfriend. "*Ja,* the pancakes."

The first strains of "The Lion Sleeps Tonight" weem-a-wecked its way into the still of the Norwegian twilight. Looking back over her shoulder, Pix saw that Jan was asking Carol Peterson to dance and Carl was heading toward Helene Feld. She was impressed again with their healthy good looks, albeit a bit disheveled in Jan's case. As usual, they were wearing matching Norwegian sweaters, issued by Scandie Sights, she imagined, and she decided to pick up some in the same patterns for her own children. And maybe Sam. He'd wear it for skiing. Even as she pictured her family Nordicly garbed, she realized she'd always be seeing these two. It would not be an unpleasant reminder. It was nice to be taken care of, instead of always taking care. She sighed and left the room.

The Dahl sisters were sitting in the lobby, drinking coffee, of course. Pix was not surprised, since Norwegians carry an extra gene, the caffeine gene, which means it has absolutely no effect on their ability to go to sleep or on their nerves, whether drunk at one o'clock in the afternoon or one o'clock in the morning. Just looking at the cups of steaming-hot dark brown liquid made her feel jangled—or maybe it was the Coca-Cola. In true Viking fashion, neither woman took cream.

"Isn't it fun!" Erna exclaimed. "They were playing some traditional Norwegian folk tunes earlier—dances we learned when we were little girls." She was wearing what Pix believed was called "a fascinator" in bygone days—a little wispy chiffon scarf pinned to her curls. Both women had "Norwegian Ladies Club" gold necklaces and large enameled pins. Erna's was a daisy, Louise's an elegant curving emerald green leaf. From the richness of the enamel's color, Pix assumed they were from David-Andersen, *gullsmed,* the premier jeweler and silversmith in Norway with tantalizing stores throughout the country.

"Good night. See you in the morning," Pix said. "I'm going to relax in the sauna and then head off to bed." And break into a closet on board our Viking fjord cruiser. It was hard to resist a perverse temptation to blurt it out and watch their faces.

"Sleep well. Won't it be fun to visit the farm tomorrow? And the weather is supposed to continue to be fine," Louise said.

Pix thought she'd heard enough about this farm virtually to replace the visit, but she agreed cheerfully.

"We may get some rain tonight, but we'll be asleep," Erna said happily. "It's all turning out perfectly."

Pix thought of her mission. Maybe for them.

★ ★ ★

Pix got towels at the desk and followed the arrow down the stairs. Soon she was pushing the sauna's solid wooden door open. The force of the heat and the steam took her breath away for an instant, but she slowly exhaled for what seemed like a long time and sat down on the lowest level of the benches. It felt wonderful.

The sole other occupant stood up, girded his towel securely about his loins, and strode down from the top level. He nodded in passing and left. It was their captain, Nils Hagen. His dark beard and hair had been glistening. She wondered if he'd gone to shower and would be back, although he didn't seem the chatty type.

Her thoughts turned to Marit's revelation about Hanna's birth but did not linger long. It was Kari who was insistently occupying center stage. Sonja's words kept echoing in Pix's mind: "Kari liked to tease the boys." The Scandie Sights steward hadn't known the English word for it, yet Pix was pretty sure it was the same. A tease was a tease. A very different view of Kari from the one Pix held, but then, how well did Pix really know the young woman? Pix remembered Kari as a delightful, happy child, then later, a delightful, happy teenager. Their contact had always been during the summer, vacation time, when judgment tends toward the benign.

Yes, the older Kari had had strong opinions and did fly off the handle a couple of times, but all teenagers did. Pix could not recall Kari acting provocatively with any of the boys around, but then, there weren't too many eligible ones. Kari had been content to fit into their life, complete with much younger children and much older adults. There had been no mistaking Sonja's antipathy, though. Her preference for Erik was clear. They had worked together the summer before—without Anders. Had Sonja fallen for Erik? Was it the jealousy dance?

Or was the older Kari, undeniably a beauty, something more than a flirt? And what had this led to? It was not the sort of thing a grandmother picked up on. Pix realized that she had been so caught up in the tour and its multiple personalities that she had been losing sight of the two most important personalities of all—Kari and Erik. The key to finding out what had happened just might lie in figuring out who the young people actually were—or, in Kari's case, she reminded herself vehemently, she hoped still was.

Wide-awake, with a troubled mind, there was no danger of falling asleep in the sauna this time. She got up, filled the dipper from the bucket, both made of pine, and flung the water on the rocks. She almost wished there was a snowbank to jump into and someone to flail her lightly with birch branches, all die-hard sauna practices. She would have to content herself with the deeply satisfying hissing sound the water made and the equally satisfying sense that all her impurities were draining out with her sweat.

Captain Hansen had a dark beard. The man on Jennifer's balcony at Stalheim had had a dark beard. The man driving the car so swiftly away from the Stalheim Hotel just after she had overheard the argument on her walk—he had a dark beard, too. But many Norwegians had beards, light and dark. Sven had had a beard, or maybe still did. Sven, Kari's father. He would be in his early or mid-fifties. Pix returned to her thoughts about Kari, about where she could be. Kari had definitely wanted to find her mother's family. Had she picked up some clue about them on the trip, or one relating to her father? Was that where she was? Depressed, confused by Erik's death, whether she witnessed it or not—for, if she was still alive and in Norway, she couldn't have escaped the news of it—had she gone in search of her past? Her mother's past? Her father's? Were some newly found relatives even now sheltering her? Hiding her? Kari again. Pix wished she had a better idea who Kari was. Now, were Samantha missing, God forbid, Pix could put herself in her daughter's shoes—not that they'd fit exactly. There are vast uncharted areas in every child's life, as unknown to a parent as Amelia Earhart's crash site. But Kari's shoes... Pix didn't even know the brand.

The door opened, but it wasn't Captain Hagen. It was an elderly Japanese gentleman wearing underwear that revealed nothing and carrying a towel. He gasped and tottered to the bench, looking at Pix, looking at the door, then looking at Pix again. For a while, he did nothing but breathe heavily and make some small throat-clearing noises.

After a moment, he started to speak to her in Japanese. She nodded and smiled, yet that only seemed to increase his agitation. Finally, she picked out some English words—*sorry* and *Japanese*. At last, a sentence. "I am so sorry. I am Japanese. From Tokyo." Obviously he had not expected to see a woman in the sauna. But what about the geisha tradition? Pix supposed that was very different and she was a far cry from it, swaddled in one of Kvikne's towels. Maybe it was her height. If they were standing, she'd tower over him.

"It's all right." She nodded and smiled some more. "No problem. It's the custom here."

That produced another torrent of Japanese; then he said in English, "I go ticky-tocky, ticky-tocky," accompanied by a fluttering hand gesture over his heart.

Suddenly, she was afraid the heat was too much for the poor man and he had, in fact, been trying to tell her all this time that he was having a heart attack. He repeated the gesture and she asked, "Are you all right?" realizing she had fallen victim to the American disease of believing you can be understood in any language if you just speak English slowly and distinctly enough in a loud voice.

She stood up, which seemed to alarm him even more, so she promptly sat down again.

After some minutes filled with grunts of diminishing intensity, *he* stood up, obviously quite all right. He repeated the "ticky-tocky" routine, bowed several dozen times, and left. Pix laughed until she thought she'd pee, except she'd oozed so much sweat, there wasn't any. Time to take a shower.

She stood up and went to the door. The temperature was 60°C, she noted, 140°F. She pulled. Nothing happened. She pulled again. Somehow, the steam must have caused the wood to swell and stick. She put both hands on the handle and pulled with all her might. The door didn't budge.

Now, don't panic, she told herself. This is ridiculous. She banged on it several times but doubted she could be heard. When she'd come in, she'd noticed how thick it was—and there was no window. She pulled at it again. Her towel slipped off.

Now she did begin to panic. How could the door have gotten stuck? The hotel would obviously have had to be very careful about the construction of its sauna and it would be checked from time to time. More than that, since this was Scandinavia.

She wrapped her towel around herself again. It made her feel less vulnerable. Had it been her imagination? She tried the door once again. This time, she was able to see into the crack between the door and the frame.

See into it and realize it was locked.

Locked? Locked!

She sat down on the bench, feeling slightly stunned. She could be in here for a very long time. It was almost 10:30 when she'd gone to her room, taken her watch off, leaving it there with her earrings and a gold chain she'd been wearing. By now, it was certainly well past 11:30. It had taken time to find the sauna; then she'd luxuriated in a long shower. It had had those jets that squirted you from all sides. Then there was her nonadventure with the gentleman from Tokyo. What with the merriment in the lounge and other nocturnal activities offered officially and unofficially on the hotel premises, unless someone had an impulse for late-night sweating, she was stuck until morning. If her mother did knock at Pix's door, she'd assume her daughter was taking a walk or kicking up her heels with the French ladies and she would go to bed. It would be breakfast time before Ursula and Marit missed her.

The feeling of panic set in again—and increased. What would sitting in so much heat do to her? Could she dehydrate? Pass out? There was only a small amount of water in the bucket. She'd planned to refill it when she went to take a shower. Should she drink it?

She went over to the bucket and stuck her finger in the water. It was hot and somehow the prospect of swallowing it made her feel queasy. The smell of the wood, so fragrant before, was also beginning to turn her stomach as she finally faced the question smack in front of her.

Who locked the door?

Was it routine? She hadn't seen any signs stating hours of operation, and like the midnight sun, she imagined the sauna never set, either. In any case, hotel workers would surely have been instructed to see whether the sauna was occupied before locking up. She had been sitting in the middle of the bench, clearly visible to anyone opening the door, as the Japanese gentleman had discovered.

The Japanese man. He was the last person in the sauna with her, but why on earth would he lock her in and where would he have found a key? He had been upset, all that "ticky-tocky" business, but he hadn't seemed to bear her any ill will.

Ill will. Given that the key was in some obvious position outside the door—say hanging from a nail—who might have wanted to keep her on ice, or rather, the reverse, for a while? With all the questions she'd been asking over the last two days, had she made someone nervous? So nervous that he or she wanted to give her a warning, or keep her from seeing something that was going on now?

Her head was beginning to ache from the heat and the stress. Her thoughts were not companionable ones. What did people in solitary confinement think about? Her brain was beginning to turn to mush, or *grøt*. Such funny words. Such a funny language, Norwegian. Those three extra letters tacked onto the alphabet after z: æ, ø, and å. Why? And that rolling *r* sound they made in the back of their throats like a cat purring. Cats. She wondered what her cat, Stan, a gray tiger with a lively personality, was doing—Stan, Stan Miller. People sometimes thought they had another child. Well, the dogs and Stan were like children, she supposed. Her children. She slapped herself lightly on the cheek a few times. It felt good. She could still feel things. The baking heat had been numbing.

She stood up and paced back and forth. Her

heart was pounding. Ticky-tocky, ticky-tocky was right. She tried to address herself sternly and calmly. Now Pix, she told her weaker sister, nothing is going to happen. You're not in any real danger. At her last physical, the doctor had told her she was disgustingly healthy. Somehow her heart was still racing, though. She didn't have a heart condition— at least that she knew of. Disgustingly healthy. At the time, Pix had felt somewhat embarrassed—it was such an odd phrase. Would she be less disgusting if the doctor had turned up a hemorrhoid or suspicious mole? More likely more.

No, she'd make it through the night. There was just going to be a lot of time to kill. She wished she hadn't thought of the phrase. She sat down again.

Captain Hagen had been in the sauna. So he knew she was here. She spread her fingers out to count the people who knew where she was. The desk clerk, who had carefully counted out two towels for her, no more, no less; the distressed man from Tokyo; silent Captain Hagen; and Mother. That took care of pointer, tall man, ring man, and pinkie. Had she mentioned it at dinner? She was sure she hadn't. But she had told Jennifer at coffee, hadn't she? Yes. Thumbkin went down and she made a fist. She looked at her right hand with its fingers still stretched out and tried to recall if anyone had been near enough to overhear her talking to Jennifer. The Dahl sisters were leaving—but she'd mentioned it to them later—and the Felds were not too far away.

Then again, the lobby had not been empty when she got the towels, and why else would she be requesting them? Their rooms were amply supplied. So any number of people knew she'd be here, the whole blasted tour. And the guides, plus the stewards. Scandie Sights—such a stupid name. Mermaids and trolls. She could use a bit less enchantment. She wiggled her fingers. Her grandmother's diamond solitaire, her engagement ring left to Pix, sparkled. It felt tight. Her fingers looked like the little sausages that had been under the dome in a large silver chafing dish at breakfast this morning. This morning—at the Stalheim Hotel. Stalheim, the swastika. She realized her left hand was still clenched in a fist. She shook her fingers free. Her plain gold wedding band—the flowers that had decorated it originally had long worn smooth— reminded her of her husband. Husbands and wives. Newlyweds. Girlfriends and boyfriends. Sonja and Anders knew she was coming here. Sonja, her dislike of Kari so intense. As intense as her liking for Erik. The jealousy dance, one face forward, one face backward.

Agitated, she stood up suddenly and felt dizzy. The heat was like armor and she must have lost several pounds of sweat. She walked slowly and deliberately from one end of the room to the other, counting her steps. It was something to do. She decided to set up a routine. She was beginning to get tired and she had to keep awake—walk, rest, walk, rest. What *would* happen if she fell asleep in here? In the morning would there just be a pool

163

of perspiration where she'd reclined? Nothing but a very damp towel, a version of the Wicked Witch of the West after she gets doused with water? "I'm melting," Pix heard herself say aloud, and she laughed. Her thoughts were definitely rambling. Maybe at some point the heat got switched off. She got up and looked at the temperature gauge. No switches.

Dehydration. That's what was going to happen to her. She wouldn't melt. Not her bones, big bones. The Rowes were all big-boned women, although not heavy. Desiccation. She'd be like one of those dried fruits she bought at the health-food store for her children's snacks, only she ended up eating them and they held out for Ritz Bits and Doritos.

Her children. Her eyes filled with tears and she quickly tried to squelch them. She needed all the internal fluids she had. But her children. Motherless. Poor Sam. How would he cope? Remarry. She sat down on the bench and thought of possible candidates, convincing herself that she was thinking rationally. She wished she had something to write with. It was such an ignominious way to go—to dry up.

Her family. Guilt washed over her so palpably, it almost felt refreshing. She hadn't thought about them much since she'd arrived in Norway. She chastised herself. What kind of mother was she anyway? It had been wonderful to be unencumbered by her daily routines. Sailing down the fjord today, she'd been very happy, forgetting everything for a time—what she'd left behind and what had brought her here.

The inside of her mouth seemed to be made of felt. Her throat was parched.

She forced herself to drink the water in the pail, taking little sips. It wasn't so bad. Damp felt now inside her mouth. She dozed off. Sleep—the sweet escape.

A hand was on her shoulder. Someone screamed. She recognized the voice. It was hers.

"Sorry we startled you, but I told you not to go to sleep in these things. Good thing we came along. The door was locked." It was Lynette. Lynette and Roy junior, both nude and carrying their towels. Thank God for honeymooners. Pix mumbled her thanks and sat up. How long had she been in here?

"What time is it?" She spoke very deliberately, like a drunk who doesn't want to slur but who doesn't fool anyone.

"Almost one o'clock," Lynette answered. Pix tried to think if she'd ever heard Roy junior's voice. As soon as he'd seen her, he'd wrapped his towel around his waist, blushing furiously. His face was pretty red, too. Lynette didn't bother to cover up.

Pix rose slowly and realized she could walk. Suddenly, she felt very, very middle-aged—no, she would not say old. She managed a weak smile and pulled open the door with relief. Outside, the air felt like the Arctic, but it brought her to her senses. She understood the point of snowbanks or icy swims now. There was a chair. She sat on it. Roy appeared and spoke.

"Lynette thought we'd better keep the key inside," he explained as he removed it from the nail it did indeed hang on, around the corner from the sauna entrance. "Are you okay?" He had a pleasant deep voice, filled with midwestern sincerity.

She *was* okay, she realized with great joy, and she offered some advice of her own.

"Definitely keep the key with you."

It was a little after one. She'd showered and dressed, drunk several glasses of water, then gone up to her room with every intent of going straight to bed when she'd remembered she had to search the damn boat.

Pix toyed with the idea of forgetting the whole thing. It was hard to believe there was a secret compartment on their Viking cruiser and even harder to believe anything illegal was in it. Yet there was never really any question. And it wasn't simply the thought of facing her mother over hard-boiled eggs and sardines in the morning. Pix had come to Norway to help Marit and apparently that meant an enormous amount of sleep deprivation. She crawled into bed and set the alarm for three o'clock.

The alarm was ringing. Pix reached for it, instantly wide-awake. She'd pulled on some corduroy pants, a heavy turtleneck, and a sweater before she realized that it was only two o'clock. The alarm hadn't gone off. She'd dreamed it.

"Damn and double damn," she said aloud,

and walked over to the window, pulling back the drapes. It wasn't dark, but the light was dim enough for a trip to the dock. The problem was, there were still a great many people strolling about the hotel grounds. Again aloud, she grumbled, "Don't these people ever go to sleep?"

She went out onto the balcony and sat down. She didn't blame them. It was so beautiful, so special—who wanted to go to sleep and miss it? The mountains seemed endless and, just as on the boat, almost within reach, a short walk at the very least. The landscape looked serene, secure even—put your trust in mountains—was that from a poem? A psalm? If it wasn't, it should be. Immovable, invariable. All day these mountain images and pieces of half-remembered phrases had filled her mind. But, she thought, perhaps the mountains would not appear so poetic in the winter, especially during the endless dark days, days of bad weather. Then the slopes would press in on one and their nearness become a weighty barrier.

The sky was starting to turn a slate gray. It was happening all at once. She hoped it didn't mean rain, as Erna Dahl had said. Two figures emerged from beneath her balcony, walking slowly down the path across the lawn to the water. She leaned forward to see who it was before they moved out of sight. They passed under one of the lights. Oscar and Sophie—Sophie sans her *cousine*! The oh-so-naughty man had continental tastes. They were headed for the benches at the water's edge.

A rendezvous by the fjord.

Next Pix heard a voice in the distance. A man's. It sounded like Don Brady. The entire Scandie Sights tour, with the exception of her mother and the farmers, seemed to be up and about. The Petersons, minus Lynette, but not Roy junior came into view from around the corner of the hotel. This was interesting, but her eyelids were getting heavy again. Trusting that the alarm would wake her, she stood up and stretched, catching sight of Sophie returning from the water much more rapidly than she'd gone, and traveling alone. At one point, she broke into a run; then, seeing others about, she slowed down. As she passed under the light again, Pix could see that she was scowling. That naughty man.

Pix went to bed.

Minutes later, or so it seemed, the alarm rang. She hadn't bothered to undress. Pausing only to make sure it wasn't raining and/or still like Grand Central Station outside, she grabbed her jacket and stepped quietly into the hall. There had been no one about and the sky was streaked with ominous bands of dark gray clouds, but the ground was dry. She'd shoved a scarf in her pocket and hoped she wouldn't need it.

Earlier, she'd made sure the door to the stairs was not locked and now she took them quickly. The sooner this was over, the better. There was no early wake-up call and she might actually get some more sleep.

The stairs ended at a hallway, leading to the lobby in one direction, a side exit to the outside in the other, she'd discovered when she'd planned her search. She'd wanted to avoid the night desk clerk—and any insomniacs wandering about the lobby.

Pix pushed the door open—it wasn't locked or alarmed—and stepped out into the brisk night air. There was no need for a flashlight, but she'd brought Faith's penlite with her, as well as the rest of her kit and camera. She was uncomfortably aware of the canister of hair spray in the pocket of her dark blue denim jacket.

It was a short walk to the dock where the fjord cruiser was berthed alongside the fleet of small pleasure boats so beloved of Norwegians, those in Balestrand no exception. All very trim, flags flying from the sterns. She passed by the huge pile of wood—odd pieces of lumber, crates, branches—that awaited the touch of a torch on Midsummer Night, St. Hans' Eve, *St. Hans-aften,* the twenty-third. They'd seen similar bonfire piles all along the fjord today. This was the largest so far, though, and people would be adding to it. She was sorry she wouldn't be here to see the conflagration.

There wasn't a soul in sight and she walked straight down the wooden dock to the boat, alone on the fjord. Or so she thought.

Just as she was about to step aboard, she heard voices from the stern and saw two shadowy figures, the tips of their cigarettes glowing in the dark. The voices stopped; then she heard footsteps. Someone was coming up on deck to have a look. They must have heard her approaching. Wildly, she looked for a place to hide and jumped into a small dinghy tied close by. There was a tarp and she crawled under it. Why hadn't the nearest boat been one of the ones with a cabin?

The tarp smelled strongly of *fisk* and she was so distracted by the pungent odor that for a moment she did not realize that whoever had been on the boat had now moved onto the dock. They were talking again, quite close to her. Pix froze. Men's voices, speaking Norwegian. Really Marit should have enlisted the help of someone who spoke the language! It was tempting to lift a corner of the heavy cloth and peer out, yet she didn't dare. Strolling on the dock or grounds could have been explained. Bundled under a boat tarp at three o'clock in the morning could not. She strained to hear what they were saying, painfully aware that her vocabulary was limited to food, greetings, requests, and bodily functions. All she could tell was that they were not quarreling. Their voices were not raised. The chat sounded companionable even. The guides? The captain? Balestrand inhabitants on a late-night— or rather, early-morning—tour of the boat?

Speculation was suddenly replaced by the realization that Erna had been right. It was raining. Heavy droplets were soon drumming against the tarp. Surely the men would leave, and she lifted a corner in time to see the two running for cover. It was pouring now and the absence of streetlights made it impossible to see who they were. They did turn in the direction of the hotel, but there were also many houses that way, as well as a large parking area. Thunder crashed. Then lightning. And again. The second flash revealed that one man had a beard. Another beard.

She huddled down under the tarp. The sailcloth was drenched and she would be soon. She was stiff, too, and the irony of having been both too hot and too cold in a relatively short period of time did not escape her. She'd have to wait a while longer to be sure that they wouldn't see her. She hoped the side door was still unlocked.

She looked at her watch: 3:30. She'd been gone from her room only a half hour! She'd wait five more minutes, then make a run for it.

The hands on her watch moved slowly and despite her uncomfortable position and the pitching of the boat as the storm hit, Pix began to fall asleep. Only three minutes had passed, but no one would be out any longer than he could help in this mess. She stood up and raced down the dock. Five minutes later, she was standing under a hot shower. No wonder Norwegians looked so clean. She hadn't had so many showers since she was a teenager.

It took awhile for her to get rid of the smell of fish that had seeped into her pores with the rainwater. How could something so good smell so bad, so *skitten*—another interesting Norwegian word. It meant "foul," "dirty," even "smutty." While sounding like a small pet, it somehow perfectly expressed the way she'd felt hiding in the boat and even now. What had she accomplished? Nothing. Kari was still missing and Pix was beginning to believe she must have drowned with Erik. Maybe someone stole her passport and money, then was interrupted before he or she could take Erik's. But, said a nagging voice, Marit had said Kari had some jewelry in her pack and that had been left.

Pix looked at her bed. It had stopped raining and it was a little past four. She sighed. She had to see this thing to the end and that meant going back to the boat. If she hurried, she could search the closet and stroll back, apparently returning from a hearty, early— very early—morning's walk.

Feeling straight out of *The Perils of Pauline,* Pix got dressed once again. Her jacket was soaked, so she put on two turtlenecks and a heavy sweater. Once more she tiptoed down the hall, descended the stairs, and slipped out the side door.

The storm had left the air with a clear, fresh feeling and the fjord in front of her was like a sheet of green glass. The sky was beginning to get light and the birds were waking up. The spire of the Anglican church, St. Olav's, was silhouetted against the wooded slopes just beyond. It had been founded by one of those intrepid British females who ranged the world, ready for a cup of tea in a bedouin's tent or Sami's *lavvo.* The architecture of St. Olav's was an interesting marriage of stave and staid—dragons and gingerbread. She walked rapidly toward the water and the path that followed the peninsula before it turned toward the center of the village, mainly consisting of a post office, small market, and two gift shops.

As she passed the last of the benches provided by Kvikne's Hotel in abundance throughout the grounds, a figure stood up. Pix was so intent on her destination that she didn't realize anyone else was around.

Not until a hand came down hard on her shoulder and a voice said, "Now where do you think you're going?"

6

It was Carol Peterson. But not the perky dancer observed a scant few hours earlier. No, this Carol's face was swollen from crying, the skirt of her cocktail dress limp, and the white sweater replaced by a sweatshirt whose KISS ME, I'M NORWEGIAN slogan seemed a pathetic mockery. Carol Peterson looked like something the cat wouldn't drag in.

She repeated her query imperiously—at least some things were constant. "*Where* are you going?"

Pix had been so startled by this sudden apparition, and the fact that it was such a dramatic shadow of its former self, that she couldn't think of a plausible excuse for a moment. She tried to marshal her thoughts and managed to say, "Ummm"

"Or, I should say, *where* have you been?"

Carol blazed. The woman was furious.

This was getting very, very weird. "What do you mean? I couldn't sleep and decided to take a walk." Pix's wits were back. Was the woman insane? Why was she so upset, and why attack Pix this way?

"Yeah, sure. I know your type, you... you easterner!" It was obviously the worst epithet she could drum up.

"Why don't you tell me what's wrong?" Pix decided to ignore the regional slur and led the way to a bench. There was no way she was going to be able to search the Viking cruiser now, and besides, she had to find out why Carol Peterson, respectable matron, was wandering the grounds, crying her eyes out at four o'clock in the morning, when surely she normally would have been long in bed, face cream applied, hair net in place.

Carol followed and slumped down next to Pix dejectedly. All the wind was out of her sails, the air out of the balloon, the stuffing from the rag doll. Her "artichoke" hairdo was down to the choke.

A snuffle, a heavy sigh, and Carol was ready to spill her guts—or so Pix hoped.

"This was supposed to be the trip of a life-time. I've been working on it for over a year. Writing for brochures, talking to the people at the Norwegian Tourist Board, comparing prices, studying the map. We've never been home, I told Roy. This is our big chance and we'll take Roy junior and his bride. It will be our wedding gift to them. A dream trip. A chance to see where we all started, of course not Lynette, but the rest of us. It was going to be perfect!" Carol started to sob again. She'd obviously been doing this on and off for quite a while. It was not a pretty sight.

"But haven't you been having a good time? I thought you told me you were enjoying yourself?" Pix hadn't heard her say exactly these words, but she hadn't heard anything to the contrary, except for the kvetching about Kari. Kvetching was not the right word. She'd have to ask Marit what the Norwegian equivalent was, although Norwegians complained so obliquely—"Do you think it was margarine in the *sandekake*? I wouldn't want to say, but what do you think?"—there probably wasn't a term.

Carol stopped crying. The sky was still gray and dawn was having a hard time piercing through. Slivers of light appeared at the horizon, then seemed to give up.

"Well, yes, I was having fun." She looked off toward the fjord, running the video of *The Petersons Return to the Land of Their Ancestors* through her mind for a moment. "Especially at the beginning. I couldn't believe I was actually here after hearing so much about Norway all my life. And everything was just right. So clean. But now this! I can't even believe it! And what if our friends should find out? Sick, I tell you. That's what it is."

But what was it? Pix had the sense not to interrupt the woman.

"And criminal. I'm sure it's against the law. I don't know the laws here, but I know what's legal in Duluth—and in the sight of God." Carol was building up a good head of righteous indignation and the train was still in the station. She continued.

"You think you know somebody." Her voice was as bitter as an unripe lingonberry. She shook her head, steam disappearing, replaced by tears again.

"How can this be happening to me! And on my dream trip!" she wailed.

"Is there anything I can do?" Pix was beginning to wonder if Carol was going to come across with any concrete information. So far, her monologue had been tantalizingly circumspect.

In the sauna at Stalheim, Lynette had said her mother-in-law wasn't going to like something that was coming. Had it arrived? But would Carol have been so reticent if the current crisis involved Lynette? Pix had the feeling any blows landed by the young woman would be met in kind and news of the battle spread far and wide. And criminal? If Lynette had broken any laws, Carol would have been the first to blow the whistle on her—and to hold Roy junior's hand steady while he filed for an annulment.

Pix repeated her request, since Carol had not replied.

"Are you sure I can't do something?"

Carol sat up straight and pulled her sweatshirt down.

"No, I think just about enough has been

done, and I'll thank you not to refer to the matter again."

It was an easy request with which to comply.

"I'm sorry you're so upset." Pix grasped for some way to keep the woman talking—and she *was* sorry to see Carol like this, obviously in a great deal of pain.

"Sorry never helps," Mrs. Peterson said. It had the ring of an off-repeated remark, automatic and a real conversation stopper. She stood up and marched off in the direction of the hotel.

Now what the hell was that all about? Pix said to herself.

The sun was rising and Pix walked toward the shore. She was exhausted, but her encounter with Carol Peterson had been unsettling and she thought she'd take the long way back, both to avoid meeting the woman again—that hand on her shoulder had sent enough adrenaline coursing through Pix's body to keep her awake for the rest of the trip—and because a stroll in the damp morning air might induce slumber. Pix could snatch two or three hours before the boat left. She'd ask Ursula to make her a sandwich at breakfast and she'd sleep in. The thought caused a yawn and she quickened her steps along the path. The tops of the mountains were streaked with gold now and the white snow shone like the enameling on a particularly fine piece of Norwegian jewelry.

At the edge of the fjord, Pix paused, unable to rush when it was so beautiful, yet telling herself she had to get going. A down comforter and pillows were calling her name. Besides, without some sleep, she'd be useless.

She looked at the rocks that lined the shore and thought of the coast of Maine—Sanpere Island in Penobscot Bay, where her family had been spending summers since before Ursula was born. People said Maine reminded them of Norway or vice versa, depending which side of the ocean one was on. The fjords are tidal, she reminded herself, although the tides are slight compared with Maine's. But the rocks looked alike, covered with rackweed. Her children had all loved to pop its slippery small balloons with their bare feet and fingers, as had she and her brother. Higher up, she noted the rocks were covered with the same yellow ocher lichen that often was the only spot of color on Sanpere's granite ledges— like splashes of paint. She had a great desire to climb down to the rocks and find a nice flat one to curl up on and nap. If it had been a bit warmer, she would have. A tern flew overhead. She stopped and looked out across the rocks to the water beyond.

The tide was out. She could see small stretches of sand. She could see—

Oscar Melling! Arms and legs spread-eagled on a ledge, face to one side. She recognized his bright blue Ban-Lon sport shirt.

Oscar Melling! Motionless. He looked

small from where she was. Small against the backdrop of the mountains and the fjord.

Oscar Melling! Dead!

It was so unbelievable that she didn't feel the least bit like screaming, hideous as the situation was. Without thinking, she climbed over the low wall that separated nature from its cultivated cousins, the lawns and shrubs of the hotel. Oscar's body was not that far away, but the rocks were covered with seaweed and it was slow going. She kept looking back to see if anyone else was up, prepared to shout for help. Although at this point, it was too late. From the way he was lying, she was certain he was dead, yet she had to make sure— though the notion of resuscitating him was one she immediately pushed far back into a distant corner of her brain, numbed by fatigue and shock.

Her sneakers sank into the wet sand between the rocks and cold water sloshed over the tops.

Melling was wearing exactly what he'd had on the last time she'd seen him. She'd noted the Ban-Lon and wondered if he'd saved the shirt all these years or had a stockpile. No jacket or sweater had been added to his attire. She reached for his wrist and, as she had suspected she would, found no pulse. The body was already giving off a sour smell that mixed pungently with the brackish rackweed, and Pix thought she might not be able to keep from vomiting. She gulped some air.

There was an empty bottle of aquavit next to the rock. The tide had either not come up this far or been insufficient to wash it away. An opinionated boozer—those telltale fine red veins she'd observed at Stalheim when he'd stopped by their table to invite Ursula to play cards were even more apparent up this close. She could see only half his face. One blue eye was open wide, a cloudy blue in old age, vacant in death. His mouth was open, drooping slackly to one side, teeth yellowed by countless cigars.

A pool of blood had collected in a hollow in the rock to the left of his body, the trail beginning to dry to a reddish brown streak. The other side of his face must have been hurt in the fall. She had no desire to assess the damage. The part of his head she could see gave no indication of injury, his baldness shiny with the morning dew, the little hair he had slightly damp.

Had the Mermaid/Troll tour been his dream trip, too? Pix felt tears welling into her eyes. Poor old man.

He'd been alive a few hours ago. Alive and enjoying himself. He must have stumbled out here with his bottle and pitched over the side. There were no railings. Oscar had been unlucky. Very unlucky. She wondered if there had been a Mrs. Melling, or maybe there still was and she'd been left at home. Where was he from? New Jersey. The mail-order Scandinavian foods, *lutefisk* in your mailbox. Exhaustion was sending her thoughts to unexpected places and she had to go tell someone at the hotel about her grisly morning discovery. It was truly morning now. The dawn had finally broken through, yet the hotel was still cloaked in sleep, the curtains closed tight against the light, guests enjoying a few more hours repose before gathering at the trough for breakfast. If last night's spread was anything to go by, breakfast at Kvikne's, Norway's signature meal, would be gargantuan.

But Oscar's bed was empty. His place at the table would be taken by someone else. She crawled up the rocks and back onto the lawn. She ought to run. A man was dead. Instead, she found herself walking slowly, as in a dream, into the hotel lobby.

The clerk looked freshly starched and greeted Pix cheerily, "*God dag, god dag*. What can I do for you?" before realizing that the woman in front of the desk, color drained from her face and swaying slightly, was not in search of stamps.

"You must get someone right away. There's a body in the fjord." Pix sat heavily in an ornately carved chair across from the desk.

"What!" The girl screeched and immediately yelled something in Norwegian, producing two other clerks from a room to the rear. After some excited talk, a young man came to Pix's side.

"Do you need some help?" He actually took one of her hands, holding it rather tenderly in both of his. He was about her son Mark's age, Pix figured. She hoped under similar circumstances, Mark would be so kind. Similar circumstances?

181

"You must think I am crazy." She couldn't help speaking apologetically. She'd thought she would get rid of this kind of emotional baggage after forty, but it hadn't happened. A man was dead. She'd discovered the body, so she must be at fault in some way. She was upsetting the hotel staff, for one thing. "But there *is* a dead man in the fjord—or rather, on the rocks. His name is Oscar Melling. We're with the Scandie Sights tour. I mean, he was and I am. You'd better call the guides, Jan and Carl. I can't remember their last names right now."

The girl at the desk was already dialing and several people had run out the door in the direction Pix had indicated. They made the journey much more quickly than Pix had and came back shouting. Her head began to ache with the sound of Norwegian swirling about her. On their trip, she and Sam had shared a train car with a ladies' choir group from Drammen and after fifteen minutes the singsong had lost its tuneful appeal, punctuated as it was with sharp intakes of breath and many *tsk, tsk, tsks*. Pix and Sam, smiling and nodding, had backed out the door and walked the full length of the train to other seats. Pix was having that same feeling now and broke in. "I'm going to my room, if that's all right. I'm a bit tired." Instantly, the young man who had been so solicitous came to her side, offering his arm. Pix took it and together they made their way to the elevator. It opened just as they got there, revealing Jan and Carl—Carl in proper pajamas and robe, Jan in sweats—both looking completely bewildered.

Pix sighed and let the young man lead her back to her seat. They'd want to question her.

She waited while the guides dashed to the fjord and back. Carl looked as if he had lost last night's dinner on the return trip and Jan was trembling. Pix thought it must be unusual for there to be a corpse of any kind on a Scandie Sights tour, the odd heart attack perhaps, but two—Erik surely counted—could only be classified as inconceivable.

"Was he alive when you found him?" Carl asked. "I mean, did he say how it happened?" Lawsuit was written bold across his face.

"No, he was quite dead. I imagine he had been lying there all night and no one happened to see him because of the position of the rocks, and also, why would someone be walking there?" As she offered this useful observation, she realized it presented an obvious question for herself, so before anyone could think to ask it, she rose, wobbling a bit— unfaked—and said as firmly as she could, "I really must lie down. This has been extremely upsetting." Her friend, as she now regarded him, once again seized her arm and cast baleful glances at the guides. She'd have to find out his name and write the hotel a nice letter. He took her to the door of her room, asked once more if he could do anything for her, and disappeared down the hall. Pix opened the door, thought of her mother, presumably asleep in her own room, and headed for bed. Bothering only to kick off her shoes, she pulled the featherweight comforter over her shoulders and fell sound asleep.

Someone was knocking on the door. Pix rolled over and poked her husband, "Get that, will you, honey?" she mumbled. She poked again when the knocking continued and, getting no response, opened her eyes. Sam was an ocean away. She got out of bed and went to the door. She felt drugged. It was Mother—Mother and Marit with a breakfast tray.

Marit set the tray on the desk as Ursula grabbed Pix, hugging her tightly.

"We've been so worried, but we didn't want to wake you. What happened!"

Pix realized that the two women thought there was some connection between her search of the boat and the discovery of the body and she hastened to correct their misapprehension.

"I couldn't search the closet. First, there were two men on board; then it started to rain and I had to come back. Since I was up, when the rain stopped, I went out again, but then I found Oscar." She eyed the tray greedily. She was starving—hence the *Reader's Digest* version of what had been a very long and complicated night.

"*Vær så god,*" Marit said, waving at the tray, using the universal phrase, a kind of Norwegian equivalent of *shalom*. It meant everything from "Come and get it" to "You're welcome," with varying degrees of "Have some more," "Go in," or "Look at anything you like" in between.

184

Pix needed no urging and was soon digging into a perfectly boiled egg, freshly baked whole-wheat rolls, farm butter, cheese, and, of course, herring and lox. There was a croissant on the tray looking totally out of place, but she wolfed that down, too. After having poured a second cup of coffee, she felt herself again, although these days that was subject to constant redefinition. She told them about getting locked in the sauna, meeting Carol Peterson, then happening upon Oscar Melling's lifeless body.

After discussing the sauna episode, which Marit was inclined to think was an accident, although Ursula, for once, was unsure, they got on to Mrs. Peterson.

"What do you suppose the woman was talking about?" Ursula asked.

"Do you think she had anything to do with Mr. Melling? Maybe she had already seen the body and didn't want to get involved?"

"But she kept talking about what someone else had done, a crime, but I think that wasn't meant literally." As she spoke, Pix recalled Carol in Oscar's arms, whirling about the dance floor. He had a certain appeal. She remembered how courtly he had been to her mother. Obviously, his manners had another side—the argument with Arnie Feld had occurred just before the dancing. Dr. Jekyll and Mr. Hyde. More likely the erratic effects of alcohol on an aging nervous system.

"Everyone is upset, of course. Carl spoke to the group after breakfast and then Marit and I went to church. The tour is sticking to the itinerary and that's why we woke you up. You can relax on the boat, but I didn't think you'd want to miss the farm. Marit's going to keep her ears open while we're gone and talk to some of the staff. Make sure this really was an accident, as Carl said."

"I'm going to be very worried and maybe a little cross." Marit smiled. " 'Are you sure it's safe to walk on that path so close to the water?' I'll ask. See what they say. The police are here, and I'll find a nice young one who will tell me more than he should."

Pix was beginning to think they should incorporate themselves.

"Okay, but I have to have a shower and wake up. When does the boat leave?"

"You have thirty minutes. Because of all this, we're not going until ten-thirty. I'll wait for you on the dock." She paused and added, "Pity you weren't able to get a look into the closet last night."

Pix gave her mother a very firm kiss and ushered the two women out the door.

Ten minutes later, she was washed, dressed, and hurriedly punching several hundred numbers into the phone. It was time to call Faith.

Faith Sibley Fairchild had spent the previous afternoon sitting in her backyard in Aleford, watching her children dig in the earth that her husband, Tom, had optimistically tilled for what he called their "market garden." So far, the only seeds sown were a row of peas, delineated by a wavy length of string. The children had been instructed to stay away from the growing plants and thus far they had been content to dig where Tom planned to put his tomato seedlings. Faith was always happy to receive fresh garden produce—the ultimate luxury was visiting friends who grew their own corn, brought the water to a boil, and dashed outside to grab the ears, stripping them on the return trip before flinging them in the water for exactly four minutes. However, Faith was not a gifted gardener. Something about compost, earthworms, and chinch bugs put her off. She preferred to do her harvesting at the Wilson Farm stand or Bread and Circus.

Now shortly after four o'clock in the morning, her dreams were filled with buds and tendrils—and soup. While she'd idly watched her children, Faith had been leafing through her recipe notebooks, looking for an alternative to lobster bisque as a first course for a wedding she was catering later in the month. The menu had been fixed—and altered—for months. The bride, apparently having nothing on her plate except wedding plans, had taken to treating Have Faith's kitchen as a kind of club, dropping in for coffee and tastes of whatever Faith was cooking, to go over things "for the last time, I promise." Yesterday, she had announced that lobster bisque was too pink and she wanted something different. Faith mulled over fresh avocado soup, garnished with a spider's web of thinned-out sour cream and spiked with a bit of white rum. In case the bride ruled it out as being too green, Faith was prepared to offer *potage de champignons sauvages* as a backup. The young woman was pretentious enough to relish the name in French, and Faith herself preferred it for the untamed flavor it promised. Wild mushroom soup sounded much more prosaic.

When the phone rang, her first thought upon sitting bolt upright in bed was that the bride had changed her mind again. "Duck consommé," she mumbled, reaching for the receiver. Tom had not stirred. The only things that woke him were a slight cough from one of his children or a whispered request from his wife.

"I know it's the middle of the night, or rather, very, very early in the morning, but I had to talk to you."

Faith was fully awake in a flash.

"What's going on? I've been thinking of you constantly." This was true. Pix and soup.

"I don't have much time—the boat is leaving in about fifteen minutes, but first you'll have to swear you won't tell Sam. He'll just get worried, and there's no reason to. Promise?"

Faith had no problem keeping secrets, especially those of her friends. And she was not a believer in telling things for people's own good under any circumstances.

"I promise. What's going on? Have you found Kari?"

"No—but I did find a body early this morning."

"Oh my God! Whose?"

"An elderly gentleman named Oscar Melling. He was a grocer from New Jersey."

To Faith, a native New Yorker, Jersey was known for only two things—its tomatoes and the place where her aunt Chat had inexplicably chosen to move after a lifetime on the West Side of Manhattan.

Pix was still talking. "He was in the fjord. Not actually in the water, but on the shore. He had been drinking pretty heavily throughout the evening and must have fallen."

"Had he hit his head? Was there a lot of blood?"

"He fell partly facedown and there was some blood, also an empty aquavit bottle. Nobody thinks it was anything but an accident, but..."

"You don't agree. Otherwise, why would you be calling me?" Faith finished for her.

Pix realized with a start that Faith had put into words what had been nagging at her since she'd found Oscar. It *had* to have been an accident. The man was drunk, yet...

"It's just that so many strange things have been happening on this tour. Starting with Erik's death and Kari's disappearance." Pix rapidly ran down some of the rest: the argument she'd overheard in the woods at Stalheim— not untoward by itself, but when linked with the sense she had of being followed and the bearded intruder on Jennifer Olsen's balcony the night before, enough to produce unease, especially as the man she observed driving away so hurriedly in Stalheim had also sported

189

a beard. Then the swastika on the grass the next morning in front of the hotel, Jennifer's sad history, Marit's revelation about Hanna, and Pix's own imprisonment in the sauna at Kvikne's. Without pausing for breath, she gave a thumbnail sketch of the Petersons, especially the newest member, Lynette, and described the strange conversation she'd had with Carol just before finding the body.

"I know it sounds like something from one of those soap-opera digests, but it's all happened since I got here."

"I believe you—" Faith started to offer some advice, but Pix interrupted.

"Oh, I almost forgot. Mother thinks she's found a secret hiding place on our Viking fjord cruiser, and that was why I was up and about so much last night. I'm leaving a lot of the details out, like the Japanese man, but we're visiting a farm today, so I don't want to be late."

"Sounds entrancing." Faith could smell the goats.

"It will be. You can't imagine how beautiful this part of Norway is. Really, the most beautiful place I've ever seen. And the food has been extremely good."

Faith didn't want to waste either Pix's time or money debating a cuisine of root vegetables, fish, and the odd berry versus French or Chinese.

"Okay. You need to start trying to make some sense out of all this. I think you're right. Tours can be ghastly, but this one is not your ordinary one from hell—whiners, clingers, and worse—it's in a category by itself. When you

190

come back from your idyllic interlude, sit down and think about it all. If you make a list, burn it afterward. Oil, drugs—remember what a long seacoast Norway has. Something's staring you in the face. Get Ursula to find out what's bothering the Peterson woman. She's good at getting people to tell her things. And above all, don't take any more saunas."

Pix hung up, then put on her jacket. She was feeling better. And maybe Oscar's death was an accident after all.

On her end, Faith put the phone down reluctantly. She was filled with conflicting emotions. Pix was a big girl, a very big girl if you considered her height, and she could take care of herself. But she was also a trusting soul and did not possess Faith's innate skepticism. This was why Faith was worried. Pix believed people. And most of the time, the trait served her well, but there had been some disasters. More than once, Sam had had to rescue her from friendships that were covers for self-centered imposition. "You have enough to do for one family. There's no reason Lydia Montgomery can't take her own dog to the vet"— and worse. Pix was always chagrined, vowed to be a better judge of character—and, she always led with her chin again the next time.

The other emotion Faith was feeling was out-and-out jealousy. Here was Pix having all the fun, up to her ears in potential international intrigue. And what Japanese man? Faith didn't know the Hansens, so it was easy for her to concentrate on the sleuthing aspects the trip afforded and not feel the pain Pix was seeing on Marit's face every day. But even if Faith took a plane that night, by the time she got to fjord country, the tour would be over and the members scattered to the winds. Faith would just have to let Pix handle it herself. She hoped she'd call again. She also hoped she wouldn't see Sam or any of the other Millers for a day or two. To put it mildly, Sam would not be at all happy that Pix had found a body. The one in Maine had been enough.

Sleep was going to be impossible now. She had too much to think about. If Oscar Melling's death wasn't an accident, it was murder.

Pix arrived at the boat, calling out apologies to the guides and stewards who were patiently waiting on the dock.

"I'm sorry to keep you waiting. I..."

Jan smiled. "Slow down. No one is in a hurry. You're on vacation, remember?"

It was hard at times. Besides, she wasn't.

Sonja and Anders pulled up the gangplank and untied the lines. Soon they were in the middle of the Sognefjord and Pix made her way below to the large cabin, where she knew she'd find Ursula. It was slightly overcast and there was no one on the upper deck. The door to the cabin that adjoined it was closed.

At least some things were predictable. At the bottom of the stairs, the farmers from Fargo were in the stern, placidly smoking their pipes. Mr. Knudsen and Mr. Arnulfson wished her a good morning. She detected a slight air of excitement among the men, anticipation. At last—dirt, farm machinery, manure.

The cabin was crowded. It seemed that the entire tour had opted for togetherness, yet there was no jollity. Oscar's death had cast a pall on the group. Even the cardplayers seemed distracted. As Pix walked past, she noticed both Golubs were staring out the window and not at their hands.

The Petersons were clustered around a table. Carol was gripping a mug of coffee so tightly, her knuckles were white. And Roy... Roy!

"Are you all right?" Pix blurted out.

Roy senior was sporting a shiner, a hell of a shiner—puffy, black-and-blue, with the promise of more colors to come—that particularly unpleasant-looking zinc yellow, chartreuse, and carmine.

"Walked into a damn door," he mumbled, and turned his head away.

Carol looked even more woebegone than she had earlier, if that was possible. She'd barely gotten herself together—her lilac pants suit was rumpled and her hair uncombed. Her lipstick was crooked. Lynette, on the other hand, looked almost obscenely gorgeous, radiating the beauty a good night in bed, and just enough sleep, endowed. She was obviously pleased about something.

"Good morning, Mrs. Miller. How are you? We missed you at breakfast."

Possibly the news that Pix had discovered Oscar's body had not been widely broad-

193

cast. Well, she wasn't about to say anything. The last thing she wanted were ghoulish questions about the poor man's appearance.

"Fine, thank you. The farm should be very interesting. I hope we get some sun." Pix decided to ignore the breakfast remark. Let them think her a sluggard.

Close to the front of the boat, her mother was sitting in solitary splendor. She reached out for Pix, drawing her into the next chair. "I was afraid you wouldn't make the boat on time, but Carl said they'd hold it for you. They are rather dear, don't you think?"

Pix told her mother she'd stopped to call Faith; then she gave Ursula her assignment for the day. It wasn't going to be easy to get Carol Peterson alone, but Mother had her ways. Once cornered, Carol had no more chance of holding on to her secret than Pix had in days of yore—actually, not so yore. Something about Mother looking one right in the eye— it had the effect of instantly causing the mouth to open and tell all, like pushing the correct spot on an old desk to reveal the hidden drawer.

"It's so quiet in here," Pix commented.

"Of course it's quiet. There's been a death," Ursula said.

Pix wondered how long it would take for Oscar Melling to move from "rotten apple" to "poor, unfortunate elderly gentleman," "one of the old school," "a character, but you had to hand it to him, built his own business from nothing," et cetera, et cetera. All those neutral platitudes that got said once someone was dead. She gave a little shudder. Her sound sleep, then talk with Faith and the race for the boat had effectively suppressed the image of that grotesque form on the rocks. A stranger. She hadn't known him, but they had formed an intimacy. She was the first to know he was dead—perhaps.

She hadn't even said a prayer for him. What would Tom Fairchild, not just her friend but also her minister, say? He'd say it was fine. Tom, the least judgmental person she knew. Tom, whose gentle guidance had helped her over a particularly rocky place some years ago. Rocks. That brought her back to Oscar again, and she commended his soul to whatever heaven he might have believed in. Would there be many who mourned him? A loss to whom? Loss, lost. She'd always thought that terminology woefully inadequate. "I lost my father, my mother, my husband." As if the beloved had been misplaced. It sounded so careless.

"Pix, what are you thinking about? You look so sad," Ursula said. "Sonja's making *vafler*. Let's share some."

The fragrant smell of the waffles seemed to restore some unanimity to the tour group and the hushed conversations became almost normal. Carl took the microphone to describe some of the places they were passing.

"Look quickly out the right side and you will see Fritjof with his Viking sword. It is a long story, but basically he had to earn his stripes in a series of difficult quests before he could become the leader. The statue is twenty-seven meters high and a landmark of the Sognefjord, which I think we have mentioned is one hundred miles long but rarely broader than three miles wide. Fritjof has the best view around here. He was a gift to the Norwegian people from..."

Pix and Ursula mouthed to each other as he spoke: "Kaiser Wilhelm the Second."

"Obviously attracted by the noble warrior, all that rampaging and pillaging," Pix whispered softly, and Ursula laughed.

The statue was indeed a landmark, towering above the park it stood in. Fritjof seemed to like what he saw, leaning on the long sword, with his other hand jauntily at his hip.

"Now, if you look out the windows on the left side, you will see what appears to be a line of big blue balloons. This is a new way we are trying to farm mussels. There's a long line descending from each and the mussels grow there. In Norway, we think it's very important to keep our farms and save the way of life they represent, so we have to think of things for the farmers to do to make some money."

"Look at the road!" Marge Brady exclaimed, pausing a moment from busily scribbling in her journal. "You'd think people would topple straight into the fjord. Oops!"

There was a moment's embarrassed silence as everyone recalled Oscar's recent "toppling." Then the silence was broken as Carl hastily told them, "The road is safer than it looks, and again the government has paid for it in order to encourage people to live here.

In the past, the only way for the farmer and his family to travel was by water, and it was a hard life. The roads enable them to get to Vik and other places for medical care and shopping. But the farm we will visit this morning is pretty isolated still. No road, as you will see."

Jan took the microphone and said, as always with a smile, "If you think this is steep, wait until tomorrow. On the way to Flåm, we pass 'the ladder,' *stigen*. It is a sheer drop—impossible to build a road vertically. A man, his wife, and two children live at the top and keep goats. They have to tie ropes to the children when they play outside. Before them, lived an old lady all alone. When her flag was flying, that was the signal that all was well. When she died, the only way to get her out was in her coffin on the pulley wire she'd used to get her supplies. They still use this arrangement today, with rocks as a counterweight—or sometimes the farmer's wife, they say. It's called *stigen* because in the old days the way to collect taxes was by first climbing the path, then placing a ladder at the steepest part to the top, where the house is. Of course, the farmer would pull up the ladder and the tax collector could just whistle for his money."

Everyone laughed. The group was rapidly returning to normal.

"It must be very lonely in the winter, road, ladders, whatever," Ursula said when Pix returned with a plate of steaming heart-shaped waffles. Somehow, she could always eat a *vaffel* or two, no matter how recent breakfast, or lunch, had been, Pix thought as

197

she spread butter and preserves on hers.

"It wouldn't be my choice, but it's glorious now. No wonder the Norwegians are such sun worshipers," Pix said, unashamedly licking her fingers. Having gotten the group back on track, Jan and Carl were continuing their version of the borscht circuit, the *fisksuppe* act, telling a series of old chestnuts with interchangeable names and nationalities.

"Many of you are of Scandinavian descent, so you'll appreciate this one," Jan said heartily. "A long-lost brother who had emigrated to the United States came back to the old country for the first time in fifty years. He was bragging a lot about everything in the States thinking that Norway had stood still since he left. 'Surgery in America has come so far that a blind man got two plastic eyes and a battery to charge them and now he can see like an eagle,' he told his brother. 'That's pretty good,' his brother replied, 'but just last year, there was a man from here who lost four fingers. The surgeon took four teats from a cow, attached them, and now the guy is milking several liters of milk every day!' His brother was skeptical. 'That's hard to believe,' he said. 'Have you seen him yourself?' 'No,' said his brother, 'but the guy with the plastic eyes has.' "

The room exploded in laughter, the bachelor farmers, who had come in for *vafler*, hardest of all.

Pix grinned at her mother. "I'll have to remember that one to tell Danny. Very definitely middle-school humor. I think I'll go out on the bow for a bit, if that's all right with you."

"Certainly. I'll go kibitz with the card-players. How can they spend all their time playing bridge while such splendid scenery passes them by?" Ursula answered. She and Pix exchanged glances. Maybe the cardplayers were on the trip for another reason. "I want to ask Sidney Harding what it's like to work for a Norwegian oil company."

Pix took the empty plate back to Sonja. The girl's smile was automatic, yet behind it, Pix could see the steward was troubled. The entire staff must be.

"This must be hard for all of you—to keep things running smoothly when there have been so many difficulties on the tour," Pix remarked, commiserating.

Sonja was defensive. "Not so many, and I think everyone is happy." She gestured toward the group spread out around the cabin. Some were going to the upper deck. "It's sad about Mr. Melling, but these things happen to old people."

Pix decided not to pursue the matter and went out to what she now considered her spot on the bow. Jennifer Olsen was there, as Pix had expected, again in the same figure-head position, a pose that once more made Pix want to reach for the girl before she tumbled into the fathoms.

The sun had broken through and the underside of the gulls' wings were jade green, reflecting the water and creating a new species. The boat had left the vast Sognefjord and turned into a more narrow fjord. Pix would have to remember to ask Carl or Jan what it was called. The boat slowly sailed past numerous waterfalls, small and large, cascading into the sea, swollen from the melting snows of winter. Here and there, a cluster of red farm buildings stood out against the steep fields. Neither she nor Jennifer said a word until they came to a sheer rock wall. The water stopped. It was the end of the fjord.

Jennifer turned in surprise. "What a strange sensation. The fjord just stops."

"I know," Pix agreed. "Of course, it must. They only seem endless."

"It feels significant. Do you know what I mean? *Journey to the End of the Fjord.* Something like that."

"We ought to have some sort of ceremony, like when people cross the equator or the Arctic Circle."

The boat turned around slowly and retraced its course. Pix wished she was in a canoe or kayak, closer to the water. She'd like to trail her fingers in the frigid depths, really feel it, instead of just looking at it.

"After the farm, we're going to the Glacier Museum. I heard them talking. They're worried that people might think that your finding Oscar in the fjord is somehow a reflection on their organization." Jennifer was bluntly informative. So, at least one person knew Pix had discovered the body.

"Will there be time?"

"It's not far, although we may not be able to see the glacier up close. I'm still going to go back, even if we do. I hate being rushed."

It was smart thinking on the part of Scandie Sights. Instead of a free afternoon at Balestrand, keep everyone busy and throw in a little something extra. Then tomorrow, everyone would be packed off to Flåm and Mermaid/Troll tour number whatever thankfully over.

Jennifer hadn't sounded particularly bereaved regarding Oscar, and Pix recalled the woman's words from the night before: "I hate that man."

"Sad about the accident. It seems so pointless," Pix said deliberately, and then produced the result she expected.

"Sad! That old fascist! Save your condolences for someone who deserves them. The world is better off without people like him. If the opinions he expressed on this trip are any indication, there will be a lot of happy folks in his corner of New Jersey."

"Fascist?" Pix was seeing a bright red swastika in front of her eyes, pulsating, as if she'd stared into the sun too hard.

"Women, African-Americans, gays, Jews, you name it—he despised anyone who wasn't just like him. The classic bigot. And *sexist* isn't the right word. *Molester* is. There isn't a woman on this trip who hasn't been groped, at the very least. If there is a Mrs. Melling, she's shedding tears all right—tears of joy."

Pix was not surprised at Jennifer's passionate outburst. Oscar stood for the people who had killed her father and grandmother. He stood for everything Jennifer hated—and maybe feared.

"This must be the farm!" Jennifer pointed to a small dock. Three children were running toward the water, followed more sedately by a young woman. The kids were waving, and Pix expected them to call out, "The Americans are coming!" or something like that. Instead, as the boat came to a stop, they jumped up and down, shouting, "*Velkommen!*" The tour visited every week during the season. By August, the *velkommens* might be a little less enthusiastic, but today anyway, the children greeted them delightedly.

Ursula unfolded her cane and joined the group, bachelor farmers in the lead, as they wended their way up to the farmhouse.

The farmer's wife did the talking, whether because her English was better or she was more at ease speaking in public. Pix recalled reading a newspaper article that listed the things people feared most. Public speaking was number one, death second.

"This used to be a community of sixty families; now we are only one—but there are four generations living on our farm, and one hundred goats. We will walk around, and please ask all the questions you want. Just to tell you a little more about us, we make our living from selling our goat cheese, which you will have a chance to taste, operating a small water taxi, and greeting people like you. Our children go to school not so far from here, by water. I take them in the morning and get them in the afternoon. In the winter, I usually stay to have coffee with my friends and do errands."

It didn't sound like such a bad life—when the sun was shining.

"My husband is in the barn and will show you how the cheese is made."

She was very pretty, tall, with short, shining blond hair. She was already deeply tan from being outdoors so much. She and her children radiated good health. After scampering after the group like puppies, the children had stripped off their clothes and were swimming in the fjord.

"It's not so cold as it looks," their mother told the group as she led the way into the barn.

Pix and Ursula first walked over to the herd of goats, scattered across the field, contentedly nibbling at what would become *gjetost,* that goat cheese so far removed from chèvre that it seemed to be produced by a completely different animal. Partisan as she was, and becoming even more so, Pix preferred the *fromage.*

The Rowes and Millers had a friend in Maine who raised Nubians and took a blue ribbon every year at the Blue Hill Fair. Ursula was evaluating the Norwegian goats with a practiced eye. "Mountain goats, sturdy, and these have been well tended."

Before her mother became overly immersed in goat husbandry, Pix suggested, "Come on, let's go see how they make the stuff."

They entered the dark barn, blinking for a moment. The farmer was embroiled in an argument with one of the Fargo farmers. Angry Norwegian was reverberating in the rafters. Pix translated it as "Call this a milking

203

machine!" or something along that line. The Norwegian-American was gesturing contemptuously at the equipment and surroundings. His fellow Sons of Norway were "*ja, jaing*" in agreement, a rude pastoral version of some Greek chorus.

The farmer wasn't giving any ground. He was older than his wife. Around her own age, Pix thought. Yet more in the nature of an aging hippie. He had a long black ponytail, streaked with gray, pulled back with a leather thong. Instead of farmer's overalls, he wore jeans and a faded tie-dyed T-shirt. His dark beard was flecked with gray also. Pix closed her eyes and listened intently. She was almost positive it was the man she'd heard at Stalheim, in the woods surrounding the folk museum. He'd been angry then. He was angry now. His accent was distinctive, especially when compared with the American's. He had a peculiar way of chopping off the end of a phrase.

"Are you asleep?" Her mother tapped her arm.

"No, just concentrating." Pix opened her eyes.

Yes—she was certain it was the same voice.

7

The farmer's wife had set up long tables covered with bright checked cloths. There were platters of open-faced sandwiches, not all of them with *gjetost,* bowls of salads, and pitchers of beer and lemonade. At one table, there was a tempting array of the sweet pancakes, as well as fruit and *pepperkaker*—crisp ginger cookies (see recipe on page 350)—and a large bowl of some kind of *grøt,* with a pitcher of heavy cream standing by to block any parts of one's arteries the rest had missed. The North Dakota farmers were still in the barn, shouting at their host, having a fine old time, but the rest of the tour descended upon the tables with all the appearance of people who have not eaten for days. Pix took a cautious bite of the house specialty and found that this goat cheese was not as sweet as the kind she'd tasted before. She wasn't crazy about it, but she finished her sandwich. She was thinking about the farmer more than his product. Given that it was the same man who had been at Stalheim, what had he been doing there at such an odd time? Was it also the man she'd glimpsed running through the rain from the boat last night? She couldn't swear it was the same voice. She'd been under the tarp, and the two men hadn't been arguing. And what about the bearded man on Jennifer Olsen's balcony? The same person again?

"What do you think of our cheese?" her hostess asked, causing Pix to start guiltily, although she wasn't sure why. Maybe the woman's husband had been delivering cheese to the hotel and arguing over the price or some such thing. It *had* still been light, and perhaps that was the best time for him to get away. As for the possibility of his being on the balcony—well, that was really a stretch.

"I think it's an acquired taste," Pix answered diplomatically.

"You are brave even to try it. Most people stick to the Jarlsberg I get from the supermarket."

"It must be difficult to live in such an isolated place. When I run out of something, I jump in my car and run to the store. You can't do that."

"No, not really. But we buy what we don't raise in large quantities. I haven't had too many problems, and this is a good way for the children to grow up."

"You said there were four generations here. There's you and your husband, the children, and—"

Helene Feld joined them. She had steered clear of all the cheese and was contentedly munching on some salad.

"Yes, I was wondering about that, too."

"My parents and my grandmother live here, too, but they leave in the summer for their *hytte* in the mountains. We were all born right over there"—she pointed to a small house—"and will die here, I suppose." Her contented smile made that event seem a very, very long time away.

"And your husband? Is he from the area?" Pix was curious about the husband.

"Oh, no." His wife laughed. "He is a city boy from the east coast. I don't know how my parents ever agreed to the marriage!"

"Your farm is lovely. I can see why he might have wanted to leave the city," Helene told her. "The buildings are so interesting."

"This one is called a *stabbur*. In the past, people stored their food for the winter there. Below you see the cellar. That was for the potatoes. But the *stabbur* held the dried meat and other things high up."

There was a remnant of old paint on the door to the sod-roofed *stabbur,* perched above the cellar dug into the side of the mountain. Weather had worn most of the design away, but there was a faint tracing of a man on horseback. The lower door still showed herringbone stripes.

"I suppose you must have some furniture and other things that have been in your family all these years," Helene commented. Her neutral tone may have fooled the farmer's wife, but knowing what she did, Pix easily detected the underlying obsession—those objects of desire—if not to own, at least to see.

"We do, but I'm not so interested in old things."

This seemed to spur, rather than dampen, Helene's ardor. "Would you mind if I had a look in the house? I wouldn't touch anything, of course."

"You are welcome to, except I'm afraid there isn't enough time." She waved to someone, and turning, Pix saw Carl with his hand up.

"Your guide is calling you now. Perhaps you will come back to see us another day. We will be here," she added graciously.

As they walked toward the group, Helene grumbled, "So many people don't appreciate what they have. I've seen beautiful old pieces that have been painted over or had the legs cut off to fit into another space. You name it. In one kitchen, the people had put their television set on top of a two-hundred-year-old chest. It was so blackened with soot that you could barely see the rosemaling!"

"I thought the *folkemuseums* had been recording the furniture and old buildings," Pix said.

"Well, yes, but they can't keep track of everything," Helene responded peevishly.

Recalling how difficult it was to take antiques out of the country, Pix wondered about Helene. The woman had obviously wanted to discover a hidden gem. But for what purpose? To inform the museum in Bergen or Oslo? Or to try to get it to Mount Vernon, New York, home of the Felds? Not a chest, of course, but things like the wedding spoons Jan had described might not be so hard to hide in one's luggage. And if they were stopped, they could plead ignorance—once anyway. The other thing that struck her was Helene's obvious familiarity with ferreting out country antiques. She'd been to Norway before, she'd mentioned, but she hadn't described scouting the countryside for antiques, unless she'd been accompanying a Norwegian dealer or antiquarian. Kari's last known request had been the phone number of her friend at the Museum of Decorative Arts in Bergen. Pix thought she'd give Annelise a call and ask her about the antiques market and what the laws were more precisely. Faith had said something was staring her in the face.

Maybe it was an ancient ale bowl.

Pix went over to Ursula, who was standing at the head of the path. As they started down to the boat, the farmers emerged from the barn, all smiles. They grabbed fistfuls of sand-wiches, drank hasty glasses of beer, and shook hands with the farmer, who seemed to be expressing genuine regret at their departure.

"Obviously a good day for Ole Knudsen and Henry Arnulfson. Now they finally have something to talk about when they get home," Ursula said dryly, the corners of her mouth twitching. "I think I just might play pinochle with them after all. It's been years."

That reminded Pix of Oscar Melling. Cer-tainly the farmers weren't mourning him.

"Did you learn anything about the oil busi-ness from Mr. Harding?" she asked her mother.

"I'll tell you about it later, dear. Wasn't that fascinating? And do you see what's over there? Such a shiny new boat. It must be their fjord taxi. What fun for the children to ride in."

Pix looked over her shoulder. The guides and Jennifer Olsen were almost on their heels."

"Yes, it does look like it would be fun to ride in, and business must be booming for them to buy such a spruce little craft." She felt as if she was reading from a script.

Jan reached for Ursula's arm and helped her aboard. Sonja and Anders appeared to cast off and soon they were in the middle of the fjord again.

Carl addressed the group before they had a chance to scatter to various parts of the Viking cruiser.

"We hope you will enjoy the special trip we have arranged for you this afternoon to the Norwegian Glacier Museum at Fjærland. To get there, we will sail back to the Sognefjord and into the Fjærlandsfjord. It's a very beautiful cruise and you will see the glacier just in front of you the whole way. The museum was designed by Sverre Fehn, our most famous architect. He calls it 'an altar in a landscape.' You see if you agree. It's only a short bus ride from the quay, and if you have any questions, please ask me or Jan."

Pix wanted to know why they were going to the museum. She was curious about what they'd say, but she decided not to ask. The somber mood of the group had changed entirely and her question would only make the guides uneasy. Besides, they'd probably just answer that they were doing it to make the Scandie Sights experience just that much more memorable for everyone. And maybe they were.

She was eager to find out what Ursula had talked about with the Hardings and the Golubs, that inseparable quartet. Her mother had apparently not had a chance to get Carol Peterson alone. Carol and Roy senior were the exceptions to the general lifting of spirits. The two elder Petersons were still obviously on the outs with the world. Carol had returned to the boat long before everyone else and Roy had moped about the shore after viewing the lunch distastefully.

It was definitely an odd sensation. Pix was walking through the model glacier at the museum. Technology had created authenticity and she truly felt she was beneath the glacier—the *bre*. She could hear the ice breaking and rocks falling above her, then a series of high-pitched creaks—the ice, in constant motion, alone. It was chilly and the glistening fiberglass maze that had been created looked as if it could freeze one's fingers off. The tunnel was dark, with occasional spots of light for safety; the ground beneath her feet was spongy, simulating clay. She stepped carefully, avoiding a pool of water. All very, very real.

They'd found two buses waiting for them at the quay and arrived minutes later at the museum, which was surrounded by walls of mountains on three sides and the fjord on the fourth. It was an altar, an altar to the powerful, massive glacier, which was so close that when one ascended the staircases to the museum's roof, the *bre* would seem deceptively within reach. Ursula and Pix had been the last ones off the bus and, with several others, became separated from the rest of the group. Attempting to rejoin their comrades, they were imperiously pushed to the rear of a very long line by a guide from another tour. "My lot already has tickets," she announced in English. Pix was annoyed at the way the woman had literally wedged her "lot" in front of them, but she had no idea whether Scandie Sights had tickets or what she should do. As she was about to explain to the woman that they were part of a group farther ahead, a lean figure jumped over the rope and, taking Ursula by the arm, led her and the rest of them to the front of the line, unleashing a torrent of invective—in Norwegian—at the other guide as they passed. It was Carl, a snarling sheepdog, protecting his flock. The woman responded. They obviously knew each other, but it was Carl's day, and soon Pix found herself in the movie theater, staring at five screens and slightly out of breath.

"Quite a passionate young man when roused," Ursula observed, unruffled. "The other leader didn't have a chance."

"We *all* have tickets," he'd said—in English—pointedly, perhaps for the benefit of her group, which was regarding the Scandie Sights stragglers with undisguised venom. Jumping the queue just isn't done, you know.

Once inside, the film, on five screens, was breathtaking. Pix instantly resolved to come back to explore the glacier, the *bre,* itself with Sam and any family members who would still take a vacation with parents and siblings. Mark had made it clear that destination was everything, and she had the feeling he was thinking of Hawaii.

One group in the film was hiking across the glacier in pleasant, gentle stages—picnics in the sun, a hearty, happy throng of children and adults. The other glacial explorers provided the drama, wielding picks and dangling into dangerous-looking crevasses, their ropes taut. They started out tanned and fit and emerged yet more so at the end. Even the oldest, who looked Ursula's age, could have qualified for a Ray•Ban ad. The film ended and everyone filed out to explore the center's exhibits.

"Makes it seem as if you really are two feet below the surface, with tons and tons of ice on top of your head." It was Marge Brady, well informed as usual. For a moment, Pix resented the intrusion, both for its quantification and because it marked an end to her solitary fantasy. She'd deliberately waited until the model seemed empty to experience it alone.

"It's remarkable," she commented. Marge, undeterred by brevity, continued Pix's private tour. "It was designed by the same person who designed the special effects for the *Star Wars* sets. The Norwegians call the glacier 'the roof of Norway.' Pretty big roof! I'm not sure I'd want to walk on it, even with a guide. How can they be sure you won't fall through?"

Pix did not have an answer. "I'm sure they're very experienced." She made a mental note to check out the accident rate before they returned.

The two women emerged into the main hall. Marge was heading for a stationary bike, ready to test her ability to generate energy. Pix was sure she'd do well and ducked behind a large photo of a woolly mammoth. It was hard to concentrate on the displays, excellent as they were, when she kept seeing Oscar's body on the rocks. The question uppermost in her mind was not why the ice was turquoise blue, but how had the man died?

Ursula was buying postcards.

"Do you think Danny would like this one of the polar bear?" she asked.

Pix started to respond, "Danny who?" but fortunately she remembered that she did indeed have a twelve-year-old. She told her mother he'd love it.

Marge came sailing by. "We're going to have time to visit the glacier after all!" she called, off to spread the news to others.

"I'm glad you'll have the chance to see part of it. It really is extraordinary," Ursula said. Then, lowering her voice, she added, "They certainly don't seem anxious to get back to the hotel."

"I think they're counting on arctic memories to obliterate any other, less pleasant ones from the 'Dear Scandie Sights' evaluation forms I'm sure we'll be filling out tomorrow," Pix remarked.

They both headed for the ladies' room, then rejoined the group. Jan was counting heads when someone from the museum came up to him and spoke into his ear. An anxious look crossed his face, quickly replaced by a neutral one. "Carl," he called to the other guide, who was answering a question for Marge Brady.

Pix wasn't taking much note of what was

going on, but Ursula poked her in the ribs. "Follow them," she whispered. "Something's up. They're not smiling."

Pix slipped away from the tour and pretended to be looking at one of the exhibits—weather on the glacier. Carl and Jan were going toward the phone in the small gift shop. She hastened toward a postcard rack, grabbed one, and went to pay the cashier. Carl was speaking and she didn't understand what he was saying, but it was clear that something serious had occurred. He hung up, pulled Jan to one side, and spoke to him. The other guide's face paled and he put a hand on Carl's arm. A few more words and they went back to the group. Pix was out the door, as well.

"Wait, you've left your card." The clerk was running after her.

"*Tusen takk,*" Pix said, and was in time to hear "So we will be returning to the hotel for a pleasant afternoon." Carl was smiling. Jan was smiling. At least their mouths turned up at the corners. Their eyes told a different story.

"What did I miss?" Pix asked Ursula.

"Apparently, we have to get back to the hotel because of the dinner schedule. We won't have time to see the glacier, but Jan told everyone the museum is better."

"Dinner schedule!" Pix was positive that when the tour was supposed to eat would not have caused the reaction she'd just observed. But what would have?

Marit was sitting on the small dock in Balestrand, next to the huge Midsummer bonfire pile, which had grown even more since they'd arrived. She spied Pix in the bow and waved her arm back and forth. Why would Marit be down here, so obviously waiting for them, abandoning her cover? Pix jumped to her feet and started toward the door of the cabin.

"What's your rush?" Jennifer asked. She was stretched out on her back, looking up at the sky.

"I—I have to check on my mother," Pix answered, and went straight inside to Ursula.

"Marit's on the dock. She waved to me."

Ursula understood immediately.

"Go see what's happened. I'll be fine."

Pix grabbed her jacket from the chair she'd hung it on—the sun had made it unnecessary—and went to the upper deck.

As the boat drew closer, she could see Marit's face was tense. She sat looking toward the fjord like some figure from Norse mythology. Pix thought she ought to be knitting a shroud or something. Shroud! Dear God, let it not be bad news about Kari.

Pix was the first off the boat. She went directly to her friend.

"What's wrong. Is it Kari?"

"*Nei.*" Marit stood up and took Pix's hand, pulling her in the direction of the hotel. "You've got to come. The man you found—it wasn't an accident. Everyone at the hotel is talking about it and the police are here."

"You mean Oscar Melling *was* murdered!" She—and Faith—had been right.

It was upsetting, yet why was Marit reacting this way—so fearfully? The older woman was setting a rapid pace.

"Murdered, *ja*," she said, "and someone saw you from a window out near the place where he was lying."

"Well, of course they did. I found him."

Marit stopped and shook her head. "Saw you before that. Saw you at about the time the police think he was killed."

Now fear filled Pix, too, like the tide rushing in. A cloud passed in front of the sun. She slipped her jacket on. It was cold.

Entering the lobby of the Kvikne's Hotel alone after Marit went to meet Ursula, Pix debated the merits of approaching the police herself versus being approached by them. Her instinct was to find them as quickly as possible and tell all, but then again, this might seem suspicious. Why was she so anxious to speak with them? they might wonder. And of course the first thing they'd ask would be how she knew they were looking for her. Her long association with Faith Fairchild had taught Pix that her own instincts were not always to be trusted, whereas Faith's were. Pix could not recall an instance in Faith's own numerous investigations where the lady had gone to the police to share what she knew. Rather, Faith felt it was completely legitimate to hold out on them. "They wouldn't listen anyway" was her oft-stated rationale. Pix decided to adopt it now. In any case, she had to think of Marit. She had no idea how Marit had found out so much—Pix recalled mention of pumping one of the younger, less seasoned veterans of the force—and she had to protect the older woman. But how could she tell them anything without involving Marit? For instance, why she had come to Norway on the spur of the moment? It was a hopeless dilemma.

In the end, she did not have to agonize over her decision for long. Almost simultaneously, a clerk from behind the desk and a uniformed policeman stopped her before she could get on the elevator. After saying something in Norwegian—the two words "Fru Miller" needing no translation—the clerk withdrew hastily, leaving Pix with the young officer.

"Mrs. Miller?"

"Yes?" She unconsciously mimicked his questioning tone.

"Would you mind talking to the inspector who is looking into the death of Mr. Melling, the man from your tour you found this morning?"

Tempted to reply, Oh, that Mr. Melling, instead Pix meekly said, "Of course," and allowed herself to be ushered into the Star Chamber. Sam would kill me, she thought. Well, if I ask to have a lawyer present, it really would look odd. Besides, her lawyer husband was thousands of miles away and need never know—at least not for a while.

The hotel had turned over a large conference room to the police. It was arranged for a business meeting, long tables in a U shape, with a pad and pen at each place. An overhead projector and screen were set up at the front, along with a television and a VCR. A smaller table and several chairs had been placed in front of one of the large windows on the outside wall. A pot of pink begonias sat squarely in the middle of each sill. With Pix's and the officer's arrival, there were exactly four people in the room.

A man got up from behind the small table.

"How do you do? I'm Inspektør Johan Marcussen," he said, extending his hand. She took it, well aware how sweaty and cold her own must feel.

"I'm Pix Miller," and I've been better, she finished silently.

"Pix—this is an English name I've not heard before," he said.

She decided to let it go at that. Let him think it was a family name and—inwardly cursing her parents' flight of fancy—it was.

"Please, sit down." He pulled out a chair across the table from his. She had the fjord view. "Would you like some coffee?" This was one question that did not take her by surprise. She could not imagine anything, even a police inquisition, taking place in Norway without this beverage, and maybe some little cakes, too. Well, it would use up some time—she didn't see a tray. Plus, when it arrived, it would give her something to hold on to.

"That would be very nice, thank you." So far, so good.

The officer who had accompanied her left the room. This left Pix, the inspector, and another police officer, pad and pen—not the hotel's—in hand.

Inspector Marcussen was tall, looming over Pix, and she judged him to be in his late fifties. His hair was gray and thinning, but he was extremely attractive. She had always thought that unattractive Norwegians were the exception, and piercing blue eyes like the inspector's had held a special attraction for her since that long-ago summer visit when Olav something, a friend of Hanna's, had flashed his at a very susceptible young American girl. The police at home did not have this effect on her. She'd known Patrolman Warren since he was a runny-nosed little boy, and his sister had been in Pix's Girl Scout troop. Veteran police chief Charley MacIsaac may have had a certain appeal once, but there had been a few too many muffins at the Minuteman Café in the last thirty years. Johan Marcussen, on the other hand, would have been in the group with the ropes and picks in today's glacier movie.

She realized Inspector Marcussen was talking to her and that she had better pay attention—close attention.

"It must have been a terrible shock for you to discover Mr. Melling like that in the fjord."

"Yes, yes it was." She folded her hands

together until the coffee came, then thought it looked like she was praying, so she quickly separated them.

"Could you tell us exactly what he looked like and what you did? Maybe starting with how you came to be at the fjord at this time of the morning?"

She definitely needed a lawyer. She didn't know whether Norway was one of those countries like France where you were guilty until proven innocent. She hoped not.

The man at Marcussen's side had leaned forward. The inspector followed her gaze.

"Do you mind if Jansen here takes a few notes—to help us find out what happened to Mr. Melling? You are free to look them over before you leave."

Leave where? The room, the hotel, the country? She nodded, took a deep breath, and—the coffee arrived.

The smell was instantly calming. For a moment, they were simply four people adding cream and sugar to their cups, or not. And while there wasn't cake, there was a plate of delicious-looking butter cookies.

"Where were we?" the inspector asked jovially. "You were going to tell us about finding the body." The words were at odds with his tone.

"Yes." Pix put her cup down on the table. She was afraid it might wobble. "I wasn't sleeping." She chose her words with care to avoid as many out-and-out falsehoods as possible. *Falsehood* was the word she used to herself when contemplating a lie. It sounded so much less serious. "I got dressed and went out for a walk. It's very beautiful here." She nodded out the window. How did the businesspeople with the fjord view ever pay attention to their flowcharts?

"Excuse me," he interjected. "How did you leave the hotel?"

Obviously they already knew that no one at the front desk had seen her.

"I left by a side door. It was near the stairs."

She paused, but he didn't say anything.

"I walked along by the water, toward where the boat was docked, and met someone else from our tour, Carol Peterson." She presumed they must know about Carol, who most certainly would have gone out by the lobby—unless, like Pix, she'd been sleuthing around for an inconspicuous side entrance and exit.

The inspector nodded.

"We sat on one of the benches and talked a few minutes, maybe five."

"So, that would make it what time?"

"I left the hotel a little past four." Seeing their faces, she added defensively. "People in my family have always been early risers." Too true, too true. "It was probably ten past when I met Carol and close to four-thirty when I found Oscar."

"You saw the body from the shore, and what did you do next?"

"I climbed down to make sure he was dead— I mean, to make sure that he wasn't just injured and needing some help." Neither man said anything. "Like CPR. I don't know what it's called in Norwegian, but it's to resuscitate people when their hearts have failed."

"Yet you thought he was dead before you got to him. Why was that?"

Why indeed?

"He looked dead. He wasn't moving, and it seemed like a very awkward position to maintain." Pix closed her eyes for a second, seeing the figure sprawled on the rocks. Oh, he had been dead. Anyone would have come to the same conclusion. Her eyelids flicked open. "I'm sure if either of you had seen him, you would have thought so, too." She could not keep a slightly accusatory note from her voice.

"Anyway, I felt for his pulse—on his wrist, his left wrist. I didn't touch anything else." She shuddered slightly. "Then I came straight back to the hotel to tell them. And you must know the rest."

She started to get up. Inspector Marcussen put up his hand. He didn't say, Not so fast, lady, but he might as well have.

"Just a few more things. You must be tired."

Pix leaned back against the chair. It had a straight back, covered and tufted, as was the seat, in deep crimson. The room had elaborate brass chandeliers, she noted. This couldn't be happening to her.

"Could you tell us about your other walk? The earlier one?"

She was glad Marit had prepared her.

"I suppose I'm not quite used to the time change." Another nonfalsehood. "I got up at three o'clock and went outside, but I came in when it started to rain. I got very wet, in fact."

"Again you left by the side door?"

"Yes, I didn't want to disturb anyone."

"Did you meet anybody during this walk?" Those blue eyes were looking straight into her soul.

"No one I knew. I saw two men running from the dock to get out of the rain."

"Can you describe them?"

"They were speaking Norwegian—I could hear it as they passed me—but I didn't get a good look at them. One had a dark beard, though."

The inspector and officer exchanged glances.

"Now, you are from Aleford, Massachusetts?"

"Yes, it's a small town west of Boston."

"I have never been to the United States, but I have cousins in New Jersey. They have been here often and sometime I must go see them." If he hoped to keep her off balance with such extraneous tidbits, it was working.

"Did you know Mr. Melling before the tour?"

"No, I had never met him before."

"And your mother, Mrs. Rowe—had she met him here in Norway or in the United States?"

"No, and neither of us had but the slightest contact with him on the tour." The question implied knowledge of Ursula's trips to Norway. It certainly indicated that Oscar had been here before, but that was not surprising for someone who imported Norwegian food and had such a strong feeling for his homeland.

"And what brought you to Norway, Mrs. Miller, besides the fjords, that is?"

Here it was. She decided it was time to come clean, at least somewhat. If it came out later, it would look very peculiar, and besides, she had nothing to hide, except her hair spray and skeleton keys.

"My mother has a childhood friend, Marit Hansen, who has been very worried about the disappearance of her granddaughter, Kari."

Both men sat up straighter and exchanged a few words in Norwegian. At this rate, Pix would really have to learn the language if she was going to find out anything at all.

"Kari Hansen? You knew her?"

Pix did not like the inspector's use of the past tense.

"Yes, and Marit wanted us to come on the tour to see if we could discover anything about where Kari might be."

"And have you?"

"Well, not really anything concrete. Some odd things have happened." Pix told them about the man on Jennifer Olsen's balcony and the swastika on the lawn at Stalheim. When she got to that, the two men gaped.

"Swastika! Are you sure?"

"Of course I am. I saw it myself. Ask the hotel—and the guides must know. Lots of people of the tour knew, too. What's the significance? I mean, I know what it has to do with the hotel, but what could it have to do with Oscar Melling's death?"

"Oscar Melling—rather, Oscar Eriksen—was one of Vidkun Quisling's most loyal adherents during the war. Eriksen was born and grew up in a small village near the hotel."

Jennifer Olsen had been right. The dead man *had* been a fascist. A Nazi. A traitor.

Marcussen poured them some more coffee. It was getting close to dinnertime, but Pix took a cup and ate a cookie anyway. She told them about the men in the woods at Stalheim and was about to reveal Ursula's find on the Viking cruise ship when the inspector rose and thanked her for coming.

"I am sure that the men you overheard, and maybe the ones who were about as early as you this morning, were involved in the illegal liquor market." He grinned. "You know what a drink costs in Norway, and people find all sorts of ways around it—brewing their own. You can get the supplies in any market. Flavoring for scotch and cognac are on the shelves with cardamom, salt, and pepper. There are also many rural stills. As for the business with Kari, you can assure your mother and your friend Fru Hansen that the police are doing everything they can to find out what happened to Kari. We care deeply. Why don't you just enjoy the rest of your tour and leave it to us?"

Pix was annoyed. She hadn't even gotten a chance to tell them about Sophie and Oscar, the dirty old man—or his argument with Arnie Feld. Or that he cheated at cards. She was being dismissed. But she wasn't going without getting one answer, at least.

"Why do you think Oscar Melling's death wasn't natural? The man had been drinking heavily and could easily have fallen."

"I'm sorry, but we can't tell you that." Inspector Marcussen didn't look one bit sorry, Pix thought. She supposed it was fair. She wasn't telling him everything, either.

Both men saw her to the door.

"Try not to take any walks after, say, midnight, will you, Mrs. Miller?"

Jansen chuckled, but Pix didn't think the inspector was joking.

Ursula and Pix had abandoned any pretense of not knowing Marit and the three women walked into the dining room together.

"I'm hungry," Pix announced. "I intend to eat a great deal of fish in many guises, then go to bed."

"Pix, dear," her mother said, "do you know these people?"

A group of Japanese tourists were leaving an earlier sitting in the dining room and they stopped, giggled, and bowed to Pix. She realized that she had given Marit and her mother only an abbreviated account of her ordeal in the sauna, omitting to mention the gentleman from Tokyo. He had apparently not been as silent.

Another group passed and bowed. Pix found herself reflexively bowing back; then the man appeared himself, wreathed in smiles and patting his heart. The tour leader, or so Pix assumed from the trim navy blazer he wore, insignia above the pocket, bowed and addressed her.

"Mr. Yoshimuro is very anxious that you were not offended in any way." He seemed to be searching for words to describe the incident.

"Oh, no, I hope I did not offend *him*. It's the custom in Norway for saunas to be shared by men and women, but we were both quite decently clothed."

Marit and Ursula were staring at Pix, wide-eyed. Pix saw her mother's mouth tremble and knew that in a moment she would be roaring with laughter.

"Please, do not think any more about it," she said, and bowed.

The man translated Pix's words and Mr. Yoshimuro spoke rapidly, pointing toward all three of them.

"Would you mind if I took a picture of you with your friends and Mr. Yoshimuro? He would deem it an honor."

What was to mind? Pix Miller, the new pinup of Japan? She thought not.

"Of course," she answered, and repeated to her mother and Marit, "They want to take our picture."

"Whatever for?" Ursula asked.

"I'll tell you later," Pix promised, falling into position between Ursula and Marit, Mr. Yoshimuro next to her mother.

With a few final ticky-tocky gestures and bows, the men left and the women proceeded into the dining room.

"I didn't know you spoke Japanese, Mrs. Miller," Jan said admiringly as they entered.

He had apparently witnessed the entire event and had been fooled by the expertise of Pix's bows.

"I don't—and it's a long story." She laughed.

"Whatever you say. You can sit at any table, except those at the windows. It was our turn last night."

"Is it all right for our friend Fru Hansen to sit with us?" Ursula asked. "She is a guest at the hotel."

"Of course. There's plenty of room," Jan replied.

There was one extra place for sure, Pix thought. Her mother and Marit had dismissed the police questioning rather perfunctorily. The idea that Pix might be a suspect in Oscar Melling's death seemed ludicrous to them, although Marit had been initially upset when she'd overheard the clerks talking about Pix's early-morning wanderings. Pix had given them a report on her conversation with Inspector Marcussen and they had figuratively patted her on the head for being such a good girl with the police. They were not surprised that Marcussen had not been interested in a possible link to Kari and Erik. That was their job—theirs and the *hund*.

Carl came forward to shepherd them a bit more as they searched for the little Mermaid/Troll flags indicating their tables. He looked concerned. She was sure he had heard about the police questioning and the reason why. The entire hotel must have, those who were not preoccupied with her sauna escapade.

"Sit anywhere, ladies, and enjoy your meal." Was Carl being a little too welcoming? A kind of "Eat up—the food in Norwegian jails is good, but not like Kvikne's" underlying message?

Now he definitely was addressing her, and her alone. "Is everything all right?" He lowered his voice, "This has been a most upsetting day for you, Mrs. Miller, and Scandie Sights is well aware of it. Anything we can do, just let us know."

Pix could think of a number of things, like possibly posting bail or finding Kari and solving Oscar's murder, but she merely thanked him and said she was fine. "I'm going to turn in early. A good night's sleep is what I need." Then, impelled by her usual curiosity, she asked him, "What do you do after tomorrow? Pick up another tour? Or do you get to rest in between?"

"We don't start another one until Tuesday."

Jan had joined them, hearing Pix's question and Carl's answer. "We always get a few days off," he answered. "I usually go home to my parents and let my mother make a fuss."

"And sleep half the day," Carl teased.

"*Ja*—and, as usual, you'll go see your father in London, I suppose. Although"—he winked at the women, seated now—"I have my doubts about this 'father.' I think it may be someone a bit younger and of the opposite sex."

Carl flushed. It made him even more attractive. "My father *is* British, although I was raised here. Maybe I just happen to like London. All right, maybe it has some charms, besides his nice flat."

The guides went to their own table, where Captain Hagen was stolidly consuming a mounded plate of each *smörgåsbord* course and the stewards were doing a fine job on the *reker*, peeling the shells off and dipping each shrimp in a mayonnaise sauce.

"I can never eat enough *reker*," Pix said, glancing at the captain. "And I want a glass of white wine to go with it. Will you join me? It's the last night of the tour." They had nothing to celebrate. If anything, things were more confused and the outlook for finding Kari alive bleak, but Pix felt they needed to keep their spirits up. Marit and Ursula agreed.

As she ate the shrimp, Pix remembered her mother hadn't mentioned what she'd found out about Sidney Harding. The room was filled with noise and their small table was set against a pillar with a serving station on the other side. They could talk softly, unde-tected.

What Ursula had to say was interesting.

"He really didn't want to talk about what he does. They had taken a break from cards, believe it or not, and were having a snack. I asked him whether his work brought him to Norway much and he was very evasive. His wife was the one who answered—bitterly. Seems he's away from home a good deal and this was to have been a solo business trip, too, but she insisted on coming this time, and then he had the idea of inviting their bridge friends to come along. 'I'm glad he did,' she said, 'because otherwise it would have been very boring.' There was not much to do in Norway so far as she could see."

Marit frowned. "Didn't they visit the museums in Oslo, Frogner Park with its Vigeland statues? Maybe they don't like scenery, but still..."

"I think she likes to shop and play bridge, period. Things are too expensive here, so that leaves cards. I did notice Sidney was wearing a Rolex and a diamond pinkie ring, so he must make some money."

Mother is getting as label-conscious as Faith, Pix reflected. She wouldn't have thought Ursula could have told the difference between a Rolex and a Timex.

"But what about oil secrets? Is he passing them on to the Russians? Did you work that into the conversation?"

Ursula gave her daughter a "Now, don't be silly" look.

"Actually, he *is* in research and development. I found that out. And he spends weeks in Bergen and Stavanger. I'm also pretty sure he speaks Norwegian. Anders walked by, saying something to Sonja, and Harding said to us, 'I guess I'd better go wash up. We'll be docking soon.' How would he know that unless he'd been able to translate what Anders had said? His wife complained about the number of business meetings he'd had to attend during the trip and he reminded her that for him, it was not a vacation. She started to say something about telephone calls and meetings at all hours, but he told her that people weren't interested in hearing about his boring life, then asked, 'Are we going to play cards or what?' "

The three left their dirty plates and moved on to the next course—and the next subject. Oscar Melling. It was Marit's turn. Marcussen had not been revealing state secrets when he told Pix Oscar's real name and what he'd been up to during the war. That had been all over the hotel, too, along with the fact that Pix was a suspect.

"There has to be a connection with Stalheim and the swastika. Yet how does it relate to Kari and Erik?" Pix asked.

Marit replied, "I have been thinking of nothing else. Kari might have discovered that Oscar was connected with the *Lebensborn* home. He lived in the area. Maybe he supplied the groceries or was somehow connected. The Nazis did not permit Norwegians to work in places like that, only Germans, but there were always exceptions. Could it have been this that she wanted to tell me on the phone?"

Pix was deep in thought. Could Oscar have been Hanna's father—Kari's grandfather? If Kari had discovered this, it might have upset her so much that she ran off. But to stage an elopement? Plus, it still left Erik's death unanswered. She sighed.

"I'm going to have some of that applesauce dessert layered with the toasted crumbs—what is it called, anyway?—but no coffee. Maybe a slice of the cake with the almonds on top, too."

"It's called *tilsiørte bondepiker,* which means 'veiled country maidens,' " Marit answered. "I have no idea why. The whipped cream on top could be the veil, but as for the rest..."

"Whatever it means, it's one of my favorites. Bring me a little, will you?" Ursula asked.

The two older women fondly watched Pix leave. A big hungry girl.

She returned with the cake and pudding, plus some fruit compote with vanilla sauce. With only a fleeting thought to what Faith would think of this plebeian dessert plate, she dug in. Norwegian food was the ultimate comfort food, lacking only macaroni and cheese to be complete.

"The police wouldn't tell me why they think Oscar was murdered, but they seem pretty sure."

Marit was surprised. "It's because he was hit from behind with something before he fell. He had an injury on his shoulder that couldn't have come from the fall, given the way the body was found."

No wonder Ursula and Marit were such friends.

"Who told you this?" Pix asked admiringly. When she grew up, she'd like to be just like them, but she wasn't too sanguine.

"Some of it was from the policeman, who was so reassuring about my safety, and some was from the maid who tidied my room. We decided it must have been a full bottle of something, because they didn't find any broken glass, and an empty one would have shattered."

"It could have been something else like a piece of wood, but that's not so easy to come by," Ursula added.

This was true. The grounds were manicured and unless one trekked up into the mountains, a cudgel of this sort would be difficult to locate. It would have helped that Oscar was blind drunk, and maybe the person hadn't planned to kill him, but a blow to the rear, precipitating a fall on the jagged rocks below, suggested a strong desire for at least grievous harm. The actual outcome meant the killer was either lucky or unlucky, depending on the intent.

Intent. Pix looked at her watch.

"I'm going to the gift shop to get something for the kids and Sam, then bed." She kissed both women good night and headed off to the tempting array of handicrafts, silver and enameled jewelry, and shelves of hideous-looking trolls. Forty minutes later, her Visa card having made it altogether too easy to acquire some gorgeous ski sweaters, Pix was in her room, eyeing her bed longingly. She had spent so little time there. But first she wanted to call Annelise, Kari's friend in Bergen, and ask her about how hard it was to smuggle antiques out of the country. Helene Feld was a collector, and collecting can be an obsession. And obsessions can lead to other things. Marit had had the number with her and, thanks again to her phone card, Pix soon heard ringing and a voice: "Annelise Christensen *her.*"

"You do speak English, don't you? This is Pix Miller, an American friend of the Hansens."

"Yes, yes, of course. Is there news? Have you found Kari?"

"No, I'm sorry. Nothing has changed. Marit is with my mother and me at Kvikne's in Balestrand. We joined the tour to see if we could find anything out the police may have missed."

"Marit's idea?" The girl sounded impressed.

"Yes, but we haven't discovered anything, except there is a woman with quite a passion for Norwegian antiques, and that started me wondering how difficult it would be to get them out of the country."

"Very difficult indeed, and a heavy fine if you are caught. There was a big case last year and both the buyer and seller had to pay a stiff penalty. Still, it does happen, and that's why we have such an elaborate security system at our museum. Even security systems aren't foolproof, though. You can have human error. Like when Munch's *The Scream* was stolen from the National Gallery in Oslo. Maybe you remember?"

Pix did. They'd used a ladder from a nearby building site, climbed in an open window, and were out again with the painting in sixty seconds. The guard thought the alarm, which went off, was malfunctioning, but it was all recorded on video and the painting recovered unharmed in two days. Since then, security in all the museums had increased.

"In terms of the world market, are these antiques worth a great deal?"

"In a way, because our laws are so strict, the value has increased. But the average tourist would not be able to buy anything over a hundred years old, so I'm not sure I follow you."

Pix wasn't sure she did, either.

"Just a thought. Well, thank you, and if we hear anything at all, we'll let you know." She was about to hang up when she recalled her sauna musings about Kari's personality, so she asked Annelise on the spur of the moment, "You know Kari well. How would you describe her?"

If Annelise thought the question odd, she didn't say so. "Well, she is very loyal to her friends and very sure. I'm not saying this right, but sure of herself and what she thinks is the right thing. Sometimes this annoys people."

"What about Kari and Erik? Did you think it was a good match?"

Annelise hesitated. "That is not for me to say. It was their business, but they had fun together and I think they probably would have been married someday. They weren't in a rush. My generation isn't, I think. Maybe we're too picky."

"Did Kari have other boyfriends?" Pix had married her high school beau the week after she graduated from Pembroke, and the generation gap suddenly seemed an abyss.

Annelise gave a little laugh. "Boys, men always wanted to be with Kari, but she has been with Erik for quite a while. I am sorry I have to go now. I'm supposed to meet someone and I'm late already."

"I'm so sorry and won't keep you any longer. Thank you for all your help," Pix said.

"*Ha det bra.*" As Annelise hung up, she reverted by habit to the Norwegian equivalent of "Have a good day." Pix hoped she would "have it good," too, wherever she was going at this time of night—a time she knew from her son Mark was the mere shank of the evening to that generation, despite its being bedtime for those on either sides.

Bed—at least for a while. She changed into corduroy slacks and a turtleneck, putting out a warm sweater next to her jacket. Ursula would certainly not approve of the number of times Pix seemed to be sleeping in her clothes these days, but then her mother had been the one who had drawn her to one side before disappearing into the Dragon Room for coffee and hissed in her ear, "Be sure to set your alarm. Do you want me to call you?"

Pix had refused. She knew what she had to do. The inspector hadn't said she *couldn't* take a walk after midnight. He had said "try not to." And if she didn't go to the fjord cruiser and search her mother's fabled closet, there would be no rest in this life. Forget "try not to."

She was about to check the pockets of her coat to make sure her kit was intact when there was a knock on the door.

It was Mother, the glint of victory in her eye. "Marit's still with her, but I wanted to tell you before you went to sleep." She came in and sat down.

"Tell me what?"

"We decided it would be pleasant to invite Carol Peterson to have coffee with us on the porch. I thought she might like to talk with a native Norwegian. Perhaps tell Marit a bit about Duluth. You know, Hans's brother settled in the Midwest."

Pix did not know. What she did know was that Carol had as much chance of talking about Duluth once she was on the porch as a fly trapped in a web would talking about aerodynamics with a spider.

"We chatted for a bit and then began to talk about the tour. Poor woman. It hasn't been much fun for her. She seems to have a daughter-in-law she doesn't much care for and then her husband made an indecent proposal to her."

"A what!"

Ursula grinned. "You'll never guess!"

Pix conjured up a mental image of Roy senior. "Indecent" and the personification of white bread didn't seem to go together. But something must have turned his thoughts from the missionary position to the wilder side. Maybe it seemed that his son was having a little too much fun with Lynette.

"Okay, I'll never guess. Wait—he wants Carol to sleep in the buff."

"I don't know about that, but what he does want is for her to sleep with Don Brady—and he gets Marge."

"Wife swapping! No wonder Carol was upset—and now we know how Roy got his black eye. I think she's wrong about it being illegal, yet that doesn't prevent it from being a crime in her book! And the Bradys! Don't tell me Marge was willing."

"I'm telling you." Ursula was laughing now, as she couldn't when Carol had poured her heart out to the two older women, unable to keep her guilty secret anymore, wanting sympathy, and secure in the knowledge she'd never see them again after the tour.

"Marge! But she seems like such a little mouse, a mouse with a cold." Marge apparently had allergies or had picked up a germ somewhere. She was constantly reaching for a tissue and her turned-up little nose was either red or about to drip. Pix had not thought of the woman as either a sex object or a libertine, but she was trim and not unattractive otherwise. Sensible shoes, denim skirts, turtlenecks, and sweaters—attire not unlike Pix's own. Her hair was short, a bit wispy, and the color mousy brown. Yes, a mouse— a well-organized, inquisitive, energetic little mouse. Inquisitive—that was it.

"She must have another list like the one of the places she wants to go—'Unusual Things I Want to Do.' "

"I'll let you get to bed and I have to help Marit. That Peterson woman is really terribly upset, but she's also a bit boring." Mother never believed in mincing words.

"Good night," Pix said. "Thank you for clearing up one mystery at least."

"I thought you'd want to know. Now, be careful tonight."

"Don't worry."

"And remember, we'll be leaving tomorrow, so this is your last chance."

Thank you, Mother, Pix said silently as she closed the door firmly.

All she had to do now was make sure she had everything she might need in her pockets and she could go to bed. She'd emptied them after she'd come in dripping wet from her first attempt and draped the jacket on the heated towel bars in the bathroom to dry. Then this morning, she'd been in a rush and hadn't bothered to transfer everything back from where she'd stashed it in her suitcase. Penlite, keys—she dropped them in and was about to add the hair spray when she realized there was a piece of paper in the bottom of the pocket. She didn't remember putting anything in. It must be her ticket stub from the Glacier Museum. She pulled it out. It was a folded-up piece of newspaper.

"Now where did this come from?" she said aloud. "Strange." Strange to be talking to herself, too. This was why people had pets.

She unfolded it. It was from a Norwegian newspaper and she was about to throw it away when she saw that single letters had been circled in red. She sat at the desk, took out a sheet of the hotel notepaper and a pen, then started copying the letters. There weren't many and put down in order, they read: "stopasking?" Although it seemed to be another Norwegian word, Pix, veteran of crossword puzzles and word jumbles, quickly deciphered it.

"Stop asking questions."

8

Pix was startled, but she was not scared. As anonymous letters went, it was pretty tame. No threats, no imprecations, merely a request. Were there time enough and words, she was pretty sure a "please" would have been inserted. No, she wasn't alarmed, but caught up instead in contemplating the odd turn her life had taken in recent years, for this was the second such missive she'd received. The other, however, sent via the U.S. mails and delivered through the slot in the front door in Aleford made this one look like a birthday card.

But it wasn't. "Stop asking questions"—the "or else" implied.

She looked at the bed. She looked at the clock. She looked at the newspaper clipping. There was no way she could fall asleep now. Wearily, she took out another piece of notepaper. It was time to make a list.

"Stop asking questions"—who had been threatened and who had access to her jacket pocket? She'd been asking questions ever since her arrival in Voss and obviously had not been as circumspect as she imagined. But, Mother had been inquisitive, too.

Her head jerked up. Dear Lord, had Mother gotten the warning, as well? It was one thing for Pix to reach in her pocket and pull out a viper, but Mother! Ursula was probably still nodding away at Carol Peterson out on the porch—which reminded Pix that if anybody should have been her unknown correspondent's target, it should have been Carol. Nobody asked more questions, and more stupid questions, than that woman. She felt a bit resentful.

The idea of going to join the threesome was unappealing. If her mother found anything like this, she would knock on Pix's door. If she had not received one—or didn't find it, not having occasion to search her pockets for a night's mission like Pix—then why upset her?

That settled, Pix turned back to her list. She was tempted to call Faith and run through the possibilities. It would be late afternoon at home, a more considerate time to call than the middle of the night, but she felt stubborn. Faith had plenty of good ideas and the kit she'd prepared had been a thoughtful, though unnecessary, gesture. Pix took up the pen. She could certainly handle this alone.

Means, motive, opportunity. Opportunity was easy. Her jacket had hung on the back of a chair in the main cabin of their Viking fjord cruiser for most of the day. Anyone on the tour could have put the piece of paper in her pocket. Even Captain Hagen, who came into the room when the boat was docked at the farm. Pix had seen him through the window as she was leaving.

A Norwegian newspaper. Anyone could buy an *Aftenposten*. The fact that this paper was used didn't mean it had been someone who knew the language. The *International Herald Tribune* was available, too, but in limited supply. Sidney Harding had guarded his copy each day, refusing to lend it to Arnie Feld, saying he had to save the financial section and he'd been lucky to get it. So, *Aftenposten* it was. No clues there.

She began to put down names, starting with the Petersons, for no other reason than they came to mind first. In a distant corner, she was still picturing the scene in which Roy senior proposed switchies to his wife and her reaction. Walked into a door. Yeah, sure.

She jotted down their names and let her thoughts roam—any connections to Kari, Erik and the murder of Oscar Melling?

Carol and Roy Peterson, Sr.: Carol was very upset at the bench by the side of the fjord this morning. Was it just her husband's indecent proposal, or had she seen Melling's body? She had been dancing with him earlier and was out and about late. She was still wearing the same clothes she'd donned for the evening's revelry and had apparently not been to bed. Had Oscar continued to pursue her? Had she had to push him to get away from his lecherous clutches, or was there an angry shove from hubby—either sending Oscar to his death? Carol had also been outspoken about her dislike for Kari. Pix wrote, *Strong connections to O.M., Kari?* As to whether the Petersons were up to anything that Kari and Erik had stumbled upon, the family group was a great cover. Drugs, oil secrets? The Petersons had secrets. That was sure.

Lynette and Roy Peterson, Jr.: Lynette was planning a nasty surprise for her mother-in-law. Like? Framing her for murder? Pix tried hard in everyday life not to be overly judgmental and ascribed most of the ills of civilization to the rush to differentiate, unlike her friend Faith, who felt it was an essential skill. With this in mind, Pix was still forced to admit to herself that even on the basis of only brief encounters, she did not like Lynette. At all. The young woman seemed to delight in tormenting her mother-in-law, flaunting her sexual powers over Roy junior. Okay, this was not a dream honeymoon, but she could have said no. Instead, she was storing up points for the future. What else could she be up to? Pix was sure Lynette would do anything for money and/or power. Pass some papers to someone, deliver a package. Kari and Erik might have discovered what she was up to. But then what? Hard to think of nebulous Roy junior, drooling at the mouth, as an accomplice. Yet, caught between two powerful women, maybe he had hidden depths. Or depth charges. Carefully she wrote, *In the running* next to their names.

Marge and Don Brady: She already knew that they had been hiding something under their TV-sitcom exteriors. Pix could not remember any episodes where the TV Bradys cruised the neighborhood. Don was retired from the oil business, a company that did business in Norway. Was he doing a little under-the-table consulting now? He had not hidden his strong dislike of Oscar Melling, though. The rotten apple. Had Oscar done something to him, or found something out? Maybe Oscar was blackmailing someone and that was why he'd been killed. Had Kari and Erik found the same thing out? Blackmail would fit in with Oscar's personality. *Too good to be true,* she wrote by the Bradys.

Erna and Louise Dahl: The twins from Virginia. Pix paused. She didn't have anything much to write. Knowledgeable about Norwegian customs? Surely the two sisters were what they seemed. Only, Faith was always telling her the whole point was that people weren't. She put a big question mark next to their names: ?

The French cousins, Sophie and Valerie: Sophie had had an encounter of the close kind with Oscar shortly before his death. Struggling to resist, had she sent him tumbling over the rocks below? The cousins took a trip someplace every year. Couriers? Their clothes looked expensive and both wore a lot of gold jewelry. But then, Faith had pointed out to her that Frenchwomen made all their clothes look expensive, and maybe the jewelry was fake. She wrote, *Possibilities,* giving a nod to her absent friend. Faith might not be here, but her maxims were proving useful.

Helene and Arnie Feld: Helene had been the last person to see Kari and Erik. Could she be lying about what she had observed? But why? She was certainly an avid antiques collector. Was Helene hiding some painted bowls, the rosemaling by the Sogndal painter, in her Samsonite? Was this what the two young people had discovered? And had Pix's own questions struck a nerve? Arnie had had an argument with Oscar Melling, but that was probably not much of a distinction. Next to the Felds, she put: *O.M.—Nil. Other possibilities.*

Sidney and Eloise Harding: Sidney Harding knew Norway very well and, Ursula was virtually certain, knew the language. Maybe he knew some other languages, too—Russian, for instance. He had a perfect cover. For a businessman connected to the oil industry, there would be nothing suspect in frequent trips to the country, as well as extensive travel within Norway's borders. This time his wife had pushed to go along and he had promptly invited their friends. A jolly bridge foursome. Could they all be in it together? But surely if they were, they would fake a bit more enthusiasm for the scenery and play cards a little less. Maybe Oscar had been blackmailing Harding. Ursula had reported Eloise's complaint about calls and meetings at all hours. Carefully, she wrote, *Yes on all counts,* crossing off Eloise's name.

Paula and Marvin Golub: Unless they were in on the scheme with Sidney Harding, providing cover for a price, she couldn't think of anything. All four of them had had little or no contact with any of the other Scandie tourists that she had observed. She wrote, *Zip,* then moved on.

Jennifer Olsen: This would take some deliberation. Pix got up, stretched, and walked toward the balcony. She was feeling a little peckish, but she did not dare eat the Belgium chocolate candy bar that Faith had tucked in unless she was in a tight situation, and this did not qualify, despite the fact that she had received a journalistic threat a short time ago. She thought she'd tell Marcussen about it in the morning. It might raise her credibility— or maybe he would think she manufactured it to further divert suspicion away from herself. Well, she'd sleep on it.

Mother tended to get hungry at odd hours, Pix had learned on the trip, so she had prudently stocked her bag with a roll of *kjeks*— cookies—several boxes of raisins, and plenty of Kvikk Lunsj, a candy bar to which both she and Ursula were devoted. It was the Norwegian version of a Kit Kat bar and she eagerly tore off the yellow-red-and-green paper wrapper, thinking as usual what a waste it was to throw away the pretty silver paper underneath, its surface subtly decorated with the Freia company's emblem—a crane standing on one leg. Norwegians were inordinately fond of chocolate in any form and edged out the United States in per capita consumption. She bit into the *sjokolade* and gazed at the fjord. It was sparkling in the bright, clear summer night—silent and motionless, the mountains omnipresent, looming over the deep waters. She should be reading Ibsen, listening to Grieg, or thumbing through some Norse folktales. There was decidedly less activity than the night before. She saw a few couples and groups strolling about the grounds, but not many, and none from the tour. It was as if by common consent, they'd all gone to ground, battening the hatches, which was possibly the most mixed metaphor she'd ever produced.

She sat down in one chair, savoring the sweet, soft air, and propped her legs up on another.

Jennifer Olsen. Had there really been a man on her balcony that first night at Fleischer's, or was that intended as a ruse? She was certainly the most likely person from the tour to have painted the swastika on the lawn at the Stalheim Hotel. Her bitterness about the war ran deep and she had referred to Oscar Melling as a fascist long before they had learned he had been one. Had she known earlier? Was the swastika meant to frighten him? Cat and mouse? Had she planned to expose him? Even if nothing could legally have been done against him, it would surely have affected his business. They were both from New Jersey, she recalled suddenly, even though Jennifer lived in Manhattan now. Was there some previous connection?

The letter q in the Norwegian alphabet

exists solely for the purpose of spelling words taken from abroad—*quixotic* becomes quite charmingly *don-quijotisk*. Vidkun Quisling had added a new word to the English and Norwegian languages—and in this case the resulting name for a traitor had found its way into the lexicon of virtually every other country: *quisling*. And Melling—rather, Eriksen—had been one.

Pix finished her chocolate bar, crumpled the papers, and stuffed them in her pocket. She walked back into the room and sat down at the desk. The list looked somewhat skimpy, yet it would serve as a mnemonic.

Jennifer Olsen was in excellent physical shape. Oscar would be no match for her. Had she somehow determined a direct link between him and her father's and grandmother's deaths? Had she waited for her mother to die before seeking revenge? Pix thought that someone like Jennifer would feel getting rid of Oscar Eriksen was morally justified. The law might not be able to get to him, but she could. Jennifer had been upset at Erik's death and Kari's disappearance. Upset at the tour's response. Pix didn't see any links there or links to any kind of smuggling, although there was the man with a bag on her balcony. Had they thought he had been spotted and decided Jennifer better cry wolf? Fatigued now, Pix wrote hurriedly, *O.M.—yes! The rest iffy.*

Had she missed anybody? The bachelor farmers, but Pix felt safe in crossing them off.

They might have descended like a hoard of their Viking ancestors on the man for cheating at cards, beating him to a pulp, but slipping out at dark to give the miscreant a helping hand to whatever the opposite of Valhalla was did not seem their style.

Everyone else on the tour had either arrived at Voss when Pix and Ursula had or were, like the farmers, such far-fetched possibilities that even suspicious Faith would have eliminated them—such as Mrs. Fields, with her malfunctioning hearing aids and inhalers, all too genuine, Pix had observed. She was spunky, though.

The guides had been with the tour since the beginning, the stewards since Kari and Erik had disappeared, but they had been in Bergen, ready to take their places, Pix recalled. The country was narrow, only exceeding a hundred miles across in the south. It didn't take long to get from one place to another. Presumably, Captain Hagen had been on the west coast, waiting for the tour to arrive and board his vessel. Pix couldn't think of any ties any of them would have had to Oscar Melling, but they all knew Kari and Erik. She wrote down their names under *Staff* and wearily decided to call it a night. Sonja's antipathy toward Kari and her preference for Erik had been obvious. Who knew what else had been going on within the Scandie Sights staff? The weight of the two deaths pressed on her. Erik's, so untimely, especially ironic in this country, which had one of the world's highest life expectancies. Erik was supposed to have seen many decades come and go. She was beginning to feel she had—and very recently.

Pix folded up the cryptic notes and put the paper in her passport case with the pictures of Kari and Erik, Hanna and Sven. She took the one of Kari's parents out and held it in front of her. She had never asked Marit if she knew what had happened to Sven—if she knew where he was now. It was a stupid oversight. All this time, she'd been imagining Kari on an identity quest involving both parents, but perhaps she already knew where her father was, although Pix had never heard any mention of him. She must remember to ask Marit in the morning whether Marit had ever known Oscar Eriksen, although surely she would have mentioned this.

Pix opened the list one last time. Only Lynette and Roy junior were too young and far removed not to have been directly touched by the war. Others besides Jennifer might be nursing secret wounds—and hatreds, including the staff.

She filled her pockets with everything Faith had thought she might need, added her camera, and went to bed. Just before climbing in, she took the torn piece of newspaper and put that in her passport case, as well, then slipped it into the bag she carried with her wallet, guidebook, and treats for Mother.

She didn't bother to pull the light-obscuring drapes. She didn't need to. Pix set the alarm, put the clock on the table, and fell promptly, deeply asleep.

When the alarm rang at three, it pulled Pix from a troubled sleep of twisted dreams. She swung her legs over the side of the bed in the half dark and tried to recall some of the images, but in the way of dreams, the harder she struggled to visualize them, the more elusive her memories became. Marit had been there, but a stern Marit. Pix had been trying to get to a child, a child who was crying. At one point, a vivid picture of herself shouting reappeared and vanished. Giving up, but unsettled, she went into the bathroom and splashed cold water on her face, peed, ready to face the inevitable. The trip ended today. It was now or never. Never sounded pretty good, but then, it also meant she'd never know.

Well aware of her laden pockets, she closed the door behind her after looking up and down the empty corridor an unnecessary number of times. She fully expected a hand on the shoulder again, but this time it would be the *inspektør*, or one of the other members of the Norwegian *politi*, not Carol Peterson.

She moved slowly down the stairs and then more quickly to the door to the outside. She put her hand on the long horizontal bar and pushed. It didn't move. Damn Marcussen! Forget about trust. He'd locked the door. What was worse, the glowing red light above indicated the alarm had been set. There was a sticker—SECURITAS—that she hadn't remembered seeing before, although from the prevalence of these elsewhere, Securitas seemed to be the security system of choice throughout the country. So much security, so little crime. She could hear the *inspektør*'s views now. "Try not to take any walks," he'd said. Well, he was making absolutely sure she, for one, wouldn't.

The idea of lowering herself from the third-floor balcony occurred to her; however, it was fraught with not simply the danger of discovery but the danger of falling and breaking an essential bone or two, which would be an enormous inconvenience and certainly counterproductive. No, she'd have to go out the front door. There was no other way. Coming back wasn't a problem. By that time, she'd either have a tale to tell or could once more use the "couldn't sleep" line and let them think what they wished. She crept down the corridor to the door that led to the lobby, just before the gift shop. The door had a window in it and she could see that there was only one person on the desk. Marcussen had stationed a man by the front door, but his head was lolled over in sleep. She could hear his snores even through the door. The clerk disappeared into the back room and Pix catapulted out, running noiselessly in her soft Reeboks to the bar, crouching down behind the substantial mahogany.

The clerk returned with a magazine and seemed to be arranging herself for the night. There was no way Pix could leave without being seen. For a moment, time froze. The policeman slept, the clerk seemed transfixed by the printed page, and Pix's muscles began to ache from the awkward position she was in. The phone rang. The night clerk spoke rapidly in Norwegian, her cheeks turning pink. A boyfriend? A tryst? Please, please, please. The young woman hung up and took a compact from under the counter, then a comb. Definitely an assignation. But where? Pix felt the balls of her feet growing numb. She tried carefully bouncing up and down to keep the circulation going. The compact was snapped shut and comb thrown down. The clerk ran her fingers through her hair and fetched a large pocketbook from a drawer. She disappeared again into the back room. More work needed to be done apparently, and what Pix was counting on was that a larger mirror was needed. She had to assume this is what the clerk was headed for, which would give Pix enough time to get out the door. But if that was not what was up and she returned right away, Pix would be stymied.

She had to take the chance. She crawled out from behind the bar and continued on all fours, passing close to the somnambulant officer of the law. She couldn't stand up. There might be one of those mirrors showing someone in the back room exactly what was going on in front. Her heart was beating rapidly and, despite the cleanliness of Kvikne's, her hands and knees were beginning to feel *skitten*.

She was almost at the door. Now, she'd have to stand up to open it. The light seemed glaring and surely someone would spot her. A quick twist and she was outside. Glancing behind her, the scene looked impossibly serene. A cop in the arms of Morpheus and an absent clerk dreaming of more active arms. Reassured that she hadn't been seen, Pix didn't waste any more time in contemplation, but took to her feet and sprinted across the lawn, taking care to stay well away from the lighted path. Every dark bush suggested a figure, yet she reached the village, still apparently the only person up and about.

Cautiously, she clung to the shadows of the few buildings and made her way to the dock past the towering Midsummer bonfire pile. This time, there were no voices issuing forth from the Viking cruiser, and so Pix hurriedly climbed on board and went downstairs to the lower deck. Piece of cake. She was feeling pretty cocky—until she realized the door to the main cabin was locked, too. "I thought Norwegians were supposed to be so honest," she mumbled to herself. "All these locked doors."

She didn't see any indication of an alarm, no telltale stickers. She had also looked for an alarm system during the day, without finding any signs of one on board. Anyway, she had no choice. Taking the skeleton keys from her pocket, she patiently tried them one by one, and before long, the door opened. Thrusting thoughts of what could only be termed *breaking and entering* from her mind— she was, after all, a member of the tour and maybe she wanted to retrieve something she'd left on board—she stepped into the main cabin and closed the door behind her, turning the lock to discourage any interruptions. It was pitch-dark and she took the penlite from her pocket to avoid colliding with tables and chairs. Faith *had* known what she was about.

In the small room behind the galley, she had no trouble locating Mother's closet. Aware of how little time she had, she emptied the contents and set to work tapping on the walls. Her mother had been right. The rear wall did sound hollow, yet there didn't seem to be any way to get into it. She shone the light along the edges, all the way to where a shelf had been built at the top. She took out her Swiss army knife and opened the thinnest blade. She ran it where the shelf met the wall and where the sides of the closet met the rear. Nothing. She pushed with all her strength along the bottom of the wall, just above the floorboards. Again, nothing magic happened. No springs sprung. Sesame wasn't opening. Poor Mother. She'd be terribly disappointed. Pix had to keep trying. She began to tap again—lightly at various points, then making a fist and pounding when the first method didn't work.

Dead center, just below the top shelf, the miracle happened. She hit it squarely with her fist and the entire back of the closet popped out, falling forward, one flat piece of wallboard held in place with clips on the inside.

There was a compartment—a secret compartment! And it was full!

Three bags had been stacked one on top of

the next. Pix removed the top one, took it into the room, and examined it. She dared not turn on a light, but using the flashlight, she could see it was an ordinary piece of soft-sided luggage, shaped like a gym bag, and bright blue. It sported a Scandie Sights tag and the Scandie Sights luggage strap cinched its girth. She went back to look at the other two bags in the closet. They were similar; one was, in fact, a gym bag, sporting the Nike logo. Both were marked with Scandie Sights identification, but no other name or luggage tags. Lost luggage from other tours? Surely they would have been missed. Perhaps a repository for lost items, things left on board?

She returned to the first one and opened it. It seemed to contain bedding of some sort. A thick quilt was on top, and reaching her hand down along the side, she felt more material. No drugs, jewels, or documents. Perhaps the closet cubbyhole was an old forgotten storage container. There was a cot in the room. The quilt even smelled musty. But the luggage looked new. She took the top piece of what she assumed was bedding out and shook it to make sure nothing was hidden in its folds. Nothing was—but this was strange. It didn't resemble the kind of quilt in use in Norway now, and she took the penlite to examine it more carefully. It was more like a rug. One of those *Rya* rugs with the long, shaggy pile that suggested the pelt of an animal. She dug farther down in the bag and realized how shortsighted she had been.

It *was* a treasure trove! Yet not what she had

expected at all. There were pieces of intricate Hardanger embroidery, obviously very old. In the dim light, she could also make out the figures of Norse gods in a fine tapestry and a pile of what she knew were old pillow covers, also woven in an intricate pattern in bright colors. They were museum quality. At the bottom, there were two plastrons, the bodice piece that was worn with the Hardanger women's costume. They were elaborately embroidered, and Pix remembered the young women at Stalheim noting that theirs were covered with beadwork, unlike the earlier ones, which were embroidered—a dying art and very expensive. Bells rang and she dashed into the closet to drag the other two bags out.

The second held wooden objects, carefully wrapped in padded cloths. There were bowls, drinking horns, dippers, engagement spoons, butter molds, small highly decorated *tiner*—boxes used to bring food to a wedding, christening, or anniversary. Pix trained the light on one bowl in particular, an ale bowl. She'd seen them in the *folkemuseums*. This one had a high collar, typical of the west coast, and was inscribed. She could make out the name Sogn and the date, 1691.

These bags did not contain lost-and-found items—or rather, they did: lost by someone and found by someone else. It wasn't a motley collection of sweaters, socks, and scarves, but Norway's heritage, objects from the past—a past well beyond the hundred-year stipulation. Some of the items were painted, others carved, some in the distinctive chip-

259

carving style. Each was intact and had obviously been well cared for.

She reached for the last bag. It was much smaller and at first glance appeared to contain linens also, rolls of white pillowcases. She took one out, undid it carefully, and gasped.

It was jewelry. Catching the light, it glowed and shone—the luster of ages, years of polishing. Exquisitely worked silver brooches were pinned to a piece of felt. She recalled reading about the importance of silver to the Norwegian peasants of old in a book her mother had received from Marit. The metal was valued not just for its intrinsic worth but for far more superstitious reasons. You could only kill a troll, even the troll king, with a silver bullet. Silver buckles were used to fasten a baby's swaddling band or a silver coin sewn in his or her blankets so the child wouldn't be snatched by the trolls. Heirloom silver was passed down reverently to ensure everything from protection against illness to getting the beer to work. Marit had taken her wedding jewelry out to show them on Pix's first trip. It had been Marit's grandmother's. There was a cloth belt covered with linked silver squares, gold-plated teardrops hanging from each engraved piece. She'd brought out cuff buttons, filigree bodice clasps, and pins of all sizes. Hans had the bridegroom's traditional silver cross, worn by his great-grandfather, and the buttons from his vest. With these in mind, Pix undid the remaining rolls. There were more brooches, buttons, amulets, and crosses. One roll contained a single piece, an enormous many-tiered brooch with golden dangles hanging from the larger pieces of silver that made up the tiers. Red and green stones had been set in the center of the largest forms. She unpinned it and held it up in the beam of her light. It was magnificent. Such craftsmanship.

"Beautiful, isn't it? We are known for the quality of our jewelry."

The words coming out of the darkness took her by surprise. She dropped the brooch, spinning around toward the direction from which the voice had come, and flashed the light on the intruder. She had been so intent on the contents of the bags that she hadn't heard the door open or the accompanying soft footsteps.

It was Carl Bjørnson. He wasn't smiling.

Carl walked to the window and pulled down the shade. They were in complete darkness except for Pix's light, and after briefly flashing it on his face, she let it shine down by her side. His expression had chilled her to the bone. But she had no time for fear. She quickly switched the light off and dashed toward the door. He covered the distance in several large steps, beating her by inches. She shrank back against the wall. Taking a flashlight from his own jacket pocket, he shone it on the lock and firmly clicked it shut. He pulled a chair over, sat down, and leaned against the doorknob.

"I'll take your camera, thank you." His accent seemed markedly British now.

Pix thought naïveté was worth a try.

"Carl, I know this must look odd, but I came on board to find my mother's glasses, which she has misplaced. She's an insomniac and wants to read. Earlier, we searched everywhere, and they are nowhere at the hotel. I thought she might have left them on the boat and came here to have a look."

"In the steward's closet?" he asked sardonically, clearly enjoying himself.

"It seemed the obvious place for lost and found." He had trained his flashlight beam on her and she gestured toward the bags.

"A good try, Mrs. Miller, but not good enough, I'm afraid." He tilted the chair down and it hit the floor with a bang. "No, you will have to do a little better than that. Now the camera."

Pix handed it over and watched him open the back, exposing all the lovely shots she'd made of the fjord. She hadn't gotten around to photographing the contents of the closet. Her plan had been to pack one case up and hightail it to Inspector Marcussen, bringing him back to see the rest for himself. Otherwise, he might have suspected her of smuggling, too.

She thought about screaming. The noise Carl's chair had made reminded her of that option. The dock had been deserted when she came, but someone might hear her now.

It was as if he had read her mind.

"Oh, and please don't make any loud noise. If you do, I will be forced to kill you." He took a gun from his pocket and held it in the beam of light. It looked very real and quite deadly. "You know how deep the fjord is here. And you have established quite a reputation for eccentricity—roaming about at unlikely hours, locking yourself in a sauna. Your disappearance may cause some initial alarm, but not for long."

It was too true. Pix sat down on the floor. It was that or have her knees buckle under her. Murder? Over some antiques? More had to be at stake.

"My mother knows where I am. She's waiting for me to come back now," Pix said bravely. She was about to add that her mother knew about the closet, but fortunately she stopped herself in time or she might have had a companion.

"Your mother is sound asleep and so is Fru Hansen."

Pix realized there was no way Carl could let her go—not until he got away. Was that what was going on? Was he waiting for someone? Someone in a boat or car who would take him and the treasures away?

He'd said "locking yourself in a sauna."

"So it was you who locked the door of the sauna!" She was beginning to feel less terrified and more angry.

"Yes, but I wouldn't worry about that right now if I were you." He sounded amazingly cool. She couldn't see much of him behind the light he steadily trained on her, and his voice emerged disembodied out of the darkness, every nuance emphasized by the lack of facial expression to go with the words.

It was on the tip of Pix's tongue to ask what exactly she should be worrying about now, but instead, she said, "And you are dealing in stolen antiques." She might as well get the whole story.

"Absolutely not!" He was righteously indignant. "Nothing has been stolen. Everything you see was purchased fair and square."

She began to get the picture. Fast cash for great-grandmother's carved bread platter and a new satellite dish instead. He had to be taking the stuff out of the country, though. If he was simply selling to Oslo or Bergen antique dealers, why the hidden chamber and all the Scandie Sights tags? The tags— ingenious. Mix them in with all the rest of the tour's luggage.

She opened her mouth to ask another question. She wished he'd lower the beam. It was making her head ache—or maybe that was due to the uncertain nature of her current position.

"Did Kari—"

"Shut up!" He stood up and seemed to listen for something. She couldn't hear a thing. He sat down.

"I must warn you, Mrs. Miller—may I call you Pix?—it is better if you do not discuss certain subjects. Healthier for you."

"No, you may not call me Pix," she retorted instantly, ignoring the threat. The arrogance of the man. "I think this has gone on long enough. Please unlock the door immediately!"

He laughed. It didn't sound as pleasant

as it had in prior days. What was it Mother had called him, and Jan—"dears"? Talk about lack of judgment. Faith was right. People wore masks, and Carl's had been diabolically deceptive.

"Not just yet. We need to wait some more. Would you like some coffee? I have a thermos here," he offered.

It was too much. What no cakes, no *vafler*? She didn't bother to refuse.

She felt utterly defeated. It was all staring her in the face now—the trail that started with Kari and Erik. Oscar Melling must have been onto Carl and Carl had taken care of the old man. Pix shuddered.

"He was an old man. Surely, you didn't need to..." Her thoughts were grim. Carl hadn't *needed* to kill any of them, but he had.

"What are you talking about? I had nothing to do with that old fart!" He nursed his grievance for a moment and added, "You have been such a nuisance since the beginning." Carl was reaching for the thermos as he scolded her. Not a typical Norwegian by any means, he did have that scolding tone down perfectly. The combination of sorrow and sternness that resonates so loudly in one's breastbone—just where one is supposed to be beating oneself. His British accent had diminished.

"Questions, questions! Poking your nose in other people's business! We tried to be nice-... to warn you, but you paid no attention. What kind of woman are you? Didn't you get the newspaper?"

Pix nodded. She was waiting for the right moment. He'd have to put the light down to open the thermos and pour the coffee.

"And what do you do? Ignore it! I pity the man who is married to you! And always by yourself! What were you doing in the woods in Stalheim! You're supposed to come on these trips to make friends! But then, that's not why you came, was it, Mrs. Miller? Pix."

She sprang forward and grabbed the thermos from where he'd placed it next to his chair just after pouring a cup and flung the steaming-hot contents directly into his face. He screamed and lunged for her, blinded. She fumbled in the dark for the lock and heard a satisfying click.

She turned the knob as he grabbed her, and for a moment they rolled across the floor, barely avoiding the precious contents of the bags. Pix brought her knee up squarely into his groin. She was in good shape and almost as tall as he was. He groaned and released her. Pix indeed!

She ran out the door, slamming it behind her, and headed straight for the bow. It was the quickest way off the boat. He was behind her. She threw down chairs as she went. She was at the door and wrenched it open. The air, the cold night air, was sweeter than any fragrance she could imagine. She stepped over the threshold, avoided the coils of rope, and climbed up on the dock.

Carl yelled something in Norwegian. She recognized two words—*stoppe* and the name

Sven. Then there was nothing.

"I don't want to get up yet, Mother." Pix firmly kept her eyes closed and pulled the down comforter under her chin. Then she realized her head was aching, and everything came rushing back. She opened her eyes. Where on earth was she? It certainly wasn't Kvikne's Hotel.

Sun streamed through the wavy glass in two small windows. She was tucked into a bed built into the wall, like a box. She sat up slowly, her head pounding more fiercely as she moved. She reached to the back and felt a lump the size of a fish cake. She'd been hit, hit with something hard. But Tylenol would have to wait. She had to get out of here and get some help. Carl was probably long gone, yet the sooner she raised the alarm, the better the chances were of catching him and finding out what had happened to Kari and Erik—both, she was sure now, dead.

Except she couldn't move. She was still clad in everything she had been wearing last night, even her jacket, but what had been added was a chain and padlock about her waist, securing her to the bed. Optimistically, she reached in her pocket for her skeleton keys, blessing Faith over and over again. But of course they were gone, as were her knife and matches. She'd dropped the penlite herself in the struggle with Carl. They'd thoughtfully left the chocolate bar—but she wasn't hungry—and the gloves, comb, and hair spray, no doubt thinking her even more eccentric, and vain on top of that. She checked her pants pocket. A five-hundred-kroner note was still there. Either they were too honest to take it or hadn't found the cash, mixed, as it was, with several tissues.

She sank back into the pillows, cursing her comfortable prison. All she could do was wait. She occupied the time by looking at the room. From the angle of the sky, she thought she was up high, a second floor, but the room seemed to be an entire cabin. Besides the bed, there was a rustic long wooden table and chairs, an old hearth with iron fireplace tools next to it, and a stack of wood. A sheepskin rug lay in front of the hearth and shiny copper pots hung on the wall. A brass oil lamp stood on the table, apart from some iron candleholders on the wall, the only source of light. A brightly painted chest of drawers with a wooden rack filled with plates and bowls above it completed the inventory. It was someone's *hytte,* or holiday cabin, she realized. Yet whose? A cabin made from an old farm building, judging from the log walls—thick walls.

Carl. It had been Carl all along. This was what Kari and Erik had found out. That Carl was exporting antiquities. But why kill them? Granted, Annelise had said the market was good for Scandinavian antiques, inflated even, because of the scarcity, but to take two human lives, three, counting Oscar—except

Carl had said he'd had nothing to do with Oscar. But if not Carl, then who? Could the police have been wrong? Had it been an accident? But Kari and Erik. Poor Marit! Pix began to sob, and soon the pain in her heart and her head sent her to sleep again.

"You have to wake up!" Someone was shaking her. Mother? She opened her eyes and started forward until the iron girdle pulled her back. The voice was a female's, but it wasn't her mother's. It was the farmer's wife. That pretty woman with her cap of shining blond hair.

"Am I glad to see you!" Pix said. "You must help me. The tour guide—Carl, not the other one—is taking antiques out of the country to sell illegally and he's killed two people. We have to call the police right away. Oh dear, you probably don't have a phone, but maybe you have one of those cellular ones?" In Oslo, Pix had noticed these were as ubiquitous as on the streets of New York City.

"You mustn't worry now, Mrs. Miller. Just come on." The woman was undoing the padlock and pulling off the comforter. "Can you walk?"

"Of course I can walk," Pix answered, climbing awkwardly out of the bed. "But you don't understand. Is it my English? We have to get some help."

"Yes, yes," the woman replied, in the tone

of voice one uses with a child. In Pix's household, the words were usually followed by
"I'll think about it." Her children were then
apt to respond, "Why don't you say no and
get it over with."

No. The woman was saying no.

Outside the cabin, which occupied the top
story of the *stabbur* she and Helene Feld had
noted, Pix observed that the farm was empty
of children, goats, and tourists. Pix would have
given everything she owned for one of the bachelor farmers. Instead, she was being hustled
down the path to the landing. The sleek new
water taxi awaited, its engine running.

"Here are some sandwiches and coffee," the
farmer's wife said cheerfully. Pix's hopes
rose. Maybe they were taking her to Vik, to
the police. She got in the boat and sat in the
stern. She couldn't see who was driving. She
was very thirsty and poured some coffee. It
smelled heavenly. She put the sandwiches
in her pocket and sipped the brew. The
farmer's wife waved. Mindlessly, Pix waved
back and drank the coffee. It was very sweet,
but she drained the cup. Sweet, like the
farmer's wife. What was her name? she wondered. Something like Flicka, except that
was a horse, she thought. *My Friend Flicka*—
that was it. A little girl, or boy? Anyway, on
the book jacket he or she'd had dimples—the
kid, not the horse. Pix had a cousin with
deep dimples who swore she got them from
sleeping on a button, but when Pix tried it,

all she got was a round mark with two dots in the center. Flicka the horse and Flicka the farmer's wife, the farmer's daughter. That was the name of a popular china pattern in Norway, an old one made by Porsgrund. All these farms. The boat was speeding along the fjord. She wished she could take a swim. Her head still ached and she was feeling very muzzy. A man came out of the small cabin.

"Come with me, *now*," he said.

She mindlessly followed him inside, her feet tangling together. She wouldn't mind taking a nap. No buttons, though. She started to tell him. He grabbed her arm and pushed her onto a bunk. It was the farmer. The farmer with the dark beard.

The farmer with the lovely wife, who had just drugged Pix's coffee.

9

"I'm sorry for the inconvenience, but we have to do what the *inspektør* says. I'm sure everything will be cleared up quickly so you can be on your way. Yes, Mr. Harding?"

Carl Bjørnson was addressing the Scandie Sights tour in the Dragon Room of Kvikne's Hotel after breakfast on Sunday morning. He had informed them that the police had requested no one leave Balestrand. Carl and Jan had decided to break the news following the meal, not before. "Hard to be too upset after a Kvikne's breakfast," Jan had observed philosophically.

Sidney Harding, however, had not been appeased by the cloudberries in cream or the more than usually abundant herring preparations.

"I demand to speak to someone from the embassy immediately! You can't hold us here against our will. We're U.S. citizens."

"We have relatives waiting for us in Kristiansand," Carol Peterson said crisply. "I don't understand why we can't go about our business. It's not as if any of us know where the uh... woman is." Ursula gave her a piercing glance. She knew the missing word was *stupid,* or worse.

A voice was heard at the door.

"Kvikne's Hotel is not exactly a prison." It was Johan Marcussen. He was holding a cup of coffee. "And we were in touch with the American embassy immediately, of course. They agreed with us that the sudden disappearance of an American citizen following so closely on the death of another in the same tour suggests extreme caution regarding the safety of the others. Certainly we hope some of you may have an idea where Mrs. Miller could have gone, but mainly we'd like you just to stay here and relax together for a little while longer."

He made it sound like a bonus, something arranged merely for their pleasure.

"If I'm not on a flight out of Oslo by tomorrow morning, everyone from the king on down is going to know about it," Sidney Harding fumed.

"I'm sure they will," Louise Dahl whispered to Ursula, who was standing next to the sisters. They had had breakfast together, and while expressing their deep concern for Pix, both had also tried to reassure her mother. "She probably went for a hike in the mountains and got lost. It happens all the time, and there aren't so many people to ask. They'll find her. Don't worry," Erna had said.

But Ursula *was* worried. So was Marit. There was a lot the Dahl sisters didn't know.

Carl continued to speak. "We will have a walking tour of Balestrand meeting in the hotel lobby in one hour for those of you who are interested. The architecture is quite special, as this was a favorite spot not only for English sportsmen but for artists and writers from many places."

"Can it, will you, Carl," said Roy Peterson senior. "No one cares. We just want to get the hell out of here."

Jan cast a desperate look at his fellow guide. The evaluation sheets were going to be X-rated. "The hotel has—" he started to say, jumping in to help.

"Well, I want to go on the tour, and I think all of you are pigs." Jennifer Olsen didn't mince words. "Two women are missing. Two men have been killed, and what you're worried about is catching a plane and"—she gave Carol a withering look—"some relatives you've never met. Worried you won't be able to sponge off them?"

Carol started to move toward Jennifer with

obvious intent. Her fist was in fact raised.

"Ladies, ladies." Carl the peacemaker stepped between them. "We are offering the tour as a diversion, to help pass the time. The hotel has many other activities, as you know. Why don't we arrange to meet here again after lunch. I'm sure there will be some news by then." Oil on troubled waters. He nodded at Jan and the two started to leave the room.

But Inspector Marcussen had the last word. "Activities on land. No boat trips."

That morning, Ursula Rowe had awakened early, even for her. She lay in bed for a while, thinking of the pain her old friend Marit was suffering. Hans was gone—and Hanna. Kari was all Marit had left. In a country that seemed to abound in relatives, Marit had few. Her brothers had settled in the United States and they were both dead now—Marit's ties with their families reduced to a Christmas card each year. It was the same with Hans's family. When Kari was first reported missing, her grandmother had heard from some concerned cousins, but there was no one she could really turn to in her loneliness and fear. No one except Ursula. These last days, the two women had spent most of their waking hours together, talking of the past, their childhoods together. Happy times. Marit had told Ursula that she had the feeling if she could just wait, everything would be all right, but the waiting was agony. So she had known from the beginning that she needed Ursula— and Pix—with her.

Old women don't require much sleep, Ursula told herself as she got out of bed. Maybe it was because she didn't want to waste the time left to her; maybe her body didn't need it anymore. She might doze in the day and turn in early, but she wakened often and arose with the dawn.

Yes, she was worried about Pix. Perhaps it had been foolish to send her by herself to investigate the closet on the boat. Ursula should have gone, too. She put on her robe and went across the hall to tap lightly on her daughter's door. She would surely be back by now. There had been no response, so Ursula had knocked harder.

Again, the door remained shut. She went back to her room and called Pix's room number. She let the phone ring fifteen times, hung up, and tried again. Then she called the front desk for them to try. They did not receive an answer, either.

"Please have someone come up with a key immediately. I want to be sure my daughter is all right." Ursula had felt her throat constrict with apprehension, yet her tone suggested only instant compliance. A security guard had appeared and together they opened the door.

Pix's bed had been slept in, but she was not in the room. Ursula looked and quickly noted that her daughter's jacket was gone, although apparently nothing else. She had thanked the guard and then awakened Marit.

"I can't imagine that she is still at the boat, but we have to check. We'll check the grounds, too."

The two women, wearing several layers against the chill morning air, had walked straight to the dock. It was deserted, as were the grounds they passed through. The clerk at the desk had given them an odd look but made no comment beyond saying, "*God dag.*" Guests sometimes did strange things, and dawn strolls were comparatively tame.

All the doors on the Viking fjord cruiser were locked. They knocked and called Pix's name but got no response. They checked the area around the hotel. Captivated by the light, maybe Pix had decided to take some photographs of the old houses. On impulse, they went into the church, St. Olav's.

Here, Marit had turned to Ursula. "We have to tell the police." Ursula sank to her knees, said a prayer for her daughter—and Kari's safety—allowed herself a sob, then got up and followed Marit to the phone box in front of the post office. The conversation was brief. "They will find the *inspektør* and we are to wait in the hotel lobby."

Thirty minutes later, Marcussen had entered with the smell of sleep and only a hasty wash still on him.

Although he had already received the message, Ursula had needed to say it directly herself. "My daughter, Mrs. Samuel Miller, the one who found the body of Oscar Melling, is missing and we think it is very serious."

So had the inspector. After obtaining some more information, he'd disappeared into the room behind the front desk, leaving an officer with them. After a while—a wait that seemed interminable to Ursula—he had returned to tell them a search of the area would be under way as soon as possible and that he himself was going down to the boat with the captain.

Now as the tour members filed out of the Dragon Room, Marcussen motioned for Ursula and Marit to stay.

"As you must have assumed, we have nothing to report yet. I'm very sorry. Will you come with me where we can talk in private? There are some things I don't understand."

Some? thought Ursula ruefully as she followed him out the door.

Pix Miller was not a drinker. Yes, she was partial to a dram of scotch now and then, particularly Laphroaig, but hangovers had been few and far between. The one she had now, she thought, not even able to open her eyelids, unaccountably turned to lead, was the mother of them all. The grandmother, the great-grandmother. Her leaden lids flew up. Wait a minute—she wasn't sure if she was speaking aloud or not because of the pounding in her head—I wasn't drinking.

The coffee. The farmer. That sweet little flaxen-haired wife. She wasn't back in their *hytte* or whatever it was, nor on their streamlined water taxi. Where the hell had she awakened this time?

At least she'd awakened.

It was dark and cold. She moved one arm carefully, then the other, and wiggled her legs around, checking to see that everything worked. It did. Someone had thrown a blanket over her. Unfortunately, it did not afford much warmth. She still had her jacket on and she buttoned it to her neck. Her hand groped the ground next to her. It was dirt, but as her eyes became accustomed to the dark, she could tell she wasn't outdoors. She sat up unsteadily and touched the wall beside her. It was rough-hewn stone—another cabin or farm building. Pix was becoming uncomfortably intimate with Norwegian rural architecture, although the opportunity for a monograph in the immediate future was slight. In any case, she would have preferred to study the subject in a crowded *folkemuseum*.

The effects of the drug had not worn off— her headache was worse, if anything, and the thought of food was quelled as soon as it arose lest it lead to immediate vomiting. But her mind was beginning to clear. A perfect setup. The farmer with his water-taxi service was a familiar figure on the local fjords and among certain people it would also be known that he would pay a good price for Tante Inge's coffee spoons, too. Scandie Sights stopped to visit the farm throughout the summer, but the goods were probably delivered at other times. Maybe arranging the farm visit had been the source of the initial contact: like-minded people meeting one another. It must have been the farmer on Jennifer Olsen's balcony at Fleischer's Hotel, mistaking it for Carl's room next door. The argument Pix overheard the following evening at Stalheim had either been over the screwup, or maybe something more—splitting the take? And it had been the dark-bearded farmer on the boat in Balestrand the other night when Pix first tried to search the closet. Dark-bearded. Pix heard Carl's voice screaming after her as she tried to escape. "*Stoppe*" had been clear. Also "Sven." Dark hair, east coast—a city boy, his wife had said, the right age—could the farmer be Kari's father? Had she discovered his identity and what he was doing?

The ground was hard and damp, yet sitting up hurt more. She debated putting the blanket under her, then decided it would quickly absorb moisture from the earthen floor and would do more good draped across her.

She knew she should get up and start to search the place for a door or window—some way to get out—but she couldn't summon the strength at the moment. If she could sleep, she might feel better when she woke up. Next time, she'd tell Faith to put some analgesics in her survival kit—that is, if there was a next time.

Pix drifted off into a half sleep. Images of Carl laughing, his face grotesque, passed through her mind. Was Jan a part of it, too? And Sonja, Anders? The captain? Was Scandie Sights itself a front?

She thought she could sleep. It was the most sensible thing to do, and Lord knows, that was what she was. "Pix is so sensible," everyone always said. "So dependable." It sounded like a dog, a *hund.*...

Mice. She wasn't a mouse, but the place had

mice. She didn't mind mice, yet the idea of those scratchy little feet running across her midriff was not appealing. But no, not mice. Something bigger than mice. A cat? She searched her mind for recollections of Norwegian wildlife. A fox? A troll?

A person. Someone had coughed. Not an animal cough. A definite human cough. Then a voice speaking rapid Norwegian.

Pix replied with one of her few Norwegian phrases—she was really going to have to get some tapes—"*Jeg snakker ikke norsk. Snakker du engelsk?*"—I don't speak Norwegian. Do you speak English?

The person did. "Don't move. I have a gun."

Oh no, not again, thought Pix, lying absolutely still.

"There was nothing in the closet, Mrs. Rowe. Yes, it did sound a little hollow in the back, but Captain Hagen told us that the boat has been remodeled so many times in its history that half of it sounds hollow. In this section, they've made bathrooms from what were the crew's quarters—these were coastal boats, used for the mail and other deliveries. The closet backs onto a bathroom and it's probably where the pipes are, but we are continuing to search the boat. We have not seen any signs of a struggle. In fact, no signs that anyone had been there, and it was all locked up tight last night, as usual. The captain checks himself last thing."

Pix had not shown Marit and Ursula Faith's

bon voyage gifts. If she had had to say why, she would have acknowledged a recurrence of the adolescent impulse that prevents teenagers from telling their parents anything that might reflect unfavorably on a particular friend. Jeez, all Mother has to do is find out Faith gave me skeleton keys and she'll never let me go over to her house again. It was absurd, of course. Pix had also felt somewhat reluctant to share the information that the wife of her mother's spiritual adviser had slipped a can of Mace-like hair spray in for good measure. While Faith was not the leading light of the Ladies Alliance, she was a member in good standing, donating many jars of toothsome peach/cassis and wild strawberry jam to the Autumn Harvest Fair. The notion that the minister's spouse was actively encouraging malfeasance among the parishioners would not go over as big as the jams, always popular items with their HAVE FAITH labels, the name of the catering company.

"If it was locked, then she must not have been able to get on the boat at all." Ursula's anxiety increased. Pix had surely left the hotel on a mission—a mission dictated by her mother. Apparently, she'd never gotten there, let along accomplished it. How could she have disappeared in the short distance between the hotel and the boat? Why hadn't she returned immediately when she discovered the boat was locked?

Marit spoke her fears aloud. "But where can she be if she's not on the boat, or somewhere in Balestrand?"

281

"According to the night desk clerk, no one left the hotel until the two of you went out this morning, and she swears she wasn't away from her post, not even for a minute. They're quite strict about it here. And we had a man stationed by the door. The clerk says he fell asleep, which he admits, but between the two of them, I'd say it was impossible for your daughter to have left by that door, and the other exits were alarmed."

"Then you think she still may be in the hotel?" Ursula had had high hopes of the boat, imagining Pix, perhaps tied up, but safe and sound in the closet.

Marit gasped. "The sauna! Remember she'd gotten locked in the sauna the other night."

Ursula was halfway to the door. They were in the same large meeting room Pix had been in, only this time there wasn't any coffee or cookies.

"Mrs. Rowe, the sauna was one of the first places we checked. It was empty." Ursula walked back to the chair she'd been sitting in. If she felt like slumping, she didn't. She'd left her cane in her room, too.

"I know how hard this is—for you both." Marcussen looked at the two elderly women in front of him, each missing a loved one. Marit Hansen reminded him of many Norwegian women he knew. The set of her mouth, the way she walked. This was a stubborn woman, a strong woman. He was interested in her American friend. Both Americans had come across the ocean at a moment's notice to do what they believed the police had not been able to do—find Kari Hansen. They all had no doubt they would be successful at unraveling the mystery. Now Mrs. Miller was missing and he could see the doubt in both her mother's and Fru Hansen's eyes. They had failed—and thus far, so had he.

He infused his voice with a confidence he was far from feeling. "Let's start again. Tell me the whole story from the beginning—from Kari's call at the station in Oslo...."

Officer Jansen came in with a tray. "*Kaffe?*"

Pix was aware of movement and a shape moving toward her.

She infused her voice with as much bravery as she could muster, "I'm an American tourist and my name is—"

"Pix!" the voice shrieked. Arms were flung about her and she was enveloped in a warm, if slightly uncomfortable, embrace. "What are you doing here!"

It was Kari. At last.

"I have the same question for you," Pix said, joy washing over her—and relief. She could just make out the girl's features in the dark. Kari's face looked thinner, and older, but it had been some years since Pix had seen her.

"Wait—let me get my blanket. You feel cold." Kari bustled away, obviously much more familiar with the layout of the place. She wrapped the blanket around Pix and the two huddled close together.

"I heard them bring you in. They left food if you are hungry. But I didn't know who you were and I was afraid to find out. It could have been a trick, or someone who didn't know I was here and might not be happy to find out. It seemed smart to wait, but I got too curious."

"You don't have a gun." Pix was not in the slightest bit hopeful.

"No," Kari said sadly. "Otherwise, I would have been out long ago."

"Where are we?" Pix asked. First things first.

"I was drugged when they brought me here, but from the size and construction, it could be one of the old huts where the farmhands stayed when they brought the goats to the summer pastures, or it could be a hiker's hut on the *vidda*. Whatever it is, it must be very remote, because it has no furniture and hasn't been fixed up at all. Now people are using these as *hytter,* you know, and I would expect a table, chairs, and some bunk beds. A fireplace. There is nothing here. Because it's so cold, I think it must be the *vidda,* but if we are high up in the mountains, that would be cold, too."

"And there's no way out."

"The shutters must be barred shut from the outside and the door is locked. I tried to dig with my hands and the clip from my hair, but it was no use. And no loose stones. Believe me, I've pulled at every one of them."

Pix felt herself start to panic, but it dissipated at once. She'd come to Norway to find Kari and here she was, alive and well. Mission accomplished. Getting them out of a locked cabin God knows where would surely prove less difficult. And now there were two of them. Her headache was better and she was beginning to feel her energy returning.

"You must tell me everything. Have you seen my grandmother? Do you know about Erik?" Kari's voice ended with a sob.

"Your grandmother is fine—worried, of course, but convinced you are alive. She's with my mother at Kvikne's Hotel. And yes, I'm so sorry—I do know about Erik." Pix put her arm around Kari.

"I've cried so much, I didn't know I had any tears left, but I suppose I always will."

"Do you want to talk about what happened?" While Pix did not want to dredge up the tragic memory, she was eager to have the mystery solved. "Why don't you tell me the whole thing, starting from your call to your grandmother from the station. Erik was still alive then, right?"

"Yes." Kari took a tissue from her pocket and blew her nose. Pix resolved to find out what else the young woman had in her pockets, yet for the moment, all she wanted was to discover the events of a week ago that had led to a death and abduction.

"You must have found out about Carl; otherwise, you wouldn't be here," Kari said matter-of-factly. Pix nodded in the dark, before realizing subtle gestures were out.

"Yes. He had me—us—completely fooled."

"Me, too. Erik knew Carl from last summer. They were on the same boat then, also. You know, Erik is like me, an only child, and he never had a big brother to do things with. Suddenly, everything was Carl this and Carl that. I must admit I was a bit jealous. They were going fishing. They were going out on the town in Bergen between tours. But then I met Carl, or Charles—he uses both names. His father is English."

"I knew that, but not about the names."

"Oh yes, he loves English people—more than Norwegians. But I didn't find that out until this summer. That's what started the whole thing. He has two passports. It's completely legal. He was born in Britain. But I'm getting ahead of myself. Anyway, last winter the three of us—and sometimes he'd bring a girl along—did lots of things together. He had plenty of money. I assumed his family was rich, and it was fun to be taken to restaurants like Theatercafeen and not think about a bill. He always insisted on paying. He knew so many things, especially about art and antiques. After a few days, he'd disappear on one of the winter tours and then come back to sweep us off our feet again. I was so stupid!"

Kari started to cry again. "If I had had more sense, Erik would be alive today!"

And Erik had been lacking in judgment, too, thought Pix, but she kept her mouth shut. She could picture Carl's seduction of these two— a handsome, witty, charming older brother with deep pockets. What young person could resist someone like that? Where was the harm? How can one bite of an apple hurt me?

"This part is hard to admit. I had a kind of

286

crush on Carl, too. Erik is the only man I ever loved or ever will love, but Carl was very flattering—not in a crude way, but he made me feel special. Now I know it was all an act."

"Why was he courting you? I know he was illegally taking antiques out of the country, but I wouldn't have thought he'd want to divide his profits with anyone other than the farmer."

As she spoke, Pix thought, The farmer! Sven! Was Kari aware of this?

Quickly, she added, "The farm on the fjord that the tour visits. The man and his wife are in on this with Carl. They collect the things for him."

"I know," said Kari sadly. "I know it all. And yes, Erik was helping them, too."

Pix didn't know what to say and the two sat in silence for a moment.

"It's a very hard thing to find out someone you love, someone you planned to spend your life with, is a weaker person than you thought. Not a bad person, just a weak person. I didn't find out what was going on until this tour. I was putting my knapsack in the closet on the boat in the staff room, when it slipped from my hands and fell against the back wall. The wall fell forward and I found all these suitcases filled with antiques. I put everything back and told Erik. He told me not to say a word, that he would think what to do. I assumed it was the captain. I was always a little afraid of him, that bushy black beard, and he never said much.

"I was after Erik to tell the police and let them figure it out, but he wouldn't hear of it. He said it would be bad for the company. Finally, I decided to call my friend Annelise, who is working at the museum in Bergen, and see if she knew of any recent robberies from a museum or someone's private collection. That's why I called my grandmother."

"But you never called Annelise."

"No, when I was on the phone, Carl came to get me, and he must have overheard me ask for Annelise's number. He knows her, too, from last winter, when she was living in Oslo. He told me to hurry onto the train; then he talked to Erik and told him he had to keep me quiet. For insurance, he called Sven, who got on the train at Myrdal."

The train. The stage was set. All the characters were on board.

"Carl told us to sit in the other car. He said that there wasn't room in the tour's, but there was. Erik tried again to convince me that we shouldn't get involved, that it was none of our business. He didn't say it was Carl who was doing this. Then finally, he told me everything and we had a big fight. I lost my temper and said things I would give the world to take back. I never thought they would be some of the last words I would say to my Erik."

"What did he tell you?" Kari was going to need a great deal of time to heal. She'd had a week alone in this dark cell to obsess about it. Now Pix wanted to get the facts, then get them out.

"Toward the end of last summer, Carl asked Erik to put some things in his knapsack and give them back to him when they got to Bergen, where Carl was taking the ferry to Newcastle. You know, there is very little security on it and Carl—now Charles, with his British passport—was well known to the British customs people. They always waved him through with whatever he had. I don't know why he involved Erik. He's an evil man and I think he wanted to control Erik, have something on him, corrupt a good person. He paid him well and Erik did it again. I asked him why he didn't come to me if he needed money, not that I have much, but he could have had it all. He said I didn't understand. I said it was dishonest and that he had to stop. I told him that I was going to tell the police unless Carl gave everything back. Erik said that would be stupid—people had already spent the money Carl had paid for the things and they didn't want them anyway. What was the harm? he kept saying. I couldn't believe it. It seemed like we were talking for hours. One of the women on the tour came into our car—a nice person, Mrs. Feld—and I was embarrassed that she might have seen us quarreling. When she left, I started to cry. I couldn't make Erik understand. Finally, he said he did and he'd go along with whatever I said, but not until after the trip was over. He didn't want to upset the tour. I had to be content with that, and it might have ended there, but Carl was nervous. Sven came along and began talking alone to Erik. I had met him on the first trip when we went to his farm and I was surprised to see him on the train, but I assumed he was just coming from Oslo like everyone else."

"Then what happened?"

"Erik came back to the seat looking very pale and very scared. Sven had threatened him. Erik begged me to promise I wouldn't say anything about what Carl was doing and he, Erik, would stop immediately. He was so agitated, I got scared, too. 'What is it?' I kept asking. Then he blurted out that Sven was working with Carl and was picking up some Viking silver from someone the last day of the tour. He said if anything messed that up, he'd kill us."

"Viking silver! What would that be worth?" For Carl, it would mean a hasty retirement as tour guide and a life of ease on some nice square in London. Of that much, Pix was certain.

"It would depend on what there was, but at least a million dollars."

No wonder Sven's threat had been so severe. From his sixties mode of dress and simple life on the farm, it had appeared that he was not caught up in material possessions in the nineties, but care he did—and the fancy boat had been a dead giveaway, Pix reminded herself. He and his lovely young wife would never have to make *gjetost* again—or eat it. Where would they go? The Caribbean? So good for the children.

"But what farmer would have anything to sell from the Viking times? Wasn't it all buried in graves?" Pix was thinking of the three large ship burials on the east coast, particularly the Oseberg find, a Viking woman's tomb, perhaps Queen Åsa of Vestfold's, with its rich treasures. A find even half the size of this would have made international headlines and been impossible to keep secret.

"The Vikings did put their goods—things that would be needed in the afterlife—in the ship burials. But they didn't put in many silver ornaments or coins. These were considered part of the family's wealth, like the land. After all, what use would someone have for these things in Valhall? Or maybe that's just what they told themselves." Kari gave a slight laugh.

Practical people, like their descendants, Pix reflected—why waste a perfectly good amulet, especially when silver was a scarce commodity.

"So what did they do with it?"

"They did bury the silver, but in hoards—secret hiding places. Every once in a while, someone comes across one of these. It can be in coins, ingots, jewelry."

"And instead of turning it over to the proper authorities, this person is passing it along to Sven and Carl. No wonder they wanted to keep you quiet until the end of the tour." And that's why Kari and she had been locked up. When Carl heard Kari ask for Annelise's phone number, he'd suspected Kari was onto him, and he had taken drastic, immediate steps.

"Exactly. They will all be wealthy men. But Erik, to his credit, didn't want any part of it after Sven told him—and he told Sven this. 'Viking things are different,' Erik said. I don't think he realized that the other antiques they were taking out of the country were as important to our history as the Viking find. He thought of them as common objects that everybody had around. He really didn't know very much about it. But he thought the Viking silver should stay in Norway. Now it was a crime. Before it was just getting around a stupid law, like... well, brewing your own beer.

"When we were getting close to Kjosfossen, he had decided to slip off the train in Voss and tell the police, even though it meant he would have to confess what he had done. I was very proud of him."

Pix was glad that Kari had this last memory. Erik had been weak and foolish, yet he had resolved to do the right thing. She could always remember that.

Now they were coming close to the moment of his death. Pix wanted to find out—and didn't. She took Kari's hand. It was a lot warmer than her own.

"The train stopped so people could take pictures and we got out to answer any questions or provide help. It was also our job to be sure no one was left behind. We were always the last by the waterfall. Carl and Sven came close behind us. I was very scared, but Erik wasn't. I think it was because there were so many people and he thought, What can they do to us? He knew he was going to the police, but they didn't, and of course he wasn't going to say anything. Then it got horrible. Carl was totally crazy. I had never seen him this way. By that time, we were the only ones left. Carl began to scream at Erik for betraying him, for telling me. He said he thought of Erik as a brother, but that he was not to speak to him again, except when he had to. Then he began on me, said that I was a whore and no man would ever have me for a wife. Erik told him to stop, but he kept going. Sven just stood to the side, saying nothing."

Pix could imagine the scene very well. She remembered Carl's transformation, the sudden flare of temper at the Glacier Museum as he berated the other guide. Mother had said he was a passionate person. She had been right.

"Carl began to laugh. 'The joke is on you, Erik.'" Kari lowered her voice. "He said, 'I know for sure what she's like, because I slept with her!' Of course it was a lie, and I yelled this to Erik, only he pushed me aside and went for Carl. Sven tried to break it up, but he tripped and fell. Carl pushed Erik away. The train was starting to move. And Erik fell into Kjosfossen."

Her voice was flat and after the last words, it was hard to know what to say. As Pix squeezed the girl's hand hard, Kari began again.

"We all stood absolutely still. Then Carl said, 'Oh shit! Look what you did! to me and he ran toward the train. I started to follow, but Sven grabbed me. The next thing I knew, I was on the farm. I don't know how he got me from the train tracks there, but Carl must have called Sven's wife from Flåm. My head had a lump, so I know he hit me."

"Carl made another call, too." Pix told her about the message the stationmaster at Voss had received that they were eloping and Carl's telephone conversation with her grandmother later that night at the hotel in Bergen.

Kari stood up and paced rapidly up and down. She was incensed.

"How could anyone have believed that! The whole time I've been wondering how Carl could have covered up our disappearance, but this idea never occurred to me."

"Because, my dear, you don't have a criminal mind." Pix was angry, too. The man was a monster. "But," she reminded Kari, "your grandmother didn't believe it. She knows you."

"The police must have, then. What has been going on?"

Pix told her as delicately as possible the theories in various papers, reassuring her that it was already old news. Kari paced even more furiously.

"They think I killed Erik! And ran off someplace! How could I? My knapsack with all my money was on the train still, under my seat."

Pix told her the bad news. "I'm afraid Carl and Sven thought of that. The knapsacks were left where they were and ended up in the lost luggage back in Oslo, but yours was missing your wallet and passport."

"So, I'm guilty." Kari sat down, then jumped up again. "If I ever see Carl again, I will kill him!"

Pix needed to get something cleared up. "Why did you and Erik have your passports?"

"Erik told me to bring mine, that you never knew when you might need it."

Shades of Faith Fairchild, Pix thought. Oh Faith, where are you when I need you now!

"I think he may have been planning to surprise me with a trip at the end of the summer, after our jobs ended. Maybe to Greece or someplace like that."

Greece. Sunny places. Olive groves. Pix thought of the picture of Kari's parents. She hadn't told Kari about the newspapers dredging up the circumstances of her mother's death. She also didn't think it was the time and place to talk about Hanna's origins. She did want to know about Sven, though.

"Kari, did Sven look familiar to you? Is it possible that you knew him before? He threatened you, but he brought you here, and you mentioned they were giving you food. He hasn't harmed you. Maybe because he knew you?"

"Why do you ask? It's true he said he would kill us, but that is very different from doing it. I saw his face when Erik went into the water, and he was horrified. Why kill me? Murder is very serious, very different from what he's doing with Carl. Just before they pick up the Viking silver, they will probably bring food and water here. Enough until some hikers find us. Or maybe they'll drug us again and leave the door unlocked. I've thought about it a lot. There's not much else to do here."

Pix decided to leave the matter at that for

now. Yet Kari was being rather naïve. With that much money at stake, Pix was sure the leap from one crime to another would not be a big one.

"I don't think we can depend on their good natures. At the least, it would be just as easy to leave us here. I hope you're right and they will come one more time to appease their consciences, if they have any. Then we can be ready for them. And now we have to think of a plan."

Pix always felt better when she thought she knew what she was doing.

The day had gone by very slowly, despite the tour of Balestrand and other diversions offered by the hotel and Scandie Sights. By dinner, tempers were short and the various tour members were either sitting by themselves or in small isolated family groups. Inspector Marcussen looked at the tables as he filled his plate with *medisterkaker* from the array of hot dishes at the hotel's *smörgåsbord*. The fragrant meat cakes were accompanied by sauerkraut flavored with caraway seeds. Having already finished several helpings of herring and other fish, he couldn't think of a better Sunday-night supper. The Scandie Sights tour members, however, with the exception of the younger Petersons, seemed to have lost their appetites.

After dinner, he would tell them they were free to go in the morning. He couldn't legitimately keep them here any longer, although he was sure that both the answer to Oscar Melling's death and Mrs. Miller's disappearance was known to someone in this room. If he could, he'd keep them in this pleasant jail until that person broke and confessed. But it was impossible. Sidney Harding had besieged his embassy with calls and several other tour members had made a single protest. Marcussen was officially ordered to let them go. Also, the hotel needed the rooms. It had been a minor miracle that they had all been able to stay put for even this long. He sighed. Could he be wrong? Jansen was convinced that Oscar Melling's death had been an accident and the injury to his back somehow obtained in the fall. And Mrs. Miller? Had she given in to a sudden impulse and wandered off? His wife had once described a sensation she got at times, that she could just keep driving and not return—cross the border and eventually be in Venice. He had been shocked, then amused. Now that the children were grown and out of the house, he hadn't heard any more about it and they had gone to Venice together last fall. He tried to remember how old Mrs. Miller's children were. Some still home, but no one at that demanding toddler stage. Carl Bjørnson, one of the guides, had privately confided that he and the other guide had thought Mrs. Miller troubled since her arrival—often agitated and given to long, lonely walks at odd hours. Carl was sure she would turn up, an amnesia victim or some other such thing.

But her mother and Fru Hansen were convinced that someone had done something to her. They were seated at a table, their food in front of them, but eating nothing, deep in conversation. He knew they believed that Kari Hansen's and Pix Miller's disappearances were connected—Oscar Melling's death, too. He considered his food. The meatballs were so good, he thought he might be able to eat some more. The mother's theory was all very far-fetched. After a meal like this, he was inclined to agree with Jansen that the women had been watching too much American television. Marcussen was opposed to television and worried that his future grandchildren wouldn't be counted in Norway's 100 percent literacy rate if things continued the way they were going with all these new channels. Mrs. Rowe and Fru Hansen were leaving the dining room and stopped to speak with him.

"I hope you are enjoying your meal, *Inspektør*," Fru Hansen said, eyeing his plate. He suddenly felt a bit overindulgent.

"Everyone will be free to leave the hotel in the morning. I intend to announce it after dinner," he told them abruptly. "I'm sorry," he added, and put his fork down, leaving the rest of his helping untouched.

"We imagined that you couldn't detain people for too much longer," Ursula said sympathetically. "Of course, Fru Hansen and I intend to remain until my daughter is found."

They said good night and left the room. Another group was coming in. Marcussen looked after the two women, handbags on arms, straight spines, no ladders in their hose.

They could be here for a long time, he thought dismally, and decided to forgo dessert.

Myrtle "Pix" Miller had never been more awake and alert in her life. She could hear Kari's regular breathing from across the room. They were taking the watch in turn. Kari had shown Pix the small chink she had found between the boulders, which had been wedged tightly together during the original construction and made more impenetrable, settling into the ground over the years. They had not taken her watch, so looking at a tiny patch of sky, she'd charted the passage of time, painfully aware of how slowly it was moving.

"After Midsummer Eve, after the children are out of school, I'm sure there will be people on walking trips, but now even if we could make enough noise to be heard through these walls, there's a very slim chance that anyone would be near enough to hear us," she'd told Pix. Midsummer Eve, Pix thought dismally, was still a week away. She willed the door to open, willed them to make one last food drop, avoiding the possibility of more blood on their hands. Blood—it made her think of the swastika at Stalheim. Carl had seemed genuinely surprised at her assumption that he had killed Oscar. If Oscar had figured out what Carl was up to, he would have been more likely to offer him a North American outlet than blackmail him, Pix now thought. Yet if not Carl, then who killed the old man—and who was the graffiti artist?

Kari had explained to Pix that it was always either Sven or his wife who came to leave some food and a thermos of coffee. The door was quickly opened, a sack dropped in, and he or she was off again. It all took only a few seconds. When Pix had been brought in, Sven had his gun out, telling Kari to get in the far corner of the hut. Once more, his exit was swift. There had been no possibility of rushing out the door or overpowering either person at any time.

"Pix," whispered Kari. "Someone's coming. Get ready."

Yes, there was the sound of a car. The engine stopped. A door slammed—one door.

Someone was fumbling with the lock and then light streamed in. Pix was momentarily blinded.

It was Sven, who was carrying a plastic bag, which he hastily set down inside the door. As he turned to leave, Kari called in a feeble voice.

"The woman. The woman you brought here is dead."

"What!" cried Sven, rushing to where Pix lay. "This can't be...."

As he leaned over to check, Pix let him have it full force with Faith's superhold hair spray. He screamed and fell back. Kari was waiting with the Thermos and brought it down on his head hard, twice. The man fell to the ground. Quickly, they searched his pockets, taking his wallet, keys, matches, some coins, and a knife. There was nothing else.

They left the food. With luck, he'd be there long enough to get very hungry.

Outside, after locking the door, they fell into each other's arms, laughing deliriously. The low stone hut had a sod roof. It looked so innocuous—a flower or two sprouting amid the grass, and a well-worn wooden door.

"We did it! It was so easy! You're a genius, Pix!" Kari hugged her again.

Modestly, Pix said, "You were pretty handy with that thermos." She made a mental note to write to the company, thanking them for the versatility of their product. She had almost gotten away by throwing hot coffee at Carl, and now they had gained their freedom using the handy vacuum bottle again.

"Now," she continued, "let's see if we can retrace his route and find the nearest police station or phone."

"Police!" Kari's expression changed. "No way! They'll never believe me. We have to see this through to the end. I need to clear my name."

"But we have Sven and they'll arrest Carl. Inspector Marcussen will believe us."

"The things that were in the closet are at the bottom of the fjord or hidden in some other place. Sven's wife will miss him soon and come to investigate. They'll deny we were ever here. Say that we're crazy. It will be my word against Carl's and Sven's. They'll probably accuse Erik, if anything. Remember, the police already think I may have killed him. And there will always be a cloud hanging over me and my grandmother. Suspicion is a terrible thing."

It was late in the evening, Sunday evening, and the sun still felt warm. They were alive and free, but Pix was forced to agree with Kari. It wasn't over.

10

Kari drove like a woman possessed. Pix wondered whether this was her normal style or an aberration produced by the present situation. Whatever it was, she was going to have to tell the girl to slow down or neither would have a tale to tell to any grandchildren.

The first part of the trip had been less dramatic. They'd had to drive carefully to follow the marks made by Sven's drive across the flat expanse that lay before them when they'd emerged from the hut. The hut was the only sign of civilization as far as the eye could see. Behind them, a wall of rock stretched across the horizon; its dramatic cliffs looked seamless.

"It's Hallingskarvet," Kari had said. "The railway lies to the south of it, across the *vidda*. You came that way in the train."

"And what is that?" Pix had asked, pointing straight ahead to one of the largest snow-capped mountain ranges she'd ever seen.

"Oh, that—that's Jotunheimen, the home of the trolls and giants, but I don't think they'll bother us," she added mischievously. "It's quite far away. I'm assuming road number fifty is in that direction. If I've guessed wrong, we'll know fairly soon, because there aren't any other roads for quite a distance. But Sven had to get here easily, and he left a good track to whatever road he did take. The ground is soft now from the snow melting in the mountains."

After several trips, the car had indeed left a distinct path, one that traced an old route across the countryside. The grass was green, but the only wildflowers Pix saw were arctic varieties. In places, the ground was completely covered in heather, its pale lavenders and pinks adding color to the gray fields strewn with boulders.

"When we get to the main road, all we have to do is guess the right way to turn. It shouldn't be hard. We just head west."

"How far do you think we are from Balestrand?" Pix asked, giving herself up to the navigator.

"It's hard to say. But we will definitely be there before morning." They had driven on for a bit; then Kari complained: "What's bumping against the back of my seat? Can you move it?"

Pix twisted around to look.

"It's a suitcase. He must have planned to drop the food off and then meet Carl someplace. Damn, we didn't think of that. They were going to pick up the Viking stuff on the last day of the tour, which is today. It would be too much to hope that Carl would have stayed on in Balestrand. I would have thought they'd meet at the farm, except Sven wouldn't have his suitcase with him if that was the plan. I don't think they trust each other enough to let one person go off with the silver. They'd stay together until they got their money."

"And even without the added liability of having kept us prisoners, Carl, Sven, and his wife will have to get out of the country with the Viking silver right away. It will be too risky to stay."

Pix agreed. "Yes, so that suggests Sven was on his way to Bergen and the ferry across the North Sea to Newcastle. Do you have any idea where they'd meet in Bergen?"

"No, but we can head straight for the ferry. Unless we can come up with a better plan."

"Whatever we decide, there's something we need to do as soon as possible. It's time to call Mother."

Kari grinned. "And *Bestemor.* Now, what's in his suitcase?"

It was at this point that she saw the paved road ahead, let out a whoop, and hit the accelerator. Sven had treated himself to a brand-new BMW and it responded immediately. Pix did, too.

"Pull over and I'll get the case. I don't want to take my seat belt off." She was feeling extremely middle-aged. She used to drive pretty fast herself when she was younger. Now thoughts of mortality—and wanting to know the ends of a great many stories—slowed her down.

The suitcase yielded little except for the

knowledge that Sven favored boxers and was carrying his passport. He also had a framed photo of his wife and children.

"The rat!" Kari exclaimed, the needle of the speedometer quivering forward. "I bet he's leaving them!"

"Pond scum—or fjord scum," Pix added. Her children, she thought with a pang, would appreciate the nicety of her distinction. The suitcase, down to the box of condoms, tucked in with a flask of brandy, had all the earmarks of a future bachelor's, including the picture of former loved ones as a sweet memory. Would he have said he was a widower or what?

"I think the future Sven had planned for himself didn't include a wife and children, especially not the children." She wasn't sorry for his wife. Since Pix had arrived on the tour, so many people had been wearing so many masks, and the disguise of the happy farmer's wife, living off the land for generations, seemed particularly repellent. She wondered if any of it was true.

"Do you think Mrs. Sven really did grow up on the farm? Was it a lie, or were her parents and grandparents at their *hytte?*"

Kari flew around a curve in the road, disturbing some birds, which were searching for food along the side. They scattered into the air with much screeching and flapping of wings.

"I never saw anybody else, but I wouldn't think she'd lie that way. It would be bound to get back to somebody in Vik or one of the villages nearby. She probably did grow up there and probably hated it."

Pix thought of Sonja. She'd grown up in a tiny village, Undredal, and was definitely not going back.

"And was it just Carl from Scandie Sights, or Jan, too? Maybe the other stewards? He could have gotten to them, the way he had with Erik."

"I would be surprised. Jan will go into his family business, the oil business. Carl used to make fun of him, but I think he was jealous of his position. I know everyone thinks we are all the same in Norway, but there are some families that are maybe a little above the rest of us—a little older, and a lot more money. Jan's is like that. He does the tours because he enjoys them and his father thinks he should do something to practice his English. As for the stewards—Anders, I would doubt, and Sonja is too stupid to keep her mouth shut. Carl would never involve her."

So, there was no love lost here, as well, Pix thought.

"She doesn't seem particularly fond of you, either."

Kari tossed her head. The car swerved.

"She was after Erik all last summer. She made a total fool of herself, and poor Erik was very embarrassed. I had to go to Bergen and put a stop to it. She has Anders now. He might be nice, but nothing like Erik. Oh Pix, I can't believe I'll never see him again! And what will I tell his parents? The truth might kill them, too."

It was hard. Pix was tempted to advise a severely edited version, with the cooperation of the police, but there were too many secrets, too many lies in life—especially family life.

"You tell them what you told me. They will know that at the end Erik was doing as he had been taught, and that will be a comfort to them."

They drove in silence for a while. It was past midnight. Pix was dying of thirst and hunger. She had taken the sandwiches the farmer's wife made—what was her name anyway?—from her pocket and left them at the hut. The sandwiches she had pressed on Pix along with the coffee as she rushed Pix to the fjord taxi. They couldn't take the chance that Mrs. Sven might have added knockout drops to the *smør*.

The Côte d'Or chocolate bar! She dug it out, unwrapped it, and handed half to Kari.

"I've never tasted anything so good in my life," the girl said.

"I'll tell Faith," answered Pix, savoring each mouthful.

They finally came to a phone—and a Coke machine—outside a small gas station. Pix was charmed to note it had a sod roof. Her family, those increasingly mythical creatures, would enjoy this country. Jan had patiently explained about sod roofs the day they were on his bus. The roof framing was covered with layers of birch bark, then sod in the old days. Now people used heavy plastic sheeting under the sod and trimmed the edges with the birch to suggest authenticity. "And we don't bring our lawn mowers up," he'd joked. She hoped he was what she and Ursula had thought. Okay, his family was in the oil business, but that didn't mean he was passing industrial secrets to a tour member or anybody else. Carl had always seemed a little too perfect, too polished. Jan, she reminded herself, had on unmatched socks the first day. Kari hit the brakes and they jerked to a halt outside the station. There were no signs of life, but Sven had thoughtfully left a full tank of gas and they didn't need to fill up.

"This is a very popular place in the winter for cross-country skiing, and hiking soon of course. In between..." Kari shrugged and pointed to the dark station.

Having felt justified in taking a loan from Sven's coins as well as using his car, they headed for the phone and machine. Kari thought it best that she be the one to call Ursula—speaking to the desk clerk in Norwegian, simply asking for "Fru Rowe."

The clerk answered and put the call through to the room. She had been instructed to let the *inspektør* know if either Fru Hansen or Fru Rowe received any calls, but she didn't think he meant her to disturb him so late at night. She conscientiously noted the time and put the message in an envelope with his name on it for the morning.

Ursula picked up the phone on the first ring.

"It's me." Kari was careful not to identify

herself, and the gasp from Ursula told her she didn't need to. The clerk could still be listening in, although Kari doubted it. It would have been very rude. "I'm fine. So is the other lady, who is with me. And we'll see you soon. I don't want to take much time, so here's what we want to know—and maybe there's a little something we hope you two can do."

They couldn't drive any longer. It wasn't fatigue, hunger—or thirst. The Coke machine had taken care of that. It was the fjord—glistening, dead calm, straight in front of them—the end of the journey, or part of the journey.

"Now what?" Pix said, stepping out of the car. She had taken over the driving so Kari could rest.

"We find a boat."

Of course. Pix added piracy to the growing list of crimes—breaking and entering, larceny—she found herself perpetrating in this law-abiding nation.

No one had conveniently left their keys on board any of the craft moored at the dock, so it appeared they would have to row to Balestrand. Pix spent her Maine summers either on the water or in it, so she was a strong oarswoman. Kari, too, had learned the art on the fjords of the east coast around Tønsberg, rowing to the nearby islands.

On the way, they had driven through Stalheim, and Pix shivered when she saw the hotel perched high above the valley. From Stalheim, they had followed the twisting road down to Vangnes, on the shores of the Sogne-fjord, coming to a stop at this deserted pier. Balestrand lay directly across the water.

For Balestrand—and Kvikne's Hotel—was their final destination, after all. Odin and the others in the Norsk pantheon had smiled on them. Carl Bjørnson was still there. Everyone was still there, detained for their "safety" by the good *inspektør*. Detained so he could try to find out what was going on was more like it, Pix thought. But for whatever reason, Carl and the Viking silver were still safe in Norway, although Carl would not be safe for long if all went well. Pix had taken the phone and told Ursula what to do, carefully speaking in such a way that anyone listening would hear only a superficial conversation about getting together. Again, she had had a plan. "It's all these town meetings, having to think of ways to raise money for things, like the library and the schools. I tend to think in index cards," she'd explained to Kari, who continued to be impressed by her friend's ingenuity. And it's living with Faith, Pix added to herself, Faith the person. She was beginning to feel a little like Kari's Faith the person—and it didn't feel bad.

They had untied a lapstrake wooden row-boat, double-ended, with the long oars favored by Norwegian mariners. It was a beautiful boat, well maintained, and Pix made a mental apology to its owner, promising to have it back as soon as possible.

Pix had always found car travel conducive to serious conversation, intimate conversation.

Something about the enforced closeness, the inability to leave. Something about talking or listening to someone with his or her eyes presumably on the road. Nothing face-to-face. This had been when her father had told her things about his childhood she'd never known, sad things. It was when Sam had proposed and they'd pulled over—to be face-to-face. She had thought this car trip would be the time when she could talk to Kari about Hanna and what Marit had revealed about Stalheim, but Kari had been asleep when they passed by. Now in the boat, in the soft darkness, Pix wanted Kari to know what Marit had told them.

"You were sleeping when we went through Stalheim. It's such a beautiful place, such a wonderful hotel. It's hard to think of it in any other way, hard to imagine what it was like during the war."

"Marit told you?" Kari was rowing and she lifted the oars out of the water.

"Yes. My mother was terribly sorry that your grandparents hadn't shared this with her years ago. She wouldn't have thought anything other than how lucky Hans and Marit had been to find a baby to adopt."

"I was very angry when she told me, but I didn't let her know. Did she tell you my mother was a teenager when she found out?"

"Yes."

"If they had spoken to her sooner, she might still be alive! Remember I said unless I cleared this up, we'd always be living with people's suspicions? That was how Hanna must have felt. That to be a *Lebensborn* child was something to hide from the neighbors and family, so nobody would be raising a finger, '*tsk, tsk, tsk*—bad blood.' " Kari sounded incredibly bitter. She had said "Hanna," not "Mor"—a distant figure.

Pix took a deep breath. The girl had started rowing again, hard. The water dripped in flashing strings of beads from each oar. A single bird flew high overhead. Of course, if Hanna had known sooner, she might not have rebelled so dramatically—and there wouldn't be a Kari—but that wasn't the point.

"People make mistakes. Lord knows, I've made plenty, *especially* in child rearing." Pix and Sam had thought they'd gain expertise with each new addition, but instead, they discovered whole new quandaries. "Hans and Marit thought they were protecting your mother. It was a hard call and we weren't there. We don't know what it was like in Norway then. They did what they did out of love."

"That's no excuse," Kari shot back.

"Oh yes, it is. It's a great excuse, the best. It may not always turn out right, but it's a damned good excuse." Pix paused. "I knew your mother, remember. Adored her. She could do anything—run faster, sing better, swim, cook, write funny poems—and she was so beautiful. But, although finding out her origins must have been a shock, I think she was a victim of her own intense personality colliding with a very mixed-up time in both our societies. So many contradictory messages. And she got confused."

312

"Still…" Kari sounded less vehement, or maybe talking and rowing at the same time was wearing her out. "I am going to try to find out who her mother was. They've opened the records. I don't care so much about discovering who my Nazi grandfather might be, but my grandmother could still be alive and might tell me something about the family."

Nazi! That reminded Pix of Oscar Melling. She'd told Kari about finding his body and who he was, but she hadn't asked about the Stalheim connection.

"Do you think Oscar Melling—I can't get used to calling him Eriksen—had anything to do with the *Lebensborn* home at Stalheim? He was from the area."

"Oh Lord, you don't think he was my grandfather, that obnoxious old lech. He made things very difficult on the tour. I was sorry for nice people like the Felds and the Bradys. He always seemed to want to pick a fight with them in particular."

Pix couldn't think of anything to say to reassure her. She'd cast Oscar in the role herself, and she couldn't say they bore no resemblance to one another, what with such a common genetic background, although she'd have to see a picture of a much younger and less dissipated Oscar to find one.

"I'm sure the odds are quite slim. Why don't I row for a while." They changed places and soon Pix was enjoying the exercise, the steady in-out rhythm of the oars.

She thought of another role she'd cast: Sven. Kari hadn't seemed to know what Pix was talking about earlier when she'd asked if Sven seemed familiar to the girl.

"Do you think this Sven might be your father?" It was out.

"Oh, is that what you were getting at before!" Kari started to laugh. "My poor father is in a home for alcoholics. He came back to Norway when he was almost fifty and had run out of money and women who would take him in, I suppose. I don't have much feeling about him, except, of course, I wouldn't be here otherwise. He got in touch with my grandmother and we went to see him. He cried and said I looked like my mother. I didn't want to go back. Marit visits him. She's a much better person than I am. He doesn't have anybody else, she says, but I think she wants to hear about Hanna."

There went that theory, Pix said to herself. Maybe a couple of theories. Certainly Kari had not run off in search of her identity. She seemed quite in control of who she was. It had been a kidnapping and one kidnapper was in for a big surprise.

Pix brought the boat silently along the dock at Balestrand, relieved to see the Viking fjord cruiser dwarfing the other pleasure boats. Farther back on shore, the hotel was illuminated by several outside lights and a few shone from windows scattered across the grand old lady's facade.

They tied up and slipped aboard the bigger boat. Without skeleton keys, they had to resort to Sven's knife, which Pix adeptly used to pop the lock and enter the main cabin. As they had assumed, Carl had cleaned out the hidden storage space in the closet in the staff room. He'd been clever enough not to sweep, leaving and, Pix was sure, adding dust and dirt particles.

Kari went to the refrigerator in the galley and took two bottles of Solo, the sweet orange soda, a national addiction—Solo and *pølser,* hot dogs, every child's idea of a perfect meal: "But there's fruit in Solo, Mom!" She handed one to Pix. "Put some of Sven's money in the jar over there. I don't feel right just taking it, but I'm still so thirsty."

They sat down at one of the tables. Carl had straightened the chairs after her attempted flight the other night. Pix took a swig of her soda. "Soo Loo"—it was fun to say.

"We have to try to think like Carl. Walk in his shoes."

"English. Custom-made," Kari said.

"But of course. Now if he wanted to hide something, where..."

Several hours later, Pix rolled off the bunk she'd fallen asleep on and went to rouse Kari, who was sleeping above. They had not thought it wise to sleep on board the Scandie Sights boat, and although the boat with the tarp was still docked, Pix could not recommend its accommodations. They'd slipped into a large sailboat, assuming the owners were at Kvikne's or elsewhere in the district.

"Kari, wake up. It's time!"

The girl swung her long legs over the side and jumped down. Then they straightened their berths and went above.

Outside, it was what Pix would have called a perfect Maine day. The sun was shining. The sky was blue, with large puffy white clouds. A slight warm breeze fanned across the water and the air was clear. A perfect Maine day, except she was in Norway.

They strolled over to the front of the dock, sat cross-legged facing the hotel, the Scandie Sights boat behind them. The Midsummer bonfire pile had grown considerably in her absence, Pix noted. There was a whole new layer of vegetable crates.

Kari leaned back on her arms and stretched her face toward the sun.

"Now we wait."

The Scandie Sights tour was the first down to breakfast, hitting the immense bowls of muesli, chafing dishes of fish cakes, and mounds of fresh strawberries as soon as the doors opened. There was a manic feeling in the air. Cheeks were flushed, voices raised in false heartiness. Equally false promises to write and stay in touch were made. Hunched over, forking in nourishment, never had the group seemed more like a new species, Ursula Rowe thought as she sat before a single slice of bread, some jam, and a strawberry, not eating anything. Locusts, lemmings, they reminded her of something. Children. No, not children. Teenagers. Avoidance of eye contact. Bolting of food. Yes, definitely adolescence.

"May we join you?" It was Sophie and her cousin Valerie.

"Of course," Ursula replied. "We need to save a place for my friend Marit, who's not down yet." And where was Marit? Ursula wanted to get going.

"We are very, very sorry that there has been no news of your daughter. *Très charmante...*" Sophie's voice trailed off. Pix would be happy to hear herself so described, her mother thought, happily thinking that soon she could tell her so.

"Yes, it is upsetting, but the police have not given up hope."

"*Bien sûr!* Of course she will be found, wandering in these very thick woods, *peut-être.*" Valerie clearly thought the notion of a walk in these primordial forests madness. Lovely from afar.

Marit arrived with a similarly skimpy repast.

Ursula ate the strawberry and raised an eyebrow at Marit. Time to go.

"I absolutely forbid it!" A chair being pushed back and the sound of broken crockery accompanied the statement, a statement that everyone in the dining room had no trouble hearing even above the concomitant noise.

"Never, never, never!" Each word increased in volume and intensity, a tour de force. The four ladies looked at one another. "Madame Peterson seems upset," Sophie said, her eyes saying what her lips did not; that is, The

317

woman is completely crazy—*folle*.

Lynette grabbed her mother-in-law's arm. "It's our turn now. I've eaten enough fish to last me the rest of my life and we're going to London. That's it."

"Don't tell me you're in on this." Carol turned her eye on Roy junior, and although not turned to stone, he didn't move, mumbling, "We'll meet you at the airport in Oslo. It's only a week."

"Only a week! Only a week! Exactly! One week out of your life to do something for somebody else. What am I going to tell the relatives?"

Priorities were being set.

"We don't even know these people and we don't care. They probably don't care, either." Lynette's voice was just as loud, but her tempo was faster. "It's our honeymoon and we're going to see where Princess Di lives."

"Princess Di!" This was the last straw. This was not what people did on honeymoons. Princess Di was no role model.

The whole room had grown quiet as everyone watched the scene unfold before them. Several people were smiling. After the events of the last few days, this comedy of errors was a positive relief. Neither Carl nor Jan had appeared to break the fight up and it continued to roll forward, taking on a life of its own, a final anecdote to entertain the folks back home when they sat captive watching the video of "our trip."

"Well, don't just sit there. *You* say something!" Carol turned to Roy senior. He stood up.

"I don't have anything to say. Let them do whatever the hell they want," he said, and left.

Carol wasn't going to give up. Abandoned by husband, son, and daughter-in-law, she was going down fighting.

"I never thought I would see the day when a child of mine, my only child, would turn on me like this. You go have your little trip and miss meeting some of the nicest people you would ever have known. People who were going to take you into their home. Your Norwegian family. You go and have fun looking at all the sights. Don't forget the Tower of London, either," she shot at Lynette. "You ought to feel real comfortable there."

She'd gone too far.

White-faced, but with a slow grin spreading across her face, Lynette said, "I was saving this news for when we got home, but I think now's as good a time as any to tell you, Mother Peterson."

"No, honey!" Roy junior, suddenly mobilized, went to his wife's side. "Not now, sweetheart. Come on—you promised!"

"Promised what?" Carol liked to know things.

"Nothing, Mom. Let's all go pack and get down to the boat."

"Promised I wouldn't tell you that he's been promoted and accepted a transfer to New York City in three weeks," Lynette announced coolly.

The room braced itself.

Carol said, "New York City?" in a "Did I hear

correctly?" kind of voice. New York City? That hellhole? That crime- and vice-ridden capital of corruption? That New York City? Come again?

"Yes, New York City. We've already rented an apartment." Lynette did not bother to hide her triumphant smugness.

"I'd like to go to my room, son," Carol said regally, reaching for Roy junior's arm. "I think I'm going to throw up." Leaning heavily on him, she slowly made her way out, a battleship that had taken a direct hit but, against all odds, stubbornly stayed afloat.

"I'd say she took it rather well," Ursula said.

Marit nodded.

"*Méchante,* that girl," Sophie observed. "I'm glad I never had children."

As Ursula and Marit rapidly left the room—the Peterson scene had taken valuable time and it had been too fascinating to leave—Ursula remembered Lynette's words to Pix in the sauna at Fleischer's Hotel. She'd predicted correctly. Carol had not liked what was coming one bit.

Inspector Marcussen was in the lobby, holding an envelope that he hastily stuffed in his pocket.

"The tour group will be leaving at eight o'clock and we're going to say good-bye to some of the friends we made. Would you care to stroll down that way with us?" Ursula asked.

"I'm sure Officer Jansen would like to come, too," Marit added, nodding at the pleasant-looking rounded-faced young man.

Now what were they up to? Johan Marcussen wondered. They made it sound as if they were inviting him to coffee or some such social outing. And who had called Fru Rowe in the middle of the night? The clerk had gone home, so he didn't know whether the person had spoken Norwegian or not. But surely if it had been her daughter, she would be saying something, or betraying her obvious relief. Both women looked the same as yesterday, and the day before. Calm, slightly detached, well scrubbed.

"Yes, I'm sure we would be happy to come with you." Nothing better to do, that was for sure, and he had intended to watch the boat leave.

Ursula was carrying some envelopes. "Tips. The staff have gone out of their way to make this a memorable trip." Some more than others, to be sure, but there was no envelope with his name on it.

Outside the hotel, Ursula turned to the *inspektør*. "We have something to tell you..."

At the dock, Kari had gone to the small market and bought them some juice, rolls, and yogurt when it opened. No one seemed very interested in them and they continued to sit where they were, ducking out of sight behind the unlighted bonfire only when Captain Hagen came down to the ship.

Busboys from the hotel brought several large wagons filled with the luggage and slung it on board. Kari and Pix kept their gaze fixed on the one and only path from Kvikne's to the dock.

Safety in numbers? Virtually the whole tour, even Carol Peterson, who did look as if she'd thrown up—pale and wan—arrived at once with Carl, Jan, Anders, and Sonja—so many sheepdogs nudging the flock along one last time. Marit, Ursula, and the police brought up the rear.

Pix looked at Kari. Kari looked at Pix. "Now," she whispered.

They emerged from behind the mountain of wood and paper awaiting a Midsummer Eve torch.

"Hello, Carl—and everyone else," Kari said in English.

"I'm glad we didn't miss you," Pix said, standing in front of the young man. "Although you may not be so happy."

Carl looked about desperately and started to walk toward the road out of the village. The police had moved in close. He decided to bluff.

"Why, Mrs. Miller, Kari, you're safe! Everyone has been so worried!"

Jan joined him. "It's a miracle. But what happened? Where have you been? How do you know each other?" He had the feeling he had missed several important chapters. None of it made sense, but things were looking a whole lot better for the tour evaluations. He liked working for Scandie Sights. The oil company's office was boring.

Jennifer Olsen came running toward Pix and threw her arms around her. "I thought something terrible had happened to you, to both of you!" She grabbed Kari.

"Something did. Tell them, Carl," Kari ordered.

"I have no idea what you're talking about, and if Mr. Harding is going to make his plane, we really must leave now."

"Not so fast. Why don't you show the police what you have hidden in the closet on the boat?" Pix suggested.

Carl smiled. He looked relieved. "I have no idea what you're talking about, but of course the police are welcome to look at anything they want on the boat."

"What's going on?" Helene Feld asked.

"Are we leaving or not?" Sidney Harding complained.

"I think we'll just take the time to look in this closet and then I'm sure you'll be able to be on your way," Marcussen assured them.

Pix and Kari led the way on board, followed by Carl, who was managing to let several in his immediate vicinity know that he thought both women were clearly unbalanced. Pix looked to be of a certain age, he whispered to Don Brady. He didn't know what Kari's excuse was. Guilt over what she had done to her lover, probably.

Pix was bemused. What a superb actor. She and Kari had thought he would try to bluster through, figuring that it was his word against theirs, yet she had still expected him to falter a little. His conceit was truly awesome. That was teenspeak, but it was the only word that applied.

As many of the Mermaid/Troll tour as possible crowded into the little room and watched while Pix revealed the false back with a single blow to the wall. There was a universal gasp, then another even more pronounced as a small soft-sided suitcase was pulled out.

"I had no idea that was here!" exclaimed Carl.

"I'm sure you didn't!" Kari said sarcastically. "Yet, it has your name on the luggage tag."

"Well, I have never seen it before in my life."

"Let's have a look, shall we?" Inspector Marcussen took the bag and opened it. It was the one with the jewelry. Helene Feld elbowed her way to the front to get a better look.

"What beautiful things! And in such good condition. It's wedding jewelry, about a hundred and fifty to two hundred years old, I'd say."

Before she could launch into a description of the various regional nuptial customs, Johan Marcussen took Carl's arm.

"I think we'd better have a little talk."

"You can't prove this is mine just because it has my name on it. I demand that you fingerprint it!"

Pix smiled serenely and slipped her hand in her pocket, feeling Faith's plastic gloves. The luggage tag had been on the inside. They'd merely put it on the outside. But there was still more to come.

Marcussen announced everyone was to return to the hotel for what he was sure would be only a short interval while they investigated further. As they passed the bonfire pile, Pix said loudly, "We won't be here for Midsummer Eve and I think we all deserve some fun on this trip." She struck a match, tossed it well into a mass of shredded paper, then pulled her can of hair spray out for good measure, preparing to spritz the flames.

"No!" screamed Carl. "You lunatic! Put that away!" He reached into the middle of the papers, pulling a leather backpack from underneath a wooden crate.

Pix slipped the hair spray back in her pocket and Kari tossed a pail of water on the fire. No use spoiling all that work.

Carl had the knapsack in a death grip and in a vain effort to escape sprinted down the dock toward the boats. Captain Hagen stood squarely in his way. The police were not far behind.

"Give me the sack, Mr. Bjørnson," Inspector Marcussen said.

"A fortune! I would never have had to work another day! Never have had to listen to stupid people like them." The police grabbed the knapsack as he flung his hand, appropriate finger extended toward the astonished Scandie Sights tour. Carl was ranting in Norwegian and Kari was providing simultaneous translation. "A once-in-a-lifetime chance! Viking silver! Do you have any idea what that's worth!" His face was as red as the flag and his eyes were bulging. He was close to apoplexy.

The inspector had ripped open the bag

when Carl said, "Viking silver," and now he was carefully unwrapping the hoard—a hoard of smooth stones gathered from the shore.

Carl screamed and almost got away from Officer Jansen's grip. "You bitches! I should have killed you when I had the chance!" He continued, but Kari said, "I don't think my grandmother would approve of the rest of his language," and she stopped translating.

Good-bye, Jennifer. Au revoir, Sophie and Valerie. Farewell, bachelor farmers. Adieu, Dahl sisters. They had waved until the boat was out of sight. It reminded Pix of the time she'd come to Norway as a little girl with her mother and her brother, Arnold. Her father had stayed behind. He'd had to work, but he'd seen them off in New York. The huge ocean liner, the *Oslofjord,* had moved slowly away from the pier into the harbor, piloted by the tugboats. Everyone had thrown bright-colored streamers. Her father held one end, Pix the other. People went down below, but she clung to the paper strand, still connected to her father, until finally it tore and they were separated. Years later, she'd recalled the sensation in the days following his death—snap!

Wearily, she turned to the small group standing with her. "I could use a drink," she said.

It was Norway. Nobody said, At this hour of the morning?

After the discovery that the silver had been replaced by rocks—"We didn't want to take any chances," Kari explained—they had given the *inspektør* enough information about what had happened so he could file charges against Carl Bjørnson and arrest Sven and his wife. All the airports, ferry terminals, and railway stations were alerted. Now, an hour later, Marcussen rejoined them on the porch of Kvikne's.

The fjord looked as majestic as ever. Pix wished she had had more time—and had been less occupied. She should get home as soon as possible. School was almost over and she had to get Danny ready for camp. The scotch had left a warm, comfortable feeling in the pit of her stomach. She was tired, yet not sleepy. She had to go home, but the fjord in front of her was saying something else, something like, Sail on. The possibilities are limitless. This was no mere wanderlust. This was something deeper.

"So, you didn't trust us," Marcussen said, interrupting her confused thoughts.

It was Kari who answered. "Would you?" she flashed back. "My grandmother has been telling me what has been in the newspapers and some of the police theories."

He didn't answer. He was feeling pretty good himself, even without malt liquor. The bureau responsible for the investigation of illegally transporting artifacts out of the country had been ecstatic on two counts. They had been trying for several years to discover the source of Norwegian antiques, primarily from the west coast, that had been surfacing in British auction houses and dealerships. Carl had extensive knowledge and exquisite taste. He'd taught Sven what to look for and the two, with Carl's father, had hefty accounts in a British bank. To have broken the ring meant the return of the items, where they could be traced, and fines levied on those who had sold them to Sven in the first place. They'd found Sven's wife at the farm, anxiously awaiting word. After discovering that Sven had apparently not planned to take her with him, she was more than eager to talk—and she was the bookkeeper. After a prison term, it appeared she'd be back on the farm with the goats for a long time, dreams of wealth and glory squelched.

Then there was the elation over the discovery of the Viking silver. This was an exciting event, particularly the way it had been snatched from oblivion. *Ja,* the bureau was extremely happy.

"You should have told us what was going on. Things might not have gone the way you planned and they could have left the country with the silver, but thank you," Marcussen said.

"As soon as we knew Carl was still here, we knew everything would work out. Pix is a great planner." Kari beamed at her friend.

"I thought we ought to have two schemes, in case one didn't work. Not wanting to put all our eggs in one basket? We were absolutely sure he had hidden the Viking things somewhere near the boat or on it, so he could get to it easily. He wouldn't dare to have it in his room with maids coming in and out. Sven didn't have it, because we had searched him, his suitcase, and car. Anyway, it was being delivered here. We also figured Carl wouldn't dump the jewelry—in the fjord, say. He is really a terribly greedy person. It took awhile, but we found the silver in the bonfire and the bag with the other jewelry under the life jackets in a storage container. He no doubt planned to slip it in with the rest of the luggage, as usual."

Kari took up the story. "I really expected him to crack when he saw his secret compartment was full. He knew we had put the bag there, but people like Carl never believe they can be caught, and he just kept going. I'm sure he thought the *inspektør* was going to let the boat sail. Then, after everyone was on board, he would have made some excuse to get off for a moment and retrieved the knapsack from the bonfire."

"I wonder why he didn't let Pix spray the fire. The silver was evidence against him," Ursula said.

"I'd like to think it was his national pride, a noble instinct—remember, it was a Bjørnson who wrote our national anthem, '*Ja, Vi Elsker*'—no relation, I hope," Marit answered. "But I think he couldn't help himself. He saw all his money about to be burned up and he went a little crazy."

Pix agreed with her. There was nothing noble about Carl, and she sincerely hoped the author of "Yes, We Love," which always brought a lump to her throat, was a far-far-distant kinsman.

She didn't want any more to drink. Maybe a little lunch, but she knew her duty. She had to call Sam—and Faith. Maybe Faith first.

It had not been easy explaining to her husband that she had once again been in danger. Or that she had found another body. The police were keeping the Melling/Eriksen case open, but Marcussen had told them that the authorities were increasingly sure it had been a tragic accident.

Pix had calculated her calling time carefully and knew that Sam would be hastening out the door to drop Danny at school before going on to work. It wasn't that she wanted to keep anything from her husband; she simply didn't want to go into detail.

As it was, he went from total disbelief, to fear, to anger, to grudging acceptance in the space of two minutes. His comments were telegraphic. "Kari is alive and well. You and Ursula are safe. Those are the main things. We'll talk when you get home. You know I love you, Pix—and you love me, so why do you do these things to me?"

"I don't mean to," Pix had protested. It wasn't as if she had planned her own abduction or decided to find a corpse. She was a bit miffed. Love had nothing to do with any of this.

Her husband's heavy sigh was clearly audible across the transatlantic cable, satellite, or whatever was carrying their conversation. "I know, I know. Got to run. We'll talk."

There it was again—"We'll talk." More like a talking-to. Now she did feel tired.

The call to Faith went much better. Tom took Ben and Amy to day care and nursery school, so Pix knew Faith would be sitting in the kitchen at her big round table, perhaps with another cup of coffee, savoring the silence. Most mothers Pix knew did this. Five minutes peace. An empty house—granted, the beds weren't made, laundry done, or dishes washed—but *you were the only one there.*

Faith had listened attentively, asking a question every now and then and making many sympathetic murmurs.

"Obviously you have to stay another week."

"I can't. I've been gone too long already."

"Nonsense. They've been doing fine without you. No one is indispensable, although you come pretty close. Samantha and I can get Danny's camp stuff ready. He won't be leaving until after you're back, in any case. The big wedding we're catering is not for two weeks, so there's no reason on earth why you can't have some time for yourself. It sounds as if you've earned it."

There they were, those magic words: "time for yourself."

Throughout the trip, Pix had found herself treasuring the anonymity, the time free from domestic responsibilities—the time for herself. And this in spite of the stress of Kari's disappearance and two corpses. What would it be like without these complications?

A gift from the gods—that's what. She could spend some more time on the fjords. Take some walks. Go to Oslo, maybe Bergen. Visit museums. Eat whatever she wanted—alone.

"I'll talk to Sam this morning." Faith was already making a list. "Plan on it. You can come back the day before Samantha graduates. She's so busy saying good-bye that she barely knows you're gone. And believe me, you don't want to be around."

Which is how Pix found herself a week later sitting on the terrace of Marit Hansen's house in Tønsberg, eating more *reker* and mayonnaise, drinking white wine. It was Midsummer Eve, St. Hans-aften, and they were waiting for the bonfires to be lighted. Kari had gone off with a group of her friends to Nøtterøy, one of the nearby islands, for a picnic. They would stay by their bonfire, singing and telling jokes until morning.

Marit's Midsummer Eve celebration had transformed a huge mound of shrimp in a large green glass bowl into a heap of shells in another. Shrimp and white wine—there was nothing better. The Dahl sisters, who had stayed on in Oslo, came down to Tønsberg by train for this farewell celebration. Ursula had been particularly insistent about inviting the sisters. It had proved a congenial group and they lingered long over the meal.

"They should be lighting the bonfires

soon," Louise said. "It's getting quite dark."

Dark for the time of year. Pix had become used to the long, bright nights that made time stretch lazily forward. It was going to be hard to go to sleep at a decent hour.

Marit stood up. "Could you make some room for dessert? Kari baked some *pepperkaker* and we have *multer,* unless you're tired of them. We also have ice cream."

Tired of cloudberries? Not likely. Just the sound of the word whetted an appetite.

"Let me help you," Pix said, taking the tray from Marit's hands.

"Coffee for everyone, too?" Marit's voice went up, but it was a statement.

The Hansens had built a new house after the war—in Kaldnes, across the canal from the main part of Tønsberg, the oldest town in Norway. The house was perched high, looking in one direction across the water to the town itself, distinguished by the spire of the *domkirken* and the thirteenth-century citadel high on the hill at Slottsfjellet. Straight in front of the house, dominating the rocky ridge, high above the trees, was an enormous arrow, an iron weather vane, a landmark for miles around. It was Svend Foyn's weather vane—the man who had invented the harpoon gun and revolutionized early whaling, a well-beloved native son. He had erected it on this hill so he could look up from his house on the other shore and always know which way the wind was blowing. The arrow pointed due west at the moment and Pix thought wistfully of flying in that direction in the morning. It was time. Time to go home. Sam had called earlier to verify the flight. "I miss you terribly, darling. And we really need you." Pix focused on the first part of his statement and let the rest, with its implications of travail, lie for the moment. She missed them, too. She went into the house with the tray, lingering at the door to look back at her mother and the two Dahl sisters, comfortably ensconced around the table, Marit's deep purple pansies tumbling out of the planters, soft velvet in the increasing dark.

"It's so beautiful here," Erna said after Pix and Marit left. "Sometimes I wish we could stay in Norway permanently, except we have so many friends in Virginia—and our jobs."

Erna was a hairdresser and Louise a legal secretary, Ursula recalled. But the words Mrs. Rowe spoke had little to do with the twins' vocations or place of residence.

"Why did you do it? Were you born at the home? Were you *Lebensborn* babies? Was that it?"

Erna clutched her throat and turned to her sister, whose expression had not changed at all. No one said a word.

Louise looked up at the iron arrow, which was moving ever so slightly. The sky was Prussian blue and a few bonfires dotted the shore far below. The light hit the water in pools, creating islands where none existed.

"When we were little, Mother would wake up screaming. She seldom slept a night through—ever. But for a time, the nightmares stopped. We weren't *Lebensborn* children, but her first child was. We were born just after the war. Our father was Norwegian, but his family made him leave her when they discovered her past. She tried to find our sister—the baby had been a girl, but it was too late. She hadn't wanted to give her up, go into the home, but she had no choice. Her family had turned on her. The village shaved her head. We would hear her cry out, 'Nazi whore,' and we knew that was what she had been called."

"People can be horrible," Erna said. There were tears in her eyes.

Louise continued. "She took us to the United States as soon as she saved the money. She wanted to go someplace where she didn't know anyone and where there wasn't a Scandinavian community, but she was always homesick. Our house could have been here. We ate Norwegian food, spoke Norwegian, and kept all the customs. It made her feel better. I saw an ad for Scandinavian foods by mail from a town in New Jersey and sent for the catalog. She looked forward to getting it each month and would plan for days what to order."

"She was a seamstress and supported us. We grew up and supported her. It was a kind of life. Not happy, not sad. We knew about our sister, and when we got older, we offered to try to find her, but my mother was afraid of disturbing the child's life—she was always to be a child. 'She might not know and I could destroy her happiness. I've made enough mistakes,' Mother said.

"Then in one issue of the food catalog the conceited fool Melling put a picture of himself as a young man in *bunad,* our national dress. It was to celebrate Constitution Day, the seventeenth of May. Our *mor* looked at the picture, whispered, 'It's him,' and fainted."

Erna was wringing her plump hands. "We didn't know what had happened. She was never strong, and she wouldn't talk about it. Norwegians are very good at keeping their mouths shut," she added. "It went on for months. We watched her disappear before our eyes. She refused to see a doctor and ate only when we became so distressed, she felt she had to please us. The nightmares got worse, and finally she told us the whole story."

Louise was venomous. "She was a child herself. Barely sixteen, high-spirited, and restless living on the farm. There was only hard work and boredom. Oscar Eriksen was a neighbor, handsome and with some money. Not a jarl's family, but not a cotter's, either. He began to court my mother and convinced her to run away with him to Bergen. Once there, he took her to a rooming house. He raped her, then explained that she was to make herself available to the German officers who came. No decent Norwegian man would have her now, he said, and it was her duty to produce a child for the new world order, the Third Reich. She was terrified, but knew she could not go home. Her parents were very strict, very religious. When she did get preg-

336

nant, he arranged for her to go to Stalheim, where she received very good care. Then the baby was taken from her and Oscar himself drove her to her village, pushing her out of the car in front of the church. He'd made sure everyone knew what she had done. He portrayed himself as her rescuer, bringing her home to 'good' people."

"A sadist," whispered Ursula. It was worse than she could have imagined. How had the woman managed to keep the will to live?

"It wasn't until much later that the truth about Oscar Eriksen came out—his lucrative business in supplying healthy, beautiful young Norwegian women for this experiment. By then, it was too late for my mother."

"What did she do?"

"She ran—living in the forest for a while, then did whatever she could to earn enough to feed herself for the rest of the Occupation. It couldn't have been much. There was very little food in Norway for anyone. She was never strong afterward. She married a man from the northern part of Norway and they lived there. We were born. She thought she was safe, but it is a small country, after all, and the story came out. So she had to leave for good."

What kind of man abandons his wife and children over something like this? Ursula wondered. A proud man. A narcissistic man. A hard man.

"What are you going to do?" Erna whispered, her voice barely audible. Louise didn't ask. She sat straight and looked Ursula in the eye. It was not a challenge, nor did she beseech. It was a look of resignation.

"Do?" Ursula repeated. "I think quite enough has been done already, don't you? Evil will out."

Louise nodded. Some strands of her straight gray hair fell across her face and she pushed them back. "I believe that, but we had to do it—for her."

"And for Norway." Erna's voice was firm.

They could hear Marit and Pix laughing in the kitchen, the bright lights from inside the house streaming out to the terrace, sending their faces alternately into shadows and brightness.

Louise asked Ursula, "How did you guess?"

"I have spent the whole trip watching. I'm not as active as I once was. I leave that to my daughter. I came to Norway to help my friend find her daughter and the best way I could think of was to try to keep a close eye on everyone on the tour. You two were different. You appeared to be having a good time, caught up in the discovery of your roots, but I soon detected a carefully concealed anxiety below the surface. What are these women so worried about? I wondered. And I kept watching. In the days following Eriksen's death, the worry began to lift. You weren't euphoric, but you were calm. A job accomplished. I talked to Marit, who is also a keen observer. She told me that she had noticed red paint under Erna's fingernails and it seemed odd for a beautician. They weren't paper cuts. They had to be from the swastika, and whoever painted that was linked to Melling. Tonight I took a chance."

Louise nodded and reached for her sister's hand.

Marit came out onto the terrace, bringing an old bottle of cognac with the coffee. She carefully filled five delicate handblown glasses, so thin, the liquor seemed to quiver in the air. Ursula nodded slightly at her old friend and smiled. Marit stood up. "I wish to make a toast. To the new generation of 'Cartwright sisters.' We may not have crossed the *vidda* on horseback, but I think we have taken another kind of journey together. *Vær så god.*"

As is the toasting custom in Norway, she selected one individual and looked straight into her eyes before taking a drink.

She picked Pix.

Epilogue

"Didn't you tell me there was someone named Sidney Harding on your trip?"

Faith Fairchild, carrying a newspaper, walked into Pix Miller's kitchen late one afternoon a week after Pix's return from Norway.

"Yes. Why?" Pix had to get Danny to soccer and drop off Samantha's bathing suit, which she'd forgotten, for a pool party. She was also trying to think of something she could feed her husband for dinner that did not have red sauce or come with chopsticks.

"He's mentioned in the business section of the *Times* today."

Pix was two days behind in reading her

Boston Globe. "What does it say?"

" 'Oil Company Reels at Unexpected Exec Departure.' It looks like he suddenly decided to resign what has been a key position in the research and development of Norwegian oil fields. 'When asked the reason for his departure, Mr. Harding issued no comment.' "

"So he *was* a spy, or passing secrets, whatever! Mother is always right, but let's not tell her for a while. I think she's holding out on me about something else. She keeps giving me these looks fraught with meaning. I'll let things simmer, then offer a trade."

Pix remembered she had a meat loaf in the freezer. Her postpartum Norway blues were beginning to lift. Soon she'd set out for the summer on Sanpere Island in Maine's Penobscot Bay. It was very beautiful there, too, but the water wasn't that incredible color and there weren't any mountains. Yet she knew everybody, as she did in Aleford—and they knew her. Good old dependable Pix.

Maybe it was time for another trip.

Have Faith in Your Kitchen
by Faith Sibley Fairchild
A Work in Progress

A sign in a Norwegian restaurant:

CONSUMPTION OF ALCOHOL IS FORBIDDEN
UNLESS ACCOMPANIED BY FISH. ALL FOOD IS
CONSIDERED FISH, EXCEPT SAUSAGES. IF
SAUSAGES ARE ORDERED, MAY GOD FORBID,
SAUSAGES CAN BE CALLED FISH.

FISKEPUDDING WITH
SHRIMP SAUCE

1 tablespoon unsalted butter
1½ pounds white fish fillets (Haddock or
  a combination of haddock and sole is
  good.)
½ cup light cream
1 cup heavy cream
2 teaspoons salt
1½ tablespoons cornstarch
a buttered sheet of aluminum foil

Preheat the oven to 350°F.
  Melt the butter and coat the inside of a mold,
such as a pudding mold or Bundt pan. The
mold should be large enough to hold six
cups. Set aside. Start boiling enough water
so that the mold will be covered by water
three quarters of the way up when placed in
a large baking pan during cooking. Cut the
fish into small pieces, approximately one-

341

inch squares. Mix the creams together in a measuring cup with a spout or a pitcher. Using the sharp blade on a food processor or a blender, blend the fish with the cream, one batch at a time. Don't overfill the container of the blender or food processor. Transfer the mixture to a bowl and add the salt and cornstarch. Beat vigorously. It will be light and somewhat fluffy. Transfer the pudding into the mold. Bang it on the countertop and smooth the top with a knife. (Norwegian cooking tends to get physical.)

Seal the mold with the foil and place it in the baking pan. Pour in the boiling water and set the pan in the middle of the oven. Cook for one hour. Take the mold from the pan. Let it stand for five minutes and then unmold it on a decorative round platter. Drain off any liquid that may have accumulated. Spoon on some of the sauce (recipe follows) and garnish with whole shrimp and parsley sprigs. Serve the rest of the sauce separately. Don't forget to serve with lingonberries and boiled potatoes. Faith actually likes this dish, but she uses steamed new potatoes or fingerlings instead of the boiled potatoes.

Serves 6.

Note: This can also be made in individual molds as a first course.

4 tablespoons unsalted butter
3 tablespoons flour
1 ½ cups milk
1 thin slice of onion
⅛ teaspoon nutmeg
salt
white pepper
¾ pound uncooked small, fresh shrimp,
  peeled and deveined

The sauce can be made while the pudding is cooking. Melt the butter in a heavy saucepan. Add the flour, cooking for two to three minutes over low heat, stirring constantly. Increase the heat slightly and slowly add the milk, whisking or stirring constantly again. Add the onion slice and continue to stir for five minutes. Remove from the heat, discard the onion slice, add the nutmeg, along with salt and pepper to taste. Return to the heat and add the shrimp, reserving some for the garnish. When the shrimp are pink, serve immediately. (You can make the sauce ahead and do this last step just before serving.)

Cook the shrimp for the garnish in rapidly boiling water until pink.

CUCUMBER AND DILL SALAD

2 large cucumbers
2 teaspoons salt
½ cup white vinegar
2 tablespoons sugar
¼ teaspoon pepper
3 tablespoons fresh finely chopped dill
dill sprigs for garnish

Slice the cucumbers as thinly as possible, using a sharp knife or a food processor. One of my relatives uses a cheese slicer—an *ostehøvel*, "cheese plane," which was invented by the Norwegians. When used with cheese, it produces one thin slice of *gjetost* at a time—possibly all one may want. If you have a slicer, it produces a cucumber slice one can almost see through.

Toss the cucumbers with one teaspoon of salt, cover, and refrigerate for at least thirty minutes. Drain the excess liquid.

Combine the vinegar, sugar, remaining salt, and pepper and pour over the cucumbers. Add the chopped dill and mix to be sure it is evenly distributed. Cover the cucumber salad and return to the refrigerator.

Before serving the salad, transfer it to a bowl, using a slotted spoon, and garnish with the dill sprigs. This *salat* is particularly good with fish (of course) and game. It is a *koldtbord* standard and, once refrigerated, will keep for days.

Serves 6 or more, depending on number of side dishes.

No, this is not a joke. I am reproducing my cousin Hege Farstad's recipe verbatim, so you will know what people like Garrison Keillor are talking about. But Hege's *lutefisk* bears as much resemblance to the butt of all those jokes as does, to paraphrase James Thurber, Little Red Riding Hood's grandmother to the wolf—or the Metro-Goldwyn lion to Calvin Coolidge.

The best raw material for *lutefisk* is *torsk,* cod, split along the backbone before hanging to dry. The dried fish is usually cut into two parts and put into cold water for six to eight days. The water is change twice daily.

After the fish is removed from the water, the fish is peeled off the bones and put into *lut,* acid, which covers the fish. The *lut* consists of thirty-five grams of caustic soda and seven liters of water. The fish should stay in the *lut* until soft, usually from twenty-four to forty-eight hours—that is, when soft enough to pierce with a finger. The fish is then put into cold water for two to three days, and the water is changed twice daily. The best way to keep finished *lutefisk* is to cut it into pieces and deep-freeze it.

To serve *lutefisk* (4 people): 2 to 2½ kg *lutefisk,* 1 to 2 spoonfuls of salt, some water. Use a pan for poaching fish. Put water into the pan nearly up to the rack. Put the *lutefisk* on the rack when the water boils, the larger pieces first. Sprinkle the salt over the fish, put the lid on, and boil until you can pierce the fish with a small baking pin, about ten to fifteen minutes. The fish must be served *immediately*!

Trimmings: béchamel sauce, with mustard added according to taste; fried bacon strips and fat; steamed green peas; boiled potatoes.

Serve *lutefisk* with Norwegian beer and Linie aquavit (*NOT* that Danish stuff). Norwegian aquavit can be called *linjeakkevitt* only if it has been shipped in barrels to Australia and back—that is, crossing the *linje,* the equator, twice.

In this country, it may be more convenient to start with dry, unsalted cod. Norwegian-American cookbooks call for potash lye to make the *lut*.

Now you know.

SMØRBRØD
OPEN-FACED SANDWICHES

If you have traveled in Scandinavia, you have some idea how delicious—and addictive—these are. The point is to compose something as appealing to the eye as to the palate, and a buffet of several different kinds of *smørbrød* makes for a good party, aquavit or no aquavit.

The bread, which may be white, wheat, rye, whole-grain, or whatever you like, acts as the platform for the creation. Slice the bread thin, but thick enough to hold what you will be arranging on top. Spread it with unsalted butter or herb butter. In addition to the butter, most sandwiches start with a lettuce leaf, but you can also use other thinly sliced vegetables. *Smørbrød* are eaten with a knife and fork. Thick bread detracts from the taste of the other ingredients and is also hard to cut through.

Generally, white bread is used for more delicate flavors, such as shrimp. Heartier breads are used for things like smoked fish or roast beef.

To make Pix's favorite, spread the bread lightly with unsalted butter, add a leaf of Boston lettuce, then arrange several rows of small cooked shrimp on top. Pipe some mayonnaise (Norwegian mayonnaise is a bit sweeter than Hellman's) from a pastry tube on top of the shrimp. Cut a thin slice of lemon, remove the seeds, then cut the slice almost crosswise and twist it, placing it across the shrimp.

Other good combinations are:

• Roast beef topped with a thin slice of tomato and horseradish mayonnaise
• Thin meat patty (beef or veal) grilled, then topped with fried onions and served at room temperature
• Smoked salmon topped with thin asparagus spears that have been marinated in a vinaigrette and a final dollop of crème fraîche
• Smoked salmon topped with slices of cucumber and dill salad

- Slices of hard-boiled egg topped with anchovies or herring and tomato slices
- Smoked mussels or smoked eel on top of scrambled egg
- Sliced liverwurst topped with crisp bacon and garnished with a sliced cornichon, the small, tart French gherkin
- Jarlsberg cheese with turkey, topped with a spoonful of chutney

It is important to put enough on the sandwich so the bread is hidden. It is also important to decorate the surface with chopped parsley, a carrot curl, sprigs of herbs, capers, caviar, strips of pimento or peppers fanned to make a floral shape, or lemon.

The sandwiches are served on large trays or platters that have been covered with paper doilies.

VAFLER
SOUR CREAM WAFFLES

2 eggs
1 cup sour cream
⅓ cup melted butter
⅛ teaspoon vanilla (or substitute ⅛ teaspoon of ground cardamom to vary flavor)
¾ cup milk
1 cup flour
3 tablespoons sugar
½ teaspoon baking powder
¼ teaspoon salt

Beat the eggs and add the sour cream, whisking well together, then add the butter, vanilla, and milk, whisking again. Add the dry ingredients and stir. The batter may seem thinner than your usual waffle batter. Cook in a preheated waffle iron; one that makes heart shapes is all the better. The finished waffle should be nicely browned. Makes approximately two dozen three-inch heart-shaped waffles.

Vafler are served room temperature with jam and butter, or sometimes with powdered sugar—*never* maple syrup.

⅔ cup butter (1 stick plus 2 ⅔ tablespoons)
⅓ cup brown sugar
⅓ cup white sugar
1 tablespoon molasses
1½ teaspoons ground clove
2¼ teaspoons cinnamon
2¼ teaspoons ginger
1 teaspoon baking soda
¼ cup boiling water
2½ cups flour

Preheat the oven to 325°F.

Heat the butter, sugars, and molasses in a heavy saucepan over low heat until the butter melts. Remove the pan from the heat and stir in the spices. Transfer the mixture to a bowl and let cool for five minutes. Mix the baking soda with the boiling water and add to the bowl. Stir in the flour, mixing well to make a smooth dough. Refrigerate for at least one hour.

Working in batches, roll the dough to a thickness of approximately $\frac{1}{12}$ of an inch. These cookies are best when thin and crisp. A heart and a fluted round cutter, each two inches wide, were used for the recipe. Bake the cookies on lightly buttered sheets for eight to ten minutes. Transfer immediately to cool on brown paper or racks. Makes approximately six dozen cookies. Store the cookies in an airtight tin. The dough may also be frozen for use later.

Pepperkaker are made all year long, but

they are essential at Christmas. Norwegian families with small children have a *pepperkaker* baking day just before the holiday. The dough is cut into many shapes: hearts, stars, men, women, and pigs or other farm animals. White icing is piped onto the cooled cookies to decorate them. My cousin Hege relates that the dough is so good that at these parties, usually only half makes it into the oven!

Author's Note

Just as the smell of cardamom reminded Ursula Rowe of the Larsens' kitchen, it transports me back to my grandparents' house. My maternal grandfather, Peter Malmgreen, built it in his old age, painting the shingles red because my grandmother Alfhild was still homesick, even though they'd left Norway at the turn of the century. She used to give us "coffee milk"—milk, sugar, and an inch or two of strong Maxwell House brew. The "Good to the Last Drop" factory was not far away in Hoboken and, more important, was a sponsor of the TV show *I Remember Mama*.

My grandmother cooked the only food she knew—Norwegian—feeding a large family throughout the Depression. Some of these dishes became the favorites of my generation, too, as our mothers prepared the kinds of meals they had grown up on— lured away on occasion by the casserole cookery craze of the fifties, which was forever changed by Craig Claiborne's hefty *New York Times Cookbook* (his beef Stroganoff was de rigueur for an exotic dinner party all across the North Jersey suburbs in the early sixties). Still, our comfort foods were my grandmother's—veal and beef meatballs with a hint of nutmeg: *tilslørte bondepiker,* with its toothsome layers of sweet toasted crumbs, applesauce, and whipped cream; fruit puddings (with more cream); and our frequent

Sunday-night supper, a bowl of bread, milk, and sugar. At an early age, we also developed a fondness for herring, but we drew the line at *gjetost,* no matter how much my mother loved it.

Our *koldtbord* on Christmas Eve was, to a child's eye, more splendid even than Kvikne's Hotel's—accompanied as it was by a multitude of cousins, rousing song, and tantalizing gifts. The tree was always trimmed with strings of Norwegian flags, shiny ornaments, and the woven paper-heart baskets my grandfather made with us. The night, which lasted long, was the culmination of what seemed at times like unendurable anticipation. My mother and her sisters would start their preparations weeks before—cookies, breads, cured meat, and, of course, *fiskepudding.*

The *fiskepudding* recipe given here is my grandmother's word for word, as are those for *Julekake*—Cardamom Raisin Bread—in *The Body in the Bog* and Norwegian Meatballs in *The Body in the Cast.*

When asked why Faith Fairchild doesn't appear more centrally in this book, I've flippantly answered that Faith would never go to Norway, because there would be nothing there for her to eat. While this may have been true some years ago—and on a trip in 1975, my husband did tell me he'd go mad if he ever saw another boiled potato—contemporary Norwegian cuisine, whether in homes or in restaurants, has changed, combining tradition with innovation to produce dishes even Faith would savor. Pillaging in the spirit, though not the manner, of their ancestors, you may now be served such hybrids as gravlaks mille-feuille, sushilike marinated salmon tartares, or venison ravioli.

All this is fine with me—so long as there are always plenty of *vafler*!